The Quiet Kill

The characters and events described in this book are a work of fiction and any similarity to real persons or events, living or dead, is unintentionally coincidental.

The Quiet Kill Title and Text Copyright© 2014 by Luke Taylor

ISBN 978-0-9906249-2-9

Cover Design by Laura Gordon

Also by Luke Taylor
Evening Wolves

*This book is dedicated to my many muses
and their endless mystery*

Quiet - *adj.*

1. making no sound; with little or no noise; silent or hushed.
2. moving very little; still or calm.
3. speaking or saying little.
4. peaceful and gentle; not offending others.
5. not showy, bright, or flashy.
(syn) unobtrusive; modest

1
Beginnings

Loeb was a writer.
A dereliction.
A disgrace.

Not in anyone's eyes, but his own, and his own wouldn't stop staring at him in the mirror to say so. They had a habit of following him with their cerulean glares and glances as he walked hurriedly in front of things that carried a reflection; windows and shiny car hoods, metallic bits and bobs and even glasses of water as they guarded the elbows of diners and restaurants.

And in Los Angeles, there was no escape.

They bruised and battered, condemned and accused.

No escape.

Loeb Cohen is a hack whose pursuit of perfection can only push him to failure.

Loeb Cohen cannot write. He can barely spell and sometimes results to making up his own words.

He can only spit out page-turning pabulum like a franchised fast food chain.

He's too young.

He's flashy, he's foolish.

He's no good.

Loeb was sleepless and slightly gray-skinned and he avoided all that glinted and gleamed in the sunlight of the cursed September brightness, bunching in the corner table of his daily visit to a roadside café named *The Black Dog*. It was a busy mix of regulars; construction workers always fiddling with parking lots and side streets in the heat and traditionalist office dwellers who didn't mind walking a few blocks for the pastrami or even the griddle cakes. As day rolled into night and early morning, the clientele changed considerably, and the staff of *The Black Dog* was always engaged in some kind of Russian roulette with whatsoever walked through the door. The decor was black and tan, topped with lethargic fans that spun year-round and never pushed out much refreshment. Dark carpet hid decades of stains and spills. Strangely there were no portraits of canines on the walls, not that it would've enhanced or subtracted anything in any way.

Loeb was brought coffee by a woman named Cat because hardly anyone called her Catriona. She had stiff blue hair that was thick and furry on top and buzzed on the sides and he'd put her in a book and was condemned by it once it became a bestseller. Cat's smile was more of a snarl, splintered by slippery silver-colored stud piercings at the corners of her upper lip. Her eyes were warm and unicolor brown with indistinguishable pupils and the slick slimness of her body bound in a black apron and pants made the tattoo on the underside of her left forearm leap from her body as he only wished he'd made her leap off the page.

Cat, and those inspirations like her in diners and shops, parks and stores; anywhere and everywhere young Loeb haunted as the cerulean-eyed specter that he was, hexed him for his pathetic attempts to capture their vibrant spirits, their unimaginable intricacies.

They were so vivid, so lovely in their contradictions and conflicts.

So...*real*.

And what had he done? Stolen them from the environments in which he'd found them, flattened them with the rollers of a printing press and glued them to pages the public chewed on till they were sick as if the product of his writerly toil was discount Halloween candy.

He'd failed them, the swimming goldfish of his life's tiny existence whom he held so dear in his heart; he'd turned his muses into mistakes and no one knew the difference but him.

Could he complain? The machine was fed. Drugstores and airports sold his books, and on the covers of those books his own name was printed larger than the title he'd toiled so furiously to come up with. He was mainstream, a product of the system, making products for the system.

But Loeb knew the difference.

He knew the emptiness he alone had created and no marathon at the keyboard could remedy his plight.

And in that, he was stuck.

Soon, contract deadlines would come and the hostage negotiations would begin and unless his pulp world of action rehash where just enough cleavage was shown and just enough junk blew sky high was turned upside down and something artistic and original fell out, he would have to call it quits and be forced to live out his days on whatever royalties would roll in from his work as his star faded into the mediocrity it so generously deserved.

Loeb was slump-shouldered over his black coffee as Cat sat down across from him in the corner booth of his ritualistic daily appearance. She'd been waiting on him for nearly three years now and wished he was far more than just her well-tipping favorite regular. He couldn't stop himself from joking and flirting with her but eventually his chronic seriousness about *the craft* always sabotaged his efforts and the result of his technical and intellectual babblings endlessly humored her blunt sense of understanding. Sometimes she wished she could curl up in the booth next to him and run her fingers through his hair and say, *what about subplots, baby? Tell me, how do you come up with such great names?* To which his hands would become demonstrative and a lecture would begin, somehow rewinding all the way back to Greek archetypes just to make a small point about the human condition.

But then Cat was just a waitress in a roadside café and he was just a bestselling author who needed a sandwich. Their working relationship had a certain distance between it and as sweet and sincere as Loeb was, Cat laid her head on the pillow every night knowing Loeb's all in one publicist-agent-publishers were always trying to set him up with some Hollywood date on one of those nights he seemed to experience so infrequently, one of those cocktail party evenings where everybody laughed and lied and got drunk in hopes he'd fall under the spell of some slinky magic queen whose face needed no airbrushing and who spent more time in the gym to look *natural* than some athletes.

"Whatcha workin' on now, tiger?" She said, opening a menu of pictures before him. Slivers of juicy sunlight glossed the laminate pages and seemed to press Loeb further into the dark corner of the booth, stifling Cat's attempt to draw him into the sunny glow. Loeb's swollen pupils were weighted down by the fictitious images of idyllic diner food staples and leapt around them as if lily pads in a swamp.

"I'm broke." He said, and his voice, stilted with its own unique staccato, was bassy and rich and sold tickets whenever he was forced, by publishers, to do speaking engagements and interviews. He should've been a singer, but his obsession with poetry and writers and novels had been stealing his time since dropping out of college, something that only added another wrinkle to his *success*.

"What?" Cat frowned. "Already?"

"No, no." Loeb corrected with a hasty smile. Even though it was still untouched in his bank account, he'd just been advanced 30K for a novel film studios were in the midst of chop-shopping and sensationalizing to run for a television mini-series. He had nothing to do with it, and had sold a part of his soul to relinquish the rights to the story, but the credits would proudly state, *based on the novel "Fractures" by Loeb Cohen.*

"You mean you're not working right now? You look to me like your working. You've got that *I'm working* look."

"...I'm always working. I can't *stop* working. I'm a slave to working. I see words, *think* words...I can't even go to the bathroom without a voice in my head typing it all out in size twelve Courier New. It's like a disease..."

Then Loeb let gravity pull his head to his fist and it mussed an artistic mop of very dark hair, thick and unevenly parted down middle and falling to his shirt collar. He was young and good-looking in a plaintive yet well-balanced sort of way, in a way that Cat admired because the magazine covers kept trying to make men Loeb's age look like women and Loeb refused.

"*You're* a slave?" Cat's query was sarcastic. "Heh. Wait for it."

Loeb's stable brows hinted at a frown and then caught on. Several tables behind, as if driven by robotic internal processing chips, the maître'd was on the march. She was a short woman in a wrinkle-free pantsuit that hovered in the sun razors between sage and hunter green, whose face shone in the slightest with the grease of too much skin lotion. Her hair was an overgrown auburn bob burdened by the weight of the product it bore and her stride was militaristic and intentionally stretched to cover the most ground possible with a single step.

Loeb stuffed a smile behind his teeth and let the fist he'd been leaning on play with his earlobe as images of delicious gut bombs tickled his palate. If he made eye contact with Cat he'd laugh and didn't want to get her in trouble.

"How is everything?" They heard, two tables away. "Good." Low heels nearly indented the rough carpet. "How is everything? Good."

The march ceased but no emotion was allowed to enter the shiny face. The amount of lotion forbade it.

"Catriona, what are you doing?"

"We're going to get married." Loeb said and his face sold the farcical statement with an angelic bent as it smirked across the wideness of his closed mouth.

The maître'd whose name was Rosemary Crane said nothing and marched back the way she came.

Cat waited till she couldn't anymore and then laughed hysterically. Her face turned red and veins popped from her forehead. She laughed a choking muffle of lungs and lips until she was exasperated and fell onto the table with a sigh, and her breath unwound from a high pitch back to speaking timbre.

"Oh..." She checked her watch, a digital job that was cheap and doubled as a pedometer and proved to one of her roommates that Cat walked ten to twelve miles a day. "My shift's almost over. Order something quick so you can tip me."

She rubbed her eyes and stowed dreams of his joke statement being true and real and squeezed her hands together to make the dreams go away before they made her sad and spoke to her of the impossibility.

"Turkey on white." He said. "Light mayo. Thin tomatoes and extra lettuce, of course."

Cat took the menu from him with a curling swipe and in a flash Loeb digested her posture for study. Femininity was hidden deep in her bones in the same manner speed was buried within a lounging zoo-bound leopard; unable to spill forth in freedom and held to the cage of the black apron and messy blue hair.

By necessity, by environmental evolution.

By the unstable prism of history.

In that split second, he assumed many things, imagined what could've been, and processed the angle of her neck and her chin and the carefree hedgehog of blue hair and the way she shaved her eyebrows thus removing them altogether to give herself little to no expression which instantaneously made her that much more fascinating.

He wanted to stand up and plant one on her

and tell her how grateful he was she had been his
sole inspiration for *Fractures* and the actress they'd
selected for the upcoming show and what they'd
done with the character and the script was a
shambolic representation, so much so, he didn't
think Cat knew *Fractures* was a story about her and
Loeb couldn't work up the courage to tell her. He
wanted to hug the stuffing out of her and wondered
why, after his faithful visits, he could only wave as
he ducked out until they met again in his dark
corner table and why he never talked to her about
her personal life or why he only wanted to sit in her
station and how her eyes were so easy to look into
and other people's weren't, other people's were to
be avoided.

Even his own mother's.

Cat was light on her feet as usual to get the
order in quick and he sensed she was eager to get
out of the restaurant. He wondered how hard it was,
working in a twenty-four hour diner that pretended
to be something else by calling itself a roadside
cafe, what kind of people she dealt with and what
kind of leathery skin she'd developed to it all.

Loeb sat and toyed with the curling handle of
his coffee mug to pout over his own pity. Writing,
while consuming him to the bone and always
calling him to the mat with litanies of inadequacy
and incompetence, especially when he wrote those
overcooked plot lines in his less successful
bestsellers, was a gift of a job and he was damned
lucky to be stuck in its rut of wealthy successes,
even if he felt like a donkey yoked to a grain-
crushing millstone with one of the suits of the Max
Rayberg Group thwacking his hind end ever so
often saying, *What's your next one about? Where's
our rough draft? What's the title? Is it a trilogy?*

His coffee was cold by the time the sandwich came and Cat brought a warm up in the other hand and Loeb listened to the sloshy sound of the cup being filled.

"You're not a caged animal. You don't have to write five books a year and apologize about not having written six." She said, as if she'd thought about it long and hard and was glad he wasn't looking as gray now that he'd been in his favorite dark corner of the cafe for a good twenty minutes, inching ever closer to the shafts of sun cutting through the dusty blinds.

"I know." Loeb agreed and removed the red and blue-foiled toothpicks unnecessarily holding the flat sandwich together. "I just...need a reason to stop, but I don't want it to be because I can't think of anything new, which is what just might be happening to me. I'll be more popular than ever with *Fractures* coming out on TV, even though I don't own the rights. Solderman and Pearle say I've got two months to be normal and then I'm going to officially become tabloid material. I don't know what that means. I guess I don't care. It's all talk. At the end of the day I'm still just a writer. Sometimes I question the value of it, like if what I've given so much of my life to...*all* of my life to actually means something to somebody."

It was then Cat ran her bottom lip over the metal studs framing her top lip and gave two nervous glances to the rest of the dining floor for Rosemary Crane. An anxious flutter flourished in her belly.

"I think I have just the thing for you."

"Oh Cat, no pie please." Loeb joked. "I'm in too much despair. I just might eat the whole thing to make myself feel better. Especially the fresh mountain blueberry."

She caught his smile as she leaned over and darkened his face. The sun slivers from the window slashed across her lithe black form and she looked like a stalking tiger, like the tattoo on her left forearm.

"No. I'm serious."

2

Deepenings

Catriona paced and smoked. In *Fractures,* Loeb had described the manner in which she did so at length, or to some critics, *ad nauseum*, but he only did so to honor her and had since given up smoking himself. It made him feel light headed. More than that, he had smoked with fiddling hands and tight lips, but Cat smoked as sailors who stood on the prows of boats, like she was breathing in the brisk salt of life and the sun and the sky were in harmony with her doing so and each puff of wisp and mist streaming from her nose like a Spanish bull in the cold was a living artform as shelf-stable creamer dispersing itself in a cup of black coffee was or motor oil dripping from a used car to make the rainbow in a parking lot puddle of water.

In the armpit of the diner's garbage bins and back doors where Loeb stood and watched her pace and take drags of a Marlboro Gold, Cat was juxtaposed and glorified all at the same time. She was a great mystery to him, how she could throw a dull sweatshirt on her shapeless thinness and become anonymous to any pedestrian set of eyes in the crowd awaiting the bus, while to his own cool cerulean-blue microscopes she bounced with the poise of an unbreakable spirit and held inside of her a depth of character he was only forced to guess the limits of.

The result, *Fractures,* had sold well over a million copies in its first printing, and though he'd never told her, he wondered if she knew. She was smart in that she was sharp and was good at hiding it. He hadn't plagiarized her, but in the same token he hadn't dreamed her up.

It was a writer's plague, to become an alchemist of reality, always seeking to transform truth into fiction and sometimes forgetting which was which.

"Don't laugh when I tell you." She said, the words darting over an edgy smile as she checked the evenness of her fingernails. The stub of the cigarette near to the filter was poking from in between her pinkie and ring finger, married hand, as barren of jewelry as the opposite hand was full of it.

"I don't laugh before one o'clock." Loeb said and his arms were crossed.

She disregarded his mockery, seeing as he'd lost it at the maitre'd's frigid reaction to his joke.

"I was thinking about you, how you always come in and tell me how you've got some epic project that'll take you two years only to find you've starved yourself to do it in three weeks, editing and everything, and what you need is an unplugging."

"A what?" Loeb said, his head tilting toward the bittersweet burn of smoke ripping through Cat's nose.

"A unplugging. Completely. A vacation where you don't do anything, you don't talk to anyone, you don't think any of those writerly thoughts you're always thinking. Nothing."

Loeb's throat carried a guttural negation like a dog on a leash that didn't want to move and was being tugged away from a tree before his business was completed, the noose around his neck tightening at the hands of better judgment.

"Become a vegetable. Lounge. And do it somewhere nobody knows you." She flicked the cigarette far and smirked at him as her final drag hovered inside, waiting to be unleashed. "You said it yourself, it's only a matter of time before the paparazzi will make you a recluse, and we both know what that means."

Loeb barely got out as it was, and traded even time between the contractual obligations of champagne and canapé Hollywood shindigs where he avoided most of the guests and his haunts of inspiration in MacArthur Park and his apartment on West Third where he still maintained a form of anonymity and cherished the chance to absorb his surroundings in efforts to assimilate and dramatize the dazzlingly mundane and ever so dynamic snow globe of the Los Angelean existence that made him such a nominal success in the eyes of the populace.

"You must have something in mind. Hawaii or something. Maybe even just plain old Malibu."

Cat crossed her arms too and masked a grin with a final expellation of cig fumes.

"Nothing of the sort, Mr. Subplot."

What then? He wondered. *And why is Cat being so cryptic? She's never like this.*

"The Last Frontier."

"Alaska?" Loeb's voice nearly squeaked, but was too bassy to do so and it came out as more of a warble, like an old record being messed with as it whirled around the phonograph.

"Yeah. I was doing some catering at hotel and

they had these brochures all laid out. I couldn't help reading a few of them."

"Catering?" Loeb's stable brows folded. "*Now* who's working themselves too hard?"

Cat shrugged and stuffed her hands in the butt pockets of her tight black work jeans. A dusting of flour on her left thigh made them look faded, even though they were a recent purchase. It was the way of a low-life worker bee, nothing was too new for too long.

"I'd like to move out, you know. I've been living with these skitzoid roommates for too long now, they're gonna drive me insane. And since my repeated attempts at community college aren't working out..."

Loeb turned to start walking, hiding an understanding nod as she followed. They walked the lot in silence. Most of the cars were gray and dirty copper brown imports and their blandness was tinting Loeb's skin again, making him become heavy and acidic. The sidewalk was parched from the September sun and heedless traffic lazily drifted up and down the street.

"Do you remember any names on the brochures? Was it one of those cruise ships where everyone gets sick?"

Cat squinted and was nearly cross-eyed. Her act of trying to remember the name was just that and she knew the name like the soles of her feet, and like her feet, her knowledge of the name was just as sensitive.

"...Quill Creek. It's south of Anchorage, in the fjords."

"Sounds beautiful..." Loeb's need for sarcastic contrast was provided in the drab shoulders and litter-ridden alley behind the twenty-four hour restaurant and the nearby buildings and businesses that all sat under the shadows of the skyline and didn't really care much that they did. After all, like the traffic, the tall buildings were just accessories, tchotchkes on a fireplace mantle.

"And cold." Loeb added, considering he was California born and raised and was somewhat addicted to year-round comfort.

"They have private cabins and all the kitchy shops you could imagine, places where you can get hand carved lawn ornaments and if you like fishing…"

"Cat," Loeb's laughter was crumpled like a sheet of scrap paper, barely escaping his mouth. "I couldn't fish to save my life. The first salmon I latched onto would pull me in and I'd get hypothermia. People who live in Alaska are like action heroes. I'm just a bum who gets paid to write nonsense."

Cat mashed down on the crosswalk button and held her arms wide.

"That's exactly what I'm talking about. You've been here too long and if this place isn't a forum for self-doubt then I don't know what is. Look at me. I thought I'd get a scholarship out of high school so I wouldn't have to work in a diner my whole life and now I'm twenty-five. You just need to go somewhere that's outside of the box you've made for yourself, you need a challenge."

"A challenge? Solderman and Pearle will cut my deadlines in half when *Fractures* hits the air. They'll want to have more books, and worse, they'll want me to have options, because now that I've written something great," the light turned in their favor and the lazy cars were ambivalent as the two crossed the sweltering street. "Or at least something

critically great, they'll think they have some say so
in what direction it'll go. Don't you see I'm
screwed either way?"

"You're not getting the big picture." Cat said
and her lips curled in the snarl he cherished. A
dance wove through the skin above her eyes. He
loved her lack of eyebrows, how she intentionally
shaved them, even though he didn't know why and
had never asked.

His neck was hooked and his tone inquisitive.

"The big picture about what, Alaska?"

"Yeah, I mean, what if you say, I'm never
writing another book again and go to Alaska and
fall in love? What if you have some spiritual
experience and write the best book you've ever
written, like an American classic or something?
You've gotta go for it! You've got to give it a
chance! This place doesn't change for anybody but
it sure as hell changes them. Trust me…"

Cat's shoulders wiggled with the blankness
falling across Loeb's face.

"You're not afraid, are you?"

Loeb said nothing. Then he said,

"I think I am."

She delighted his honesty, his sincerity, and
how he would sink into candor's pitfalls head first
so she could get him back to a place of levity.

Catriona lived in a Spanish speaking
neighborhood that was always peppered with the
tinny romance of pop radio and scantily clad loiters
and their young relatives playing soccer in the
street. Loeb lived only five blocks away and though
he left her politely at her door she'd never invited
him in and he'd never asked her to come to his
place.

"Well…" They reached a thick mission-style

house on a small slope that elevated it above the others in the neighborhood. It was well kept by one of Cat's roommates, Rhonda, a person for whom her type-A personality was more of a medical condition. She had a penchant for tirades if certain *chores* weren't done to her liking and she lorded with a fastidious manner that would never be pleased. "I guess I'll see you tomorrow, then."

Loeb was distant, staring out past a bracket of palms and chain link fences. They were buried in the miasma of a hundred suburbs in search of a city.

"Loeb?"

"Yeah?"

"I'll see you tomorrow."

"Yeah." His smile was hasty and forced. "Adios."

Loeb let his hands fall in the pockets of his slacks and his head dipped as he walked. He didn't see Cat's brown eyes on him for nearly two minutes as his shape became smaller and smaller to her amidst the diorama of gray street concrete and sunshine.

Cat was quick with her keys. The place was empty and would remain empty for only a few more minutes. Another of her roommates, a poly-sci student named Kris would be home soon and with her whirlwind arrival of book bags and giant sparkling water bottles the TV would be snapped on and bags of potato chips would be rattled and munched and consumed. Then Rhonda would return from her job at the storage unit and explode at the brazen white-trash slobbery and UCLA pre-med student Tam Phan would pop in and smooth it all out while Cat kept her mouth shut, listening to heavy metal music on studio headphones and cooking dinner, because after ten to twelve hours a day around the stuff she couldn't wait to get back at it.

Ah, life...

So Cat all but rushed to her bed and laid across its stiffness as the September sun hit the amber shade drawn across the large window that ate up the wall space where, in a perfect world, she would've loved to hang black and white photography of the northern hemisphere.

Iceland. Japan. Scotland. Russia.

Alaska.

She had to think.

She had to tell herself he would go for it, for the Alaskan *vacation*, and he felt what she felt, that she wasn't confused and reciprocity, if not spoken, *was* their reality.

Only one year separated them, didn't it?

Why else would he come and see her so often if he didn't care about her and even walk her home on Wednesdays?

Cat's fingers were nearly shaking as she went for another Marlboro Gold and just put her mouth to the pack and took the one that stuck to moist lips. She sat up and lit it, reaching to the nightstand for a book she'd read cover to cover a dozen times if she'd read it once.

Fractures, a novel by Loeb Cohen.

The matte jacket, a black and white photo of a girl walking alone down a European tree-lined cobblestone street at night, was riddled with the grease of her after-shift fingerprints and a few of the crème-colored pages were even tear-stained.

And with cigarette perfume curling as incense in the ashtray, her hushed voice cut the stillness of the closet-sized room in which her messy blue twin bed was stuffed against the corner window and walled in by musty flower print wallpaper.

"Fists pounded on the door of the cell. Keys jangled and violated the lock. Her solitude was stolen at their hands and her knees squealed across the cold concrete as they trussed her up for another beating. Her face was blank as they stripped her, detached and removed. She thought about him. How she loved him."

The pages of the book became heavy and sagged in her lap. Her eyes eased shut and the long shift at the diner seemed to dissipate and slide from her bones and skin, as if caught in the smoldering curl of the cigarette's ash tip.

The smoke took her prayers to be free from the torpid ruts of life's grind to the heavens, a plea that wished with whole-hearted fervor for the unspoken to be made known.

Loeb understood her. He had written every word for her.

Hadn't he?

Or was she just another twenty-five year old who'd heard too many stories about the glass slipper?

Cat's brown eyes were closed as she kissed the cigarette for a puff and set it back, quoting the words as if passages from the Bible.

"Everyday she sat in the prison yard where no grass was allowed to grow for fear of it giving the prisoners hope. Her eyes craved the heat of unclouded sunlight. He would come for her. He would not forget her. He would bide the gray fog of war, as did the ageless sun, and pierce its muddled veil. Then, and only then, would he rescue her from the bonds and chains and cruel razor wires. Then, and only then, they would be together again."

Cat blew the smoke from her nose and curled

up in a ball on her side, leaving the Marlboro to die. The story was about World War II spies who couldn't physically love each other as they yearned to but continued in their duties, the ends of which were heroic sacrifices, not for their countries as their posthumous awards and the speeches of grateful Officers and government officials dictated, but because of what boundless, secret connection had been fused between them.

Love.

It was fiction, wasn't it? Fake, false; a forgery of real life's best elements to fashion a land of make believe.

Cat fell asleep and woke in a light sweat from the jarring tones of a yet another new reality show and Kris' assault of blue corn chips and mild salsa that would in no way steal her voracious appetite from Cat's preparation of dinner, which she still had to run out at some point and get from the store because none of the other girls had the time, according to them, to do so.

Like she did.

The thin walls of the mid fifties mission house were unbearable, like crepes or sheets of wax paper. She may've been dreaming, she couldn't tell. Even the blank darkness of sleep was a dream at this point in her life, and whatever rest she'd fallen into with the routine of work finally behind her had been sullied by a hamster wheel of a different kind. The vivid movies of unconscious rest were as far from her as the horizons of day and night and for yet another moment in time they would stay as such. Kris was in front of the TV like clockwork and the volume of the new flat screen Cat'd been forced to chip in for was close to max.

Ten incredible cities. Ten jaw-dropping

*challenges. Ten highly qualified teams from vastly
different walks of life will compete for ten
consecutive days with the chance to win up to one
hundred thousand dollars in cash and prizes.*

This is...American Challengers.

She hated the candy-coated racket of the
music, the juvenile sound effects, every single
torturous word as it punctuated the limitless
onslaught of plasticized *reality.*

It was all she could take.

Cat rushed from her bed and slammed the
door shut and crumpled down against its cheap,
laminate scratchiness and began to cry.

Tonight, they would be eating Chinese
takeout.

3
In High Places

The elevator doors spread wide.

Loeb waited till those before him departed to release a hefty sigh and chew on his lips for patience' sake. It was always hard to transition from time with Catriona and her irreverent urban armor to the bleached teeth and glossy desks of the publishers, but Wednesdays had a habit of doing that-especially with *Fractures* going to TV where hundreds of thousands were eagerly awaiting the next water cooler obsession.

Or so they said.

And the middle-aged Solderman and Pearle said a lot, so much so even Loeb with his sharp memory was always forgetting their unfiltered and unorganized mix of promises, suggestions, debates, criticisms and bad jokes.

Their offices were somewhere in the clouds close to the pass-through of 110 and if he had a dime for every time he'd listened to their arguments while counting cars he'd live in Malibu.

The secretary, whose name was Lily, a heavyset woman with small eyes and a tight ponytail, greeted him with professional aptitude. He could tell she wanted to be on lunch but the

impromptu meeting had stolen such from her. It was
almost twelve o'clock.

"Hey there Lobster." Pearle said as Loeb was
allowed in. The offices of the Max Rayberg Group
were minimalist and self-indulgent in the use of
glass and priceless Asian antiquities Loeb was
forced to wonder about the purpose of because he
always forgot to ask.

"Sods," Pearle called out and his voice echoed
in the slightest through the expanse of space.
"Lobster's here."

Loeb and Pearle shook hands and Loeb had
developed a thick skin to the squatty, gray-haired
and quick-mouthed former newspaperman, who,
because of his own heritage, though watered down,
loved to make the anti-kosher joke about Loeb's
name.

Sods was Pearle's name for Solderman, and
Pearle had a name for everybody and they had to
laugh as if they loved it even though it was
traditionally a derogatory effort to make Pearle feel
taller and more powerful. Sods, he said, was short
for Sodom and Gomorrah because Solderman was
always the one begging Loeb for more sex, more
violence, and more cursing. Sods came from the
Market and was a man of the trend. Solderman was
also Jewish. They all were, all the way up to Max
Rayberg himself, who'd had his fingers in
Hollywood since he was in a crib. In that way, Loeb
didn't think about signing with anyone else because
they took such great care of him, despite the
constant barrage of joshes, ribs, complaints,
confused faces, and attempts to make him one half
of a new power couple by marrying him off to an
attractive actress on the rise.

Solderman emerged from a small restroom,

hidden by hand painted shoji screens and a stepped series of blue Chinese vases on glossy ebony shelves. Solderman was thin and wiry and not much taller than Loeb but quite a bit taller than Pearle.

After the handshakes were over they all took to low couches, to which Solderman rose again to fix himself a drink, as if he'd forgotten something vitally important. There were four of the couches in the expanse of the cloud-reaching office, God only knew why when chairs would've sufficed.

"We wanted to ask you a few things about *Fractures*." Pearle cut to the chase.

"I thought the ghosts and the screenwriters were handling it now." Loeb said as he turned down beverages. "I don't own the rights anymore."

"Yeah yeah…" Pearle waved a splotchy reddish-hued hand and adjusted a golfing shirt that was too tight on his ever so slowly expanding midriff. "It's nothing to do with that."

"What then?" Loeb eased in his spot, warming to the idea the meeting could actually be a pleasant discussion of *the craft*, a subject of which he knew they took advantage of him and wound him up to set him loose on their cash cow seminars and speaking engagements.

"I was, well, *we* were wondering, not to sound like a prima donna here but it was my idea,"

Solderman retuned from a long bar with a gin and tonic.

"There you go again, like Cohen cares whose idea it was."

If Loeb were to describe them in a book, Solderman was the pencil and Pearle was the sharpener.

"I'm just saying."

Solderman had placatory hands that steepled

whenever he was trying to be tactful and curled into fits and sat mid thigh when he wasn't.

"Pearle wants you do write a book about writing *Fractures*. He thinks it'll be a smash."

"What the hell Sods? Why didn't ya let me lay it out for him?"

"Cohen's not stupid, he doesn't need you to do that."

"I never said he was stupid, I just wanted it to be all nice and smooth and you go in with both feet like a paratrooper."

"You were wasting time."

"We've got all day!"

"Cohen's a busy man."

"Yeah, too busy for Sasha Chung!"

They reminded Loeb of his parents back in San Francisco, so he interjected, or else he wouldn't leave till five o'clock. And Sasha Chung wasn't his type, even though they were brainwashing him into thinking so. Her personality was as flat as her stomach, and did he really want to marry an action star who lived in the gym on some crazy diet? Did they ever think about what Loeb wanted? Did they ever ask?

"A book *about* a book?" Loeb asked, clearing his throat after finding it had gone dry. "Isn't that redundant?"

"No!" Pearle nearly bounced on his couch, his flat face alive and appearing somewhat exasperated due to his naturally reddened skin.

"I think we'd risk oversaturation." Sods confessed.

"Timing, gentlemen, timing. Right after season one is done airing we'll do a sixty-five dollar package deal with the DVD. I've already run it by a few department heads and they're nuts over it."

"A *book* book about a book or like a flip-thru DVD kind of a book about a book?" Loeb asked in seeking clarity.

"No, a nice gloss five by eight, like a memoir of what was running through you when lightning struck." Pearle said as Solderman seemed to fade into thought, chewing on something small and infinitesimal in his back teeth, perhaps part of the lime rind of his aperitif. "I mean, you've done so well for your age, you're only twenty-six and you've already got seven books out there, but *Fractures* is an experience, it's the kind of thing that comes along ever so often and people are just waiting to jump into it. Once you give it to them, you have to be ready with more ammunition or else you'll cause a riot. I think this is the best route because you've said up down and sideways you won't do a sequel."

Loeb was quick.

"Season one?"

"Yeah. We just signed a deal for three."

"Three?" Loeb's throaty voice nearly squeaked. "The main characters both die at the end!"

"Prequels." Solderman said, eyes transfixed and meditating on one of the vases, molars still grinding on something invisible.

"Prequels? Why's this the first I've heard of it?"

"Small stuff, Lobster, I didn't want to worry you. Years out, you know, one day at a time."

Loeb frowned and the brightness of the glass and the windows beckoned him and he rose and walked nearly a hundred feet to gawk into the downtown beehive.

Pearle had wound himself up and rambled

about demographics and Solderman corrected him, which was a mistake because even more words rushed from Pearle's mouth about timing and Christmas and somehow a story about golfing with the Governor fell out.

"About my contract," Loeb cut in with some heaviness, "Is there any leeway?"

Pearle stopped dead in his tracks even though he was getting to the funny part about the sand trap on the fifteenth hole. Solderman stopped his aimless grinding nibble and his face became sharp and pointed.

"You're not thinking of leaving us, are you Lobster?"

"That'd be like a kid leaving his own family." Solderman added.

It was true, Solderman and Pearle went to bat for him when he'd dropped out of college and moved to an apartment in Riverside and barricaded himself in his bedroom to write. They'd found a pair of his short stories through a writing competition and knew he was a gold mine if steered the right way. He could write action, but it was action with *heart*.

Four years and some odd months later he stood before them with the pressures of success having constructed a planned forest around him and he was having trouble seeing daylight through its maze. All of his heart had gone into *Fractures*, eschewing his brand, his audience, his publishers.

Kismet.

"No, no, I mean…" Loeb crossed his arms. "If I give you guys another *Fractures*, not the same story but one just as powerful and beautiful and popular, would you let me out of having to do three of those bang bang novels?"

Loeb called them *bang bangs* because they were mindless and just required fingers full of caffeine and reference books on machine guns, exotic locations, and certain scientific technologies. Another pitfall of writing *bang bangs* was the fact that whatever stunning girl Loeb imagined up for the high-octane escapade somehow had a habit of haunting those Hollywood parties, Sasha Chung being the latest incarnation of a long list of beauties Pearle had ushered in to get his most talented writer *off on the right track.*

In the same way that selling and relinquishing control over *Fractures* removed a part of his soul, the writing of his moderately successful *bang bangs* wore him out and made it hard for him to sleep. He craved another *Fractures* and the more he thought about it the further away it became, like it was an angel that visited him as he slept, touched his forehead, and imparted to him a gift he'd never see again.

Fractures was some strange drug the high of which would never leave him.

And then there was Catriona, his muse and constant reminder, his secret crush that was an ever-evolving yin yang of living, *breathing* realities and writerly imaginations.

"What did you have in mind?" Solderman asked before Pearle could say anything. Pearle was kind of a fire hose, full on, abrasive and powerful, clumsy and hard to handle but extremely effective at certain functions.

"I'd like to get out of here for awhile." Loeb found himself saying with a near mumble. "I'd like to go to Alaska."

Solderman said nothing. Pearle's face reacted as if he'd seen a stunt explosion on a movie set.

"What a great idea. I've been there, it'll take your breath away."

"What part of Alaska?" Solderman asked, not yet willing to give up the *bang bangs* he relied on making his trans-Pacific flights bearable. He'd never let it be known he hated *Fractures* and thought it was girly and men shouldn't write such emotional garbage, even though his wife nearly melted with every word and talked his ear off about it every night before they doused the lights.

"South of Anchorage. Some dump with private cabins, the whole bit." Loeb said.

Strokes of genius spread across the redness of Pearle's face as if wiper blades were exaggerating the fact, smearing it.

"Yeah, yeah...with seaplanes and grizzly bears?"

"The whole bit."

"I like it." Solderman nodded, making a hasty business decision, even though he was pouting inside about not getting his *bang bangs* like a boy would lament a lack of dessert after toughing out a dreaded dose of garlic broccoli.

"Yeah," Pearle stood and walked to Loeb at the window. "You're definitely onto something...and I'm trying to think if the market's available..."

"The market's fine." Solderman was bland and sipped at his gin and tonic.

"How long you need?" Pearle rubbed his hands over his tummy and then wound an arm around Loeb. Pearle's arms were tanned and hairy and all of the hairs on his arms had gone gray and wooly.

"I mean," He whispered. "With the breakdown and all..."

It was true, during the writing of *Fractures* Loeb Cohen had suffered a nervous breakdown and had spent a week in the hospital and a few more weeks on sedatives with a fierce order to stay away from caffeine, sugar, and all of his nosy relatives like the plague.

And in that order.

"I'll be okay."

"You got any friends to bring along?" Pearle kept whispering. "Any...you know, companionship? It might help your book out, especially if you write what Sods is always begging for, what *Fractures* actually never had in it, if you catch my drift."

Loeb swallowed and squinted as a fender-bender clogged traffic on the 110, northbound. Pearle was just as subtle as the crunching of car plastic and broken diamonds of glass.

"I don't know." The writer's voice lost some of its resonance, and his breathing was shallow just thinking about it. He was young and somewhat inexperienced in life, but wrote from a place of instinct far beyond his years. In some ways, he wanted to keep those secrets of his young soul free from the world, lest they found that *Fractures* was more of a dream of real love in the bitter analogy of war, oppression, imprisonment, torture and duty rather than the actual, visceral, tangible memoir of such, even though Loeb had written it as the latter.

"I'll tell you what," Solderman stood and waited to say what until he reached the bar and prepared two more drinks. "I'm going to advance you seventy-five thousand for your new book as an Alaskan expense account so you can live the life you need to produce your next work of art and when they come like honey badgers to turn it into a picture or a serial, I won't sleep unless you get at least one million and two percent gross."

Solderman turned and raised his glass, pausing for the other two men to join him.

"All in favor say *Aye*."

There were *ayes* and clinks.

"Oppose no?"

Silence.

"Motion carries."

Solderman took a deep draft and drained his gin and tonic. The corner of his eye caught Loeb's cerulean-iris melancholia, to which he assumed was something other than what it was.

Loeb finished his drink and left with handshakes and a forced smile.

The secretary had gone to lunch and he was free to loaf the hall to the elevator in the tormenting peace of his thoughts.

He was afraid to embrace the love of *Fractures*.

He was afraid to experience it.

Even though it could've made them all rich and cast him a legend in the hearts and minds of American readers, Loeb Cohen was not ready for Alaska.

And he was not going to Alaska without Cat.

There'd be no *Fractures* without Cat. Without Cat he'd be chained to *bang bangs* for all his born days, and in so many ways he couldn't write another *Fractures* till his relationship with Cat progressed or another Cat entered his life.

The elevator was ponderous in its descent to the gray September concrete. Was Loeb Cohen ready to open up to Catriona and tell her he wanted to take her to Alaska, not to unplug from the shoebox of fiction he'd made for himself, but to plug in to a real, rich, living world of human experience?

He had to make a decision. A good night sleep would sort it out.

It always did.

4

Understandings

Loeb mashed the silver button. The bathroom was dingy and carried a fakely fruity effervescence. Warm air worked up the energy to blow the dampness from his hands and he returned to the black and tan floor of the diner, unable to take his usual dark corner booth. It had happened before in times past, but kismet was kind in granting him a seat in Cat's section regardless. This time, however, the time he really needed to speak with her, he found himself across the breadth of the restaurant near the bussing station and the slap-floppy pass-through door to the kitchen. He only saw her in glances and even though it was Thursday, he was going to walk her home. He'd thought about it all night, and the stagnancy of the September heat as it beat Los Angeles to a staggering pulp only further cemented in his mind what needed to be done.

In his restless fury of flipping and tearing up the bed sheets of an uncomfortable queen that was far too big for him and made him feel lost and alone, finality pierced him through and through and when dawn finally broke the window and began to creep across the carpet, he watched it, with heavy eyes, like some strange form of sundial telling him the time had come. The seclusion of sleep stolen simmered all periphery to one simple yes or no question.

Do you love her?

Loeb had already paid and was waiting for her approach and fought excitement when she finally stood at the table in cocked-hip repose, beat from being on her feet since two in the morning.

"Hey tiger." She said, her blue hair fanning like a Roman Centurion's battle helm.

"Are you off?"

"In about five minutes, why?"

She sensed it. He was poor at hiding it.

"I'll walk you home. I've got to talk to you."

"It isn't about Alaska, is it?"

"Five minutes?" Loeb asked, vision going to his coffee cup and back to her brown eyes which had a way of not moving when they wanted to and her lack of eyebrows gave her the poker face of a steel lamppost. The thinness of a smirk slipped between her bracket of upper-lip piercings and spread to fullness after she tapped the table with her left hand to say *okay, tiger* and turned with a pep in the arches of her feet to walk back to the kitchen and ditch her apron.

To hell with Rosemary and her five minutes. Cat wasn't coming back to work the twenty-four hour diner.

Ever.

Loeb was a nervous wreck. It was kind of cute.

It could've only meant one thing in her mind and she latched on to it with eagle talons.

She had her pack of cigarettes in hand and her sweatshirt was over her shoulders like a cape as she met him in the parking lot. She put the pack to her lips and nibbled on the first one to stick to them till it was in the right spot. To her surprise, Loeb had a lighter available.

"Oh…" She said through the side of her teeth. "You taking up smoking?"

"Nah." Loeb chuckled. "I'm taking up lighting cigarettes."

The subtext of the future hung in the air through the click and the dance of flame.

Loeb waited to speak till they had left the ugly twenty-four hour diner parking lot of faded white lines and littered beauty bark and shrubs and the sordid alley behind it that smelled of piss.

"I was thinking about what we talked about yesterday." He said.

"Uh huh…" Cat said after an interminably long wait.

"I…I don't know how to say it."

At the intersection Cat flicked the cigarette end over end and Loeb watched it free fall.

"Just let it out."

Loeb squinted at the oppressive sun and the not-so far off skyscrapers.

"I'm going to Alaska. I want you to come with me."

Cat's face paled and she arched her head back and let the smoke plume as if she was an old-time steam train leaving the station for good.

Then they stared at each other, Cat's brown eyes heavy on Loeb's darting and insecure glances of liquid blue.

A beleaguered honk put movement to their feet and cloth swished between them till they crossed the street and Cat's stride slowed and her hands slipped to the butt pockets of her tight black jeans.

"What if I can't?" She said, hiding her toe-curling glee.

"What do you mean?" Loeb face was rippled with confusion. It was the not response he'd anticipated and was unprepared for anything other than *yes*. It made his long night of weighing thoughts and conversations on scales seem pointless and vain. "I…I guess, let me start over."

Cat suppressed her joy as Loeb began to wind himself up for the pitch.

"I thought about it a lot, and I convinced Pearle and Solderman that I'll move to Alaska for as long as it takes to write them another *Fractures*."

At the very mention of the book she deemed a brazen love letter, Catriona felt coldness run down her spine and Loeb's mouth kept moving.

"Not the same book, but one like it, you know, a literary style, not that drugstore junk where crap blows up and the guy always gets the girl and stuff."

"Uh huh." Was all she said, her feet slowing to some form of crawl as she remembered yesterday's tears.

How much longer could she…

"And Pearle agreed, Alaska was the perfect place, so beautiful, he said he's even been there, not Quill Creek, but you know, Alaska…"

He wanted to take her with him, to write another *Fractures*?

The magnitude of possibility crushed her.

Cat's knees failed to hold her lanky one hundred and ten pounds and she took a smack of grass on the face.

Loeb's hands were quick to hoist her upright and it wasn't until she realized she had actually passed out that the hiding of her feelings toward the young writer whom she was infatuated with and was dead sure was infatuated with her scared her.

The burden of lugging the unanswered around had sabotaged her when things were going so well, it could only get worse.

He needed to know. She needed to know he knew.

She tried to speak. Her mouth was dry.

Even her feet wouldn't help her, where was the spring they'd had in the restaurant after her long shift?

"Cat, you okay?" He looked in her eyes and clarity came to them and she embraced him, tired and dehydrated and light-headed from the nicotine and even more so from the daydreams.

He hugged her back, his hands possessive against the notion of her passing out.

"It must be the heat." She chirped and rubbed her forehead. She was sweating. She brushed her fingers together to rid them of the sweat and jabbed her hand against the thigh of her jeans.

"Listen," Loeb said, sincere as ever in lieu of her wooziness. "I need help. I want to write a good novel. I consider you one of my only friends in the world, *objective* friends, and I'd like you to work for me, as weird as that sounds."

"Work for you?" Cat's eyebrow skin leapt, though she wished she'd said, *weird? No, not weird! Perfect!*

"Yeah, I'd like you to type out whatever I dictate, I think it would help free me of the voices in my head, you know, hearing myself speak the dialogue and the prose and all that. You can tell me if it's crap or not. I mean…you…"

She could sense something deep worming its way out, something older than the moment they were stuck in.

"I what?" She was still a bit dizzy.

Loeb turned and began walking again, walking away from what he could not say because of all that held him back and when she wouldn't follow he returned.

"I wrote *Fractures* for you, okay?" He blurted out. "I wrote it for you, about you, because of you…there'd be no *Fractures* without you."

Then his hands couldn't decide between an apologetic shrug and a *to hell with it* gesture and performed both.

I'm weird. He thought. *I'm twisted. This isn't how normal people are, normal people don't do this. Now she knows what you think about her, all those weird writerly thoughts you think about her, how you make stuff up in your head. You're so stupid, Loeb Cohen, juvenile and foolish. Do you have a glass slipper for her to try on, too? Or better yet, go to the library and check out some non-fiction books. Or even better, go tell Solderman you're sorry, order an extra large pepperoni pizza and a two liter of root beer and lock yourself in your apartment till you can write him a damn good bang bang with a frickin' helicopter chase and missile launchers at the end.*

He turned and pounded the pavement with thick steps until Cat caught up with him and took his face between her hands and kissed him long on the lips with undue yet vindicated fervor, which left them both a bit breathless in the sweltering heat.

Then Cat sat down on the grass of a random citizen's yard just like the one she'd previously plowed into to think about what she'd done.

How brash. How foolish. You can't do that.

But his hands were strong around her arms in

lifting her up.

"I'll take that as a yes."

A smile didn't hesitate rushing across her lips and Cat couldn't restrain herself in kissing him again.

5
North

Cat studied the airplane. The seat reminded
her of an old minivan, squeaky and plush in a dusty
way, dark blue to match the carpet. A stuffy tube of
plastic, grating and groaning with the terrible gnaw
of the engines, the Boeing 737 was something to
forget yet be thankful for all in the same stale
breath. It was only her second time in the air, the
first had been a one-way ticket to Los Angeles,
milliena ago, and now, the second was a one-way
back to the land of her birth.

Loeb was two rows ahead of her and on the
opposite side of the plane, and she could see him in
her bright window seat, but her could not see her.

The nervous energy of their new romance was
weaving its way through her thin body and every
time their eyes met it was like a cooling breeze,
stilling what had a habit of working itself into a hot
frenzy.

Leaving her roommates had been a thrill and
the joy of it was simply telling them she'd never see
them again and paying an advance of her month's
rent. She had few possessions and stuffed her
newest clothes and her favorite book in a backpack.

Rhonda was furious. Who would do the

cooking? Tam Phan cried. They never got to talk
after that one time she'd blown up on Cat about the
pressures of school and a large family. Kris waved
but didn't take her eyes from the TV. She was glued
to the season finale of a show she'd been binge-
watching.

What a relief.

And having taken to the air, Cat was now
soaring north into a brand new world.

Loeb said they'd get everything they needed
in Alaska and Cat wouldn't have to ask any
questions. He said it'd be simpler for both of them
that way, and in many regards they'd be living part
of the fantasy that would create the book.

Catriona sat by herself in the window seat
with only the piercing clouds to shine back at the
breadth of her uncontrollable smiling. It was a rare
nonstop flight from LAX to Anchorage, and Cat
pulled *Fractures* from her backpack, old and ragged
as it was.

*The leather belt would snap as it slapped her
skin. She wouldn't scream.* She read, vibrant color
refusing to leave her face despite the horrors of the
text.

Love had made itself known and brought
satisfaction to passages where, at one time, each and
every word sagged with the heavy burden of a cloud
aching to unleash torrents of rain.

The storm had passed, and now there was
freedom. In memorandum it didn't seem as long
and hard as she'd made it, the journey to finally be
desired by a man, but that was the nature of the
moment and the slow ticking of the clock as life
dripped and dripped its dreary rain-gutter dance.

*Give us the names of your contacts, you Spy,
the guards would spit in broken English as one of*

the SS men would sit and watch with crossed legs,
the light of a candle dancing across the shine of his
calf skin boots. Do you want to die a horrible death,
alone and afraid? Tell us and your pain will end!
Tell us, they begged, as leather snapped and sliced
the air. Tell us!

No, she didn't, and as long as he consumed
her thoughts, she wouldn't. It was only in
relinquishing her hopes of returning to his arms
that she would die, and though the cross-legged SS
man was determined to know her secrets her love
was a secret no one could comprehend but her love
himself.

Catriona shut the book and nodded off and
was awoken hours later by the vibrating rumble of
turbulence, and with it, the whimpering murmur of
a woman across the aisle from her.

"Hold me," She said, in a hairless dog's
shiver. "Hold me Robert."

Cat took in the scene with veiled disgust as a
frail woman who couldnt've been five years older
than her was boxed in and shattered in her crisp
slacks, flats, and cardigan. Trembles and shakes
rushed through her like electric currents.

"Hold me, Robert."

"It's okay darling." Robert said, who was a
grave-faced man with a vampire's angled widow's
peak hairline of black stubs. He simply placed a
cold fish hand on her shoulder and went back to the
lap tray and the papers spread on it.

"Take one of your pills, darling." He said, and
the physical strain of her reaching below her seat to
get said medication hurt Cat's waitressing instinct.
Cat was always reaching out in assistance as a
reaction and with the space of the empty seats and
the aisle between them, she could do nothing but

watch.

The turbulence, which wasn't more than a jiggle in the Boeing 737 subsided and the woman's breathing slowed from near hyperventilation.

"What are you doing?" She asked Robert, and Cat, now beginning to eavesdrop, caught an air of worship, as if he were out of her league and she was damn lucky to even be sitting by his side.

"Just…writing out some scales." His voice was bored, lowering whatever musical genius took residence inside of him to do so. He had drooping ears and a pointy nose.

"You're so talented." She said, and eased into his shoulder under the effects of the anti-anxiety medication until the food cart came along and both of them pestered the flight attendant for soymilk.

"Can I get you anything, ma'am?" The flight attendant asked Cat. She was a striking Asian woman and had a kind demeanor though Cat could tell the couple's demands for soymilk had been upsetting for her. They simply had none on board and the couple was talking of filing a complaint with the airline. Robert had forced his number one fan to write down the flight attendant's name on a notepad she had to dig in her purse for, even when he was holding a pen and a mess of musical notation paper.

"Yes, would it be possible for you to give the man two rows up from me on the end, the one with really pretty blue eyes, a turkey sandwich with this note."

The note was simple, a one-sided yellow sticky that said *I ♥ U.*

The flight attendant smiled and continued her work as Cat's face was becoming infectious. The woman in the cardigan gazed at her.

"What are you reading?" She asked as her hand gestured between herself and the maestro. "We're both teachers."

"You're a teacher." Robert said. "I'm an *instructor*. There's a difference."

Cat swallowed hard and fought certain revulsion. It was as if the man named Robert only cemented the fact that Loeb was one in a million, a very rare breed in the arts, the cornerstone of an ever-shrinking demographic.

"*Fractures* by Loeb Cohen." Cat said with great relish, not only from loving the work, but knowing the author, and the not so small point about being the sole subject of the piece.

"Oh, I *loved* that book." The woman laid a brittle set of fingers over her heart.

"What garbage." The man said. "Filth. I'm sick of people talking about books like that…"

The woman batted her eyes to the carpet runners and leaned as far as she could across the aisle.

"Did you hear it's coming to television?"

"I'd rather watch one of those reality shows." Robert's words were aimless as his pen worked through the Lydian scale, cogitating if Lydian contained a sharped fourth or diminished fifth.

Cat's molars ground at the thought of the obnoxious sort of *entertainment* her roommate Kris favored and the snack food consumption that accompanied it to the painfully stark yet dreamlike potential of a visual interpretation of *Fractures*. As much as Loeb griped about it not being what he saw in *the movies of his mind*, as he called them, which he then further stated were always shot in 35mm, she was very much looking forward to it.

The thought rushed through her to point two

seats in front of her and say to the woman *there he is, there's the author!* But she only nodded and knew that by the time the flight attendant carried out her simple request, Loeb would be experiencing that tender and hope-giving secret she'd just read about.

But only a handful of feet away, Loeb sat in his seat with the stiffness of a dog catching a whiff of trouble in the air. New love's fuzzies couldnt've been further from him.

He'd run a few Internet searches on Quill Creek, Alaska, and found it not only to be a breathtaking display of pristine green angles dramatically crashing straight into the sea, but the site of one of Alaska's most notable unsolved murders.

All through his quick fire of clicks and key hammers, he'd kept his posture rigid and tried to hide the small computer screen from Cat by twisting to his right and was developing a pain in his back by doing so.

He'd promised her he wanted to get a fresh, *virginal* experience with Alaska, how it would help the book, how it would help their relationship. It would be like skydiving, knowing jack nothing about the place and falling, literally from the clouds, into its arms and words would form from whatever life threw their way at the continent's northern edge.

But thoughts of their togetherness and the summer warmth of a new romance's proximity and the strange honeymoon it had the potential to be were dissipating as if caught in the smoke of one of Cat's Marlboro Gold's and blown by a cruel sea breeze.

Loeb clicked and clicked and his eyes sucked

and slurped up the information he saw with a straw.

It was the book, the new one, this unsolved murder, the one that would make *Fractuers* look like child's play, not that his genuine affection for Catriona and the muse that she was would've been a bad book, just that, each and every image, steeped in moody mists and frosty white blankets spoke to him in a nearly transcendental language far beyond Cat's initial pull three years ago.

The scope of it, the haunting chill of entering a realm sealed-off from the world and frozen in time.

It crept around his shoulders and pressed him further into his squeaky seat, phantom fingers that dug into the base of his skull and planted little ideas about a quaint seaside town and the devil's evil that it hid.

Granite peaks and trees and wild animals, men with guns and the broad and haunted spaces of evergreen trunks and fallen limbs, bandied and broken by the burden of what blood had been spilled twenty-three years ago.

The hours passed. He didn't look at the sandwich nestled up against his computer and the sweet sticky note beneath it, he didn't even remember whatever perfunctory words'd flown from his mouth at the flight attendant's gracious offering of such.

His mind was consumed with murder, rapt by the fact that Quill Creek was a stunning catacomb of secrets, a vault of the undisclosed as God had pressed two fingers into the earth to run a jut of frozen water up into the mountains.

Then, he saw the picture-the black and white of Sarah Enos the summer before her untimely death.

His breath left his body and the blood along his spine ran cold.

She was the most beautiful woman he'd ever seen and she captured him, from the grave, with the endless penetration of her eyes.

6
Anchorage

The airport was congested. Cat, wide-eyed at everything and anything, stuck close to Loeb because he knew what to do and more than that, he was her only security in this new world she'd so often fantasized about. Now that it was here, in front of her, jostling her thinness with elbows and ripping across the tops of her sneakers with the dirty wheels of rollaways and luggage carts, she sunk within the blue-helmed shell of her urban armor. Eyes of judgment were cast her way and seared her California-sunned skin, and even though she'd drawn her first breath on planet earth in a hospital not too far away from the airport, the citizens of Anchorage were making her feel she as though she were an unwanted foreigner. It was a cage of half-covered coughs and *excuse me's* and the waft of traveller's perfumes and food court deep fry that further submerged her into isolation as Loeb was ever so busy with the necessities of travel.

Unwanted…

How had long the weights of government-assigned adoption been strapped to her ankles? Twenty-two years, at least! It was a spiritual depravity, that condition of knowing one's parents weren't really one's parents and growing up the physical differences only ever drove the stake further down. Loeb Cohen had saved her from it all three years ago when he'd immediately taken an interest to her and now there was fruit.

Living, breathing, *organic* produce.

She moved to hold his hand as he secured a rental car, and he squeezed back but was preoccupied and looked past her with a busy face and she took it in and drifted. Her eyes noted all of the clocks as they symmetrically stuck to their spots on the walls and she wondered of lovers caught in different time zones, thrown into the spin cycle of life's washing machines and plastic repetitions of fate's rodent wheels.

Ted Stevens Anchorage International was one of the busiest airports in the world, most of the flights being pan-pacific cargo runs, and the buzz of the place was humming at an entirely different frequency than Los Angeles but still, far from relaxing.

Cat held onto her desire for a true, *quiet* moment, and what thanks he'd get for asking her to come with him, away from the sun and sand and empty lies of SoCal.

They'd both been in such a whirlwind, and now that it was Wednesday again, Cat was ready to slow down.

"Cat?"

She turned as Loeb approached her in some juggle of papers, envelopes and all the necessities that were in the end, needless wastes of time designed to stress travellers.

"Yeah?"

"Hold these."

She could see her presence would be a

blessing to Loeb. He may've been a master with words but it was hard for her to watch him struggle with the mess of documents he'd amassed in such a short time. Obviously, some of them were obtained before the trip for their future destination of Quill Creek, papers produced from the supposedly simplified processes of the Internet and his publisher's offices, and it was all she could do to stop herself from taking them and organizing them with her waitresses' acumen.

The papers wouldn't stop their unnerving slides and attempts to leap to the gloss buffing of the floor. She watched him fail under the burdens he'd placed on himself to handle everything and his cache of documents spilled to the floor, his rental keys and computer bag somehow leapfrogging the jailbreak of his grasp.

Harsh eyes and muffled comments assailed them, frustrations on their hogging of a central causeway with their foolish ineptitudes, and that girl with the blue hair, who invited her? Why didn't she go back to LA, Seattle, or Portland, wherever freaks like her came from?

"Baby, take it easy." She said and placed her hand on his. "I'll take the papers. You drive."

She gave him the keys that had skidded across the floor and been kicked by several clumsy pairs of feet and ended up coming back to the stability of her own sneakers.

Her face was soft with understanding about what he was trying to do and said that he didn't have to work so hard.

It was all good.

They were here. They'd made it. The novel would write itself and she was ready to take it slow. She was gone from Los Angeles and hoped to never see it again. Each minute was breaking the newborn dawn of a past life that had lived a survivalist existence in shadowed hibernation.

It's okay. Her eyes said. *Trust me.*

Loeb swallowed hard and stood to twist away the jab of pain lumped in the middle of his back, unduly placed there by his four-hour stint on the computer and the all consuming but unfulfilling research of the murder. He felt he hadn't even scratched the surface and it was running a holding pattern in the back of his brain, stealing from what processing power was needed to deal with all of the extemporaneous nonsense necessary to travel and uproot one's life from one place and plop it into another. His eyes were a bit blurry and he didn't want her to know about the mystery, yet.

He had to find a way to tell her. The right way, perhaps their first *quiet* moment.

Catriona's unicolor eyes were on him, gazing through him and his blender of reasonings with an expressionless desire.

Why is she looking at me like that? Is she thinking of a quiet moment, too?

Change the subject, Loeb, change the subject. She won't stop looking at you like that till you change the subject.

"Are you going to miss LA?" He asked, gathering up his things and pressing into the traffic of human bodies and their mouth-breathing efforts to catch connections to small bush airstrips as the seasons dwindled in September's final kick of bearable temperatures.

"Not a bit." Cat snarled her trademark smile, and it wasn't until they bunched in a small and nearly free to rent Toyota Prius to see the golden brown skyline of Anchorage glint and dapple off the

glassy waters of Cook Inlet as the soaring white and
blue knuckles of the Chugach Mountains observed,
with their ancient grandeur, from behind, that
Catriona knew in the very foundation of her
fractured heart she'd finally returned home.

7
Quill Creek

It was the end of the road. The Toyota Prius had passed nearly a hundred miles of stunning vistas too surreal for a writer who spent most of his time indoors to fathom. He could sense the magnetic and gravitational energies of the icy ranges and their massive, sky-skimming endlessness as they framed every angle that was not sea-facing, and caught in between the cold, wet horizon of the Pacific that he thought he knew so well being a Californian and the indomitable shoulders of Alaska's ancient mountain spines and shoulders, was the somnolent fishing village of Quill Creek.

It was hidden and cloistered from the highway exit in congested knots of drooping, dreary evergreens. The three o'clock sun was barely pushing the mercury above forty and Loeb urged the gimpy Prius across the town's long and uneven line of colorful yet faded wood structure facades as they seemed to stare out into the clustered marina of cheap boats bobbing in the dark and frigid wet as if they were a negligible hand in life's game of poker. In light of Anchorage's mess of desperate vacationers eager to get their frontier kicks in before the temperatures became deadly, Quill Creek was either hibernating or just plain vacant.

Other than a huddle of jeeps and pickup trucks in the town square, making itself known by tall flagpoles flapping country and state flags in the dingle dangling breeze, Loeb could see no signs of human existence.

Loeb circled the town square and the bulk of its offerings twice.

It didn't take more than ten minutes.

The town center was a rusty red and white trim three-story building linked to other one and two story jobs, all of which gave him the flavor of a gold-rush town, even though the plainness of coastal fishing villages from Alaska to Nova Scotia to the Baltic and back always held a certain similitude, and the general interpretation that Quill Creek was just another forgettable nowhere gave Loeb a great deal of satisfaction.

Though it couldnt've been further from the truth.

Catriona was silent, and seemed to slip lower in the seat as Loeb's eyes explored from the relative comfort and seatbelted safety of the Prius, taking in every single detail as she knew only a true writer could.

What did he think when he saw the garish half-painted wood carvings outside of King Minos' Wood Shop, blocky statues of gap-toothed sailors, cartoonishly fat moose in mid bray and pelt-garbed woodsmen with muzzleloaders that no one would ever *dream* of purchasing?

Or what about the rag tag allotment of tickey tack stores and trinket treasure troves trying to cop a feel for those stray interlopers from the State Parks who'd swung in for a simple meal, who'd come by sea plane, or who'd booked a whale watching tour somewhere else along the coast?

Cat had her chin buried in the top of her dark gray sweatshirt and was playing with the zipper as if it were a teething biscuit, aimlessly nibbling and thinking.

It was the same as she remembered it, in so many ways, though memory was often a lie.

"Some place." Loeb said as the main drag appropriately named *Shore Road* stretched free of civilization, and they continued on Shore Road as it wound and wrapped along the coast. The Prius ambled past the private drives of idyllically secluded dwellings, sandwiched in stilling silence between the spicy sap of firs and pines and the splash and lap of sea salt, gray beach rocks large enough to hurt oneself on and cloudy arctic water.

Cat would have to tell him soon. The atmosphere of the place was unearthly, unreasonably motionless, so much different than Los Angeles in every possible way. It was so quiet she could hear the faintest ringing in her ears, perhaps a side effect from her self-prescribed medication to combat Kris and the TV. It then occurred to Cat she hadn't listened to her beloved heavy metal since that Wednesday with Loeb and she didn't miss it, though throughout high school she'd been labeled a music freak and so many grown-ups had said she'd be deaf by the time she was their age.

She loved music. She would never stop loving it.

Cat sat up as Shore Road made a Y and Loeb veered from it to explore inland. He'd taken the path to the old abandoned mine and as the road rose in height it gave her the uneasy sinking sensation of getting ready to crest a rollercoaster.

She was back.

I guess there's no leaving Quill Creek, she thought. *Not now, not ever. It was my idea, he fell for it, now we're here, together.*

She was beginning to feel sick in a breathless way and cracked the window. Loeb's head snapped to his right at the sucking sounds of the chilly wind and he promptly fiddled with the thermostat.

"Rentals are always stuffy." He said and drove a few miles an hour slower.

Cat stared, eyes glazed in the curve of the window as the thick fortress of forest and nostalgia rippled and reflected before her distant face.

A disconcerting voice chided within.

It's what you want, isn't it, Cat? You want him to love you, don't you? You wanted him to take you away from LA and now that you know how crazy he is about you you could've chosen anywhere in the world but you chose Quill Creek.

You chose.

Welcome back.

Welcome home.

Silence hung in the air, cut by the mechanical rhythm of the car groaning up and wheezing down the low rolling hills of the forest. Loeb checked his destination address once more and resigned to the fact that addresses didn't mean the same thing in Quill Creek as they did in and amongst the lower intestines of Los Angeles.

Do you want to be in love or do you want the truth, Cat? Decide. You can't have both.

Loeb's ready for one or the other.

It's up to you.

Cat sat up in childlike wonder as Loeb began to make sense of the hooking and winding streaks of unused gray pavement and initiated their final approach.

The cabin, if it had to be called that for quaintness' sake, though it was more of a lodge it was so palatial, was a muscular feat of wood, stone, and glass on the steep angle of a sheer dirt and needle-covered slope. The ashen gray river rock entrance was subdued on behalf of the structure's surrounding body, and from the circular drive appeared to be a nice little place tucked in the woods, when in actuality it was a mansion of three stories, each with cathedral cedar-panel ceilings and gratuitous coastal views; far too many rooms, too many entrances and too many places to sit for two people.

After the car had been put to rest, the forest diffused the shutting of the car doors and Loeb whirled a slow three-sixty as he digested the fairy tale he was standing in the midst of.

His lungs filled with the dispelling cool of a new climate, a new time zone.

A new life.

His spin ended to face Cat, who was bracing crossed elbows on the hood of the Prius, her face buried in the sleeves of her sweatshirt and her brown eyes were rimmed with pleasure.

"Isn't it something?" He said.

"Feels like home." Cat said and her snarl was strong and steely as she walked around the hood to lean into open arms.

He hugged her good and sighed, rubbing her back and inhaling the tranquility. His back pocket held the keys to their new home. Because of Cat's help, all of the papers were organized and stacked in the back seat. He could breathe now, and was quickly forgetting the stress of the airport.

"It's not a bad setting for a book, huh?"

"Not bad?" She pecked his lips. "It's perfect. Like you."

The building's insides were warm, expansive and refined; what wasn't stained or clear-coated cedar was gray or tawny stone. The rest was glass.

It was clean to the eye, ripe for inspiration's quick and cutting sense of right and wrong.

The focus was the obvious view, and it poked out over the rocky shore through a parted bracket of prickly green to see the sea and the razor-carved lines of dry land in the distance as they jabbed back into the water.

It was fully furnished, geared for comfort and Cat took a few minutes in the kitchen, whistling to herself as her hands slid over the stainless-steel double ovens and granite countertops. The kitchen was larger than her bedroom in Los Angeles.

She wanted to smile like she'd never smiled before, throw her hands out wide and scream about how magnificent it all was.

But Quill Creek the portal of a dark and lurid world, the memories of which were saturated in the frosty buckets of an October night where the moon and all the stars in heaven had failed to shine down on Sarah Enos and the bastard that'd stabbed her to death twenty-three years ago.

"I'll be going back into Anchorage for some heavy-duty shopping, would you like to come?" Loeb said as clip clopping city shoes ushered him into the hollow spread of the kitchen and the open subdivisions of the up-stepped sea-facing alcove dining space and below it and behind it the depression of the forest-view sitting room and the massive fireplace that dominated it.

"No, but..." Cat said, running her bottom lip over her top. "You must be getting hungry by now.

A turkey sandwich'll only last a man so long."

She braced her hands on the countertop. Her demeanor was suggestive.

"What sandwich?" Loeb said as he passed her and didn't see her face fall.

"You didn't eat on the plane?" Cat watched him walk over to the fireplace and imagine himself leaning against it, dictating perfect poetry and prose while a nearby Cat huffed and puffed on a Marlboro Gold and typed with flourishes as if she were a concert pianist.

"No."

"Oh…" Cat stowed thoughts that were negative and accusatory. "Well, then I'll make you something nice for when you get back."

Loeb's stable face was alive as he walked to the door.

"And I'll make sure to get *you* something nice for when I get back."

He waved and she waved though he was already out by the time her hand flew up to reciprocate and the reverberation of the door's shutting rang through the emptiness of the private retreat and hit her in the flatness of her chest.

Her lips were drawn into a sullen line.

What was he doing on the plane that he didn't get the sandwich and my note?

I didn't hear him talking to anyone. I don't think he slept.

Her mind nibbled at the possibility, a fish observing an angler's bait as it bobbled along the surface where light and sound played tricks.

Was he…

No, he would've told me if he found out about the murder, it would've flown from his mouth like every other time at the diner when he'd rush in the door and tell me about his next project.

Let it go, Cat, let it go.

*Or just ask him when he comes back! Look
him straight in the eye and ask him!*

*No, don't. Don't think about it. The
opportunity will come.*

*But will he know you want him to help you
solve Sarah's murder? Does he know you're
playing both sides for the middle?*

*Which one's more important to you, Cat?
Love or truth?*

*God knows you've waited a hell of a long time
for both.*

Cat opened all of the food-filled cupboards
and took stock of the expensive cookware. She
would make him the best meal he'd ever eaten, but
her initial hopes of it being a night of romance were
backwashed and drowned with the frost-bitten tide
of Quill Creek's secrets and if Loeb Cohen knew
about the murder of Sarah Enos and had spent the
bulk of the five hour flight researching it then he
would soon have to know that Catriona was
inextricably entangled in Quill Creek and its
murderous secret and her reasons for suggesting the
place to the young, thumbtack-minded writer were
not as altruistic as he may've suspected.

Though she wanted to be his muse and typist,
to let his next novel capture the hearts of hopeless
romantics as they lived the fantasy of a lover's
escape from Los Angeles' dungeons and dragons of
commerce and humanity, she knew the pull of Quill
Creek and the rapturous woman who'd breathed her
last breaths that cursed October night was far too
strong to resist.

Cat reached in her right hip pocket for her
pack of cigarettes and lit one up as the Prius

wheeled away and the heavy foliage stole the shine of its red brake lights.

"I didn't forget you, Sarah." She said, and she stuck the cigarette in the corner of her mouth and began to cook, the smoke of it carrying up silent prayers that begged for truth and justice in a town that had, itself, twenty-three long and arduous years ago, truly died.

8
Ninth Life

Loeb returned four hours later. In that time, Cat had cooked up a storm in a somewhat unconscious manner and had given herself to the cathartic process, uncertainties and all.

Chilly air pressed through the door as Loeb swept in with an unbalanced stagger, fists full of unruly shopping bags which plonked themselves on the hardwood floor at the smells of Cat's food smacking him in the nose; garlic and toasted flour, the butter and sugar of cookies and something spicy and herbed all wrapped together to let him know just how hungry he was.

"Dear Lord." He said. "I must've died and gone to heaven."

Sixty some odd feet away, Cat snarled.

"Welcome back. Need any help?"

"No," Loeb pushed the bags away from the door with his foot. "But I should've let you know when I was coming back. I'll get one of those pay as you go phones for each of us."

"Nah." Cat lifted a paper towel hiding a fresh baked loaf of bread and began to slice. "You're here. I'm here. Besides, it's Alaska. Not LA. The town's only one street long and the street's longer than the town."

Loeb chuckled and said he'd be back and rushed out to get more bags. He must've spent thousands of dollars and Cat could only wonder at what Loeb had purchased for her.

The thought curled her lips.

Unable to neglect feelings of the best of holiday memories, few and far between though they were, Cat served Loeb proudly and they both faced the darkness of the window as the shore splashed with a hushed crash and flow of cold waters below their elevated palace of wood, glass and stone.

"This is amazing." Loeb said as he ate the soup she'd prepared with a great deal of care, verdant and chunky peas and lentils all blended up and subtly spiced. "All this stuff was in the pantry?"

"And the freezer." Cat relished buttering a thick piece of chewy fresh-baked bread. She could tell he was looking forward to the cookies.

"How'd you get..."

"Butter." She cut him off, chewing and smiling. "Lots of butter."

He smirked at her.

"You eat butter?"

"I smoke." She said, carefree. "I'm a study in balance."

"Speaking of study, I was reading some interesting facts about Quill Creek."

"Oh really?" Cat's face fought a glower and her lack of eyebrows assisted her, even though the more time she spent with Loeb the more she felt in tune with his thoughts and vice versa.

"Yes, it seems Quill Creek has fallen under the spell of an unsolved murder."

Cat's teeth ground the food in her mouth slowly as Loeb's dreary and thoughtful dictation rumbled in his chest. She'd been down this road with him before, holding a sloshy coffee pot or blank order pad and ball-point pen, enjoying his disordered spiel of potential characters, outlandish ideas, and semi-self-deprecating jokes about *the craft* and his butchery of it to make new bang bangs.

But this time, it was different. Old wounds. She didn't want to hear it. She wasn't ready.

Dammit, Cat, get over it! Right now! He knows and you've got to tell him all you know! Do you want the truth or not! He deserves it! He's here because of you!

If you love him then tell him. You don't love him if you won't tell him.

You have to let someone in at some point, Cat, you can't be alone all your life.

If he's already in then don't push him out.

"I know." She found herself saying.

"Oh really?"

Cat swallowed hard and then drained her glass of red wine and wiped her mouth with the skin of her arm. She wore a gray cap sleeve t-shirt in the coziness and her neck became hooked and bent. Before cooking she'd removed all of the rings on her right hand and her only adornment was a simple gold necklace Loeb never saw more than the chain of, though she always wore it, stuffed down in her shirt close to her skin.

"You're talking about Sarah Enos, aren't you?"

Perplexity framed Loeb's stable and symmetrical face and its artistic roof of very dark hair.

"You know?"

"God…" Cat pushed her food aside and fell to

the table, banging her head against her bony forearms.

"What, what is it?" Loeb nearly begged with concern. Cat held her left hand out, to still him, silence him, *stay back.*

Loeb finished his own wine and would have to wait for seconds on a bowl pea soup. His mind was a scatter of possibility.

When Cat finally did speak, it was in a mumble through the skin of her forearms as the deep-seeded darkness of the window cast before her the shadows of evening long since fallen and the cold and cruel emptiness of memory.

"Since you're the kind of guy that likes a good story I'll go back to the beginning." She said. Her cigarettes and lighter were in front of her but she refused them. She'd unearthed them from her tight black jeans but would not touch them.

"Should I be writing this down?"

She didn't bother.

"My father was a Russian Jew by the name of Shmuel Enovsky. He had a sister. Her name was Sarai. Shmuel and Sarai. Inseparable." Cat's face was glazed, as if she'd repeated the story a thousand times before and Loeb was sucked into her expressionless mask and the drone spilling from its trance. "They left Russia in the mid seventies, at a young enough age to remember how hard it was to be a Jew, and yet, in coming to Alaska in the same manner a Cuban would seek asylum in Miami, they faced judgment of a different kind. They may've been Jews but to Americans, they were Russian. So as they grew up and learned to adapt in the brave new world their parents had chosen for them, parents that stayed in Russia and died in poverty; they changed their names, lost their accents, and decided they would one day marry Americans and raise American children, becoming American citizens as the result of their political asylum. Or that was the plan, stillborn in its execution, I guess…"

Cat sat up, stiffened her back, and laid her right hand on the cigarette pack but still gazed into the deep space ink of the window and whatever specters of shoreline shapes it contained as the tides slipped and slid across the bony lumps of rocks and pebbles.

"I was born in 1989 in Anchorage, Alaska, Catriona Enos, no middle name, none needed, to Sam and Gloria Enos. Shmuel Enovsky didn't exist. He was now Sam. Sam Enos. He owned a restaurant near the waterfront and he made soup to die for. He married a nice young waitress there, Gloria. They were beloved, life was good…or so I tell myself, if anything to give a heart to the newspaper articles I had to track down a dozen years later. I don't remember him. I don't remember mom. I don't remember much."

Cat's nostrils flared and it made sense to Loeb in that fraction of a moment why she exhaled smoke through her nose.

Pain. Release. Habit.

Repeat.

Cat stifled her emotions and slowly began crushing the pack of cigarettes in her right hand as her left brushed the space beneath her monochrome brown eyes with two-fingered swipes.

"But I remember *her*…I remember her as if she were still alive."

"Sarah?" Loeb was almost afraid to speak.

"Yeah. *Sarah*. But she wasn't *Sarah* to me. I don't remember what I called her. I was two, you know…she just…*was*." Cat craned her neck for the ceiling to take her mind off all of it but with the food and the nearness of Loeb it was as if she was skinny-dipping her thin body into an ice-cold swimming pool one inch at a time and had nearly overcome the uncomfortable, sensitive bits.

"I saw her picture…" Loeb poured himself more wine and hesitated before pouring Cat half a glass as well, which she didn't refuse but didn't drink.

"She was something, wasn't she?" Cat smiled, blurry eyed, and Loeb gave her the fullness of his concentration, glad that she'd finally made eye contact and showed a spark of levity, if only a spark. Then she asked, "You can't see it, can you, the similarity?"

"You're both beautiful." Loeb said with all seriousness, but the twist of Cat's neck chided, as to say *come on…*

Perhaps the genetic division was in Cat's expression of pain and protection of that little girl whose life changed so drastically without her permission twenty-three years ago. With her hedgehog of blue hair and shaved eyebrows, symmetrical upper lip piercings and suntanned thinness she was nearly as far from the heart-shaped face and platinum shoulder length hair of her aunt as she could possibly be. And the purity protecting the precision of Sarah's bones and clarifying the milk of her Russian skin, as if she was an angel dipping her ankles in a hidden forest lake in some long-forgotten Nordic fairy tale, was nowhere near Cat's provocative *leave me alone* package that no one knew what beauty slept beneath the jacket of.

Except Loeb.

In their femininity, warm and desirable to any

man seeking the honest stability of a life mate and
the promise of a mother, he saw similarity; a
sweetness that demanded closeness, a gentleness
and compassion that one must've been born with
like a genetic defect because it was so rare.

Only Sarah's was unreasonably obvious in
that fact that it was impossible to hide, especially in
the newspaper photo, a black and white shot of her
face and nothing but her face that rang out with an
unending string of words as only a picture could,
crying, still to this day, *my murder was unjust!*

Cat's eyes were heavy on the wine and its
bloody color and her left hand inched toward it.

"To me," She said. "Sarah was my mother.
She was all I remember. She had the most amazing
eyes, blue and green and gold all together,
like...like God just decided to get out a brush and a
palate and go to town for his own personal
enjoyment."

"What happened to your parents?" Loeb asked
courageously, not understanding why she couldn't
remember them and cursing himself for never
asking her about her family for the *three years* he'd
known her.

Three years!

*You're a selfish bastard, Loeb Cohen. If you
didn't talk about yourself and that little world that
lives between your ears so much you'd be a lot
further down the road, don't you think?*

Bastard...

Cat took a nervous sip of the wine and then
another, longer draught so that it was nearly
finished.

"Mom and Dad both died in a bush plane
crash in the interior in April of '91. It was their
anniversary...an accident. Sarah was made my legal

guardian. She died in October." Cat drank again and
then shrugged. "It's one of those things. God knows
how I got sent to California and however many
foster homes have handled me...my driver's license
says Catriona Patrick but I go by Cat, because I had
a life, and a home, and a family, then life made me
a stray and someone new took me in."

It was then Cat smoked, one of the few
uncrushed cigarettes sticking to her lips as she put
the pack to her mouth and the cigarette passed back
and forth over the flame in some strange dance.

"So there you have it." Her cheeks hollowed
to inhale. "I'm on my ninth life now."

Loeb's squint was stinging and while pity was
as far from his heart as Cat wanted it to be, his face
was twisted as if full of it.

"I don't know what to say."

"Don't say anything." Smoke billowed from
her nose. "I baited you in to coming here...some
sadomasochistic exorcism."

Cat stood and stretched, arching her back and
walked away from the table and the dark void of
reflection the window had become. She took up
residence in a high-back chair ideally placed for a
nighttime reader beside the dormant fireplace,
across from which and perpendicular to the
fireplace was a squishy black leather couch.

Loeb left her wine at the table and followed
with hesitant steps.

"What do you mean by that?"

"You're the writer." She quipped, laughing
and coughing in a few breaths before sucking on her
cigarette again and flipping her legs over the side of
the chair and nestling into the lazy lounge of
someone who was spent and exhausted.

Loeb sat across from her on the couch.

"I'm sorry." He said. "Life's a bitch."

"It's okay…I'm here with you. That's what I wanted, you know…I never knew you'd written *Fractures* for me…*to* me. I'd always hoped, you know, in the way a young girl hopes one day a man'll love her and never leave her…but I wanted to *know*…I wanted to feel it like they do in the movies. But…I've just hopped around so much and adapted that my survival instinct was always taking over. If I could go back to those talks we had in the diner, *knowing* you had feelings for me, I would've been a lot different. I would've been freer…happier. I wouldnt've tried so hard." Cat shrugged and dragged. "That's the way of it, I guess…but that Wednesday, God, feels like ages ago even though it was only a week…that Wednesday you walked me home and I sat on my bed and read your book, I knew. I actually *knew*. I thought coming to Alaska would be perfect. We'd live on a cloud. Then I'd be able to open up about my life, like the winter melting the spring, and you'd get your book. You'd get love and redemption, you'd get pain and beauty, the real thing…I'd just melt like an iceberg and you'd catch me and filter through it all; keeping the good and tossing the bad."

Cat pressed herself from the chair and flicked the cigarette into the fireplace and walked to where he sat, darkening his face.

"But now, by God, you're gonna use everything you've got up in that computer brain of yours and we're gonna find who killed Sarah and why. Her blood still stains the dirt of this God-forsaken place and I'll be dammed if I sit up here in this palace begging for some Cinderella fantasy while injustice covers this town like a hangman's shroud. I can taste it, Loeb, it's like gravity here.

It's so damn heavy."

Her left hand rose without hesitation and ran with spread fingers through his dark hair; flattening, curling, *feeling* and stroking it to return to his chin and for a lingering cup and a prying gaze into his eyes that he didn't look away from.

Her touch was soaked with invitation.

Make me forget, the tips of her fingers urged and the bittersweet hints and breaths of tobacco on her skin were vespers of such.

Then she walked off to the darkness of the downstairs master bedroom where there was no window and shut the door, giving him the unspoken option to follow if he so desired.

But Loeb sat and digested for a few minutes before busying his hands with the dinner clean up and the organizing of his many purchases, some of which he set in the hall near the door to Cat's master and refused the magnetic force that told him to rush in.

Hours passed as night grew colder and darker and the same simple conflict knocked itself back and forth between his ears.

Quill Creek had presented him with Catriona and her two faces.

Murder and love.

And he could only indulge in one or the other. They would not mix. They were the Taoist symbol, that swirl of energies diametrically opposed to each other in every possible way.

The killing of Sarah Enos was sitting as plain as the masts and motors of the marina, waiting for him to dive into its depths and discover its flaws and contradictions; to run its rabbit trails with his own Iditarod sled, driven by the dogs of research, analysis, and time consuming patience.

And Catriona, his muse, his delight; a woman that was his secret to the world-a woman whose desire to love a man of depth and devotion sat full and heavy in the core of her belly like wet sponge aching with a full soaking of water.

Loeb cursed himself.

With the light of the morning sun he would decide which would possess his soul.

9

The Russian

Loeb sipped his coffee. Cat had made a pot just before he'd woken from a restless form of flipping and flopping around a duvet-swallowed queen that reminded him a bit of his own apartment, but she was nowhere in the house and the more he looked for her the more he couldn't find her. It wasn't that he worried about her safety, she was home, back where she'd been born, but the night had taken an unexpected turn and ended with the ball in Loeb's court. Cat was a part of the murder of Sarah Enos; Cat, the woman he wanted to fall into endless love with, she was Sarah's niece! It was a part of her life, even though she was only two and a half when it'd happened, the mystery of Sarah's death had been eating at her *all of her conscious existence!*

He had to find the truth. But he wanted to talk to her, ask her where she stood, and discourse about the not so subtle facts of their proximity and its sleepless effects.

The way she'd touched him last night, never in his life had he felt a woman's desire seep into his skin like that; it even made him question some of the romantic passages of *Fractures*. It made them seem flat and one dimensional, pale shadows of the real thing.

But Cat was gone, and would come back to the house as cats did, whenever they damn well felt like it.

So he stood with a cocked elbow on the uneven shore below their mansion and held a mug of black Arabica that wasn't that hot but was just to his liking with a touch of whole milk and stared into the muddled breath of fog hanging on the water.

It would burn off, wouldn't it?

He waited around for her until nearly eight o'clock and then decided he'd walk into town as it was only a few miles and he walked everywhere as it was and had a walker's body and good lungs, but walking rocky Alaskan waterlines and foresty dirt paths and walking the flat concrete of LA were two very different things.

By the time he reached Quill Creek and its beleaguered stretching of antiquated buildings that didn't quite sit straight as he studied them, he was winded and slowed to a stagger.

Fishermen were preparing their boats and there were less boats in the marina than when he'd drove in the day before. It was such a foreign process to him and Loeb took a chance to analyze it before a voice startled him from behind.

"Hello there."

Loeb turned to see a tall man, thick and barrel chested with a long and narrow face, the top of which was shiny, and what wasn't skin was a close crop of bristly white hairs, his beard homogenizing with the hair of his head, all the same, nearly inch-long in length. His apparent sixty-some odd years of life had greatly stressed him and his face had a sagging weightiness, as did the dense limbs of the blue-green pines and firs he seemed to appear as an apparition from.

He was in a dark puffer jacket and a wolf-like dog sat a pace behind him with an oddly intense ambivalence, as if it was staring at otherworldly figures dancing on the water.

"Oh hi." Loeb said.

"You must be our new visitor." He replied, and his voice was Russian in that it sounded as if he had peanut butter in his mouth.

"Word travels fast, I guess." Loeb said. "So much for anonymity."

"This is a most peculiar place," The Russian's eyes didn't know if they wanted to be gray or blue and were perhaps once blue but had lost their color and gazed into the morning fog and the small fishing vessels trying their luck but only filling their nets with futility. "I guarantee you everyone here knew of your coming, when you booked what residence you did, watched you drive in and whispered to each other about the purpose of your visit."

"Ha." Loeb stuffed his hands in his pockets. All of his clothes were new and he was trying to look local in hiking boots, heavy jeans, and a brightly colored fleece pullover that was a bit too big. He'd left the heavy gear back in the mansion but had second thoughts about doing so. His Californian acclimatization was working a wonder in his hundred and sixty pounds.

"Sounds suspicious." He rubbed his hands together.

"Just the thoughts of a writer." The Russian smiled weakly and offered his hand. "I am Grigory Ukaskaya."

"Loeb Cohen." They shook hands and the old

man's skin was dry and unhealthy and his grip unexpectedly nonexistent.

"I've read a few of your books." He said, turning his vision again to the fog. "I did not care for them."

Loeb tried not to smile.

"Well…" He said. "I'm writing a new one. If you help me with it I'll give you a nod in the backpages." Loeb smirked, completely snubbing the Russian as to say he'd never heard or read his work even though he had. Grigory Ukaskaya was a lesser-known contemporary of a Russian liberal named Yvgeny Yvutshenko, who wrote, among other things, "Babi Yar", which confronted and criticized the Soviet regime's treatment of Jews. Loeb wracked his mind and came up with a publication date of 1961.

The Russian was an intellectual, a theoretic student of the humanitarian condition, an observer and dissector of the animalistic nature and a man who looked down upon Loeb for his bang bangs and the fact that, in today's world, senseless bang bangs were what people pounded the table for.

"Help?" The Russian's eyes drifted back. Loeb wondered how well he could see. There was a cloudiness in him, confusion.

Maybe just the reflection of the murky fog on the water, though…how can something so thick and murky reflect? Something has to have light to reflect and everything here's so dark and…and viscid, like there's a gloopy glue holding everything in place…

Has he been imprisoned in Russia? Forced to escape for his liberal or anti-communist views?

When did he come to America?

Why Alaska? Why here?

Did he kill Sarah Enos? She was a Russian

Jew, too.

Suddenly the man was very interesting to Loeb, as was the scar he noticed down the left side of his face when he turned.

"Well, if I am to help you then you must meet my dog, Shiva."

"Hello Shiva." Loeb managed a small bow of his head and the dog didn't care. Its wolf-shape was nearly all dark brown and probably weighed more than Cat. The dog was still searching the mist for ghosts to protect its master from them. "That's not the most common name for a dog...is she the god of death, then?"

The Russian chuckled and kept the meaning of why to himself.

"So, what could I possibly do to help you? I mean, you are a very successful young writer, I imagine you already have your plot and your characters and you just have to decide now what foreign government, ideology or people group you want to defecate on to exalt your sexy gun-toting heroes."

Loeb twisted to stare, as must've been the local pastime, into the fog edging the marina as another boat chuggled out into the murk with the limp clicks of a small motor.

"I'm writing about the murder of Sarah Enos."

"Oh." The Russian's voice changed and when Loeb turned to face him the heat of the Russian's gaze, even though his eyes lacked focus, was tangible. "Well then why don't you talk to Sheriff Evans. He was on duty that night and has been ever since. He's got all the evidence locked away at City Hall."

"I'll do that," Loeb smiled, fighting a cold chill and he had no idea where it came from, just a

strike, like lightning, down his spine and he
shivered.

"And get yourself a real jacket." The Russian
smirked. He turned to leave with Shiva. "And don't
invite me to that castle of yours but you're welcome
to come to mine. It's that way."

Loeb followed the Russian's finger and saw it
pointed across town, back by the highway turnoff,
perhaps seven or eight miles from Loeb's.

"Okay, thank you very much."

"Don't mention it." He said, and then paused.
"But don't come empty handed. I like whiskey, but
vodka will suffice in a pinch."

It wasn't the time for Loeb to say wine was
his limit as anything else gave him a headache and
beer wasn't the healthiest endeavor ever invented
but he was sure beer was the state beverage and
would be forced to imbibe at some point in the
foreseeable future.

"Um...*do svidaniya*." Loeb attempted.

Grigory Ukaskaya only grunted and walked
back into the woods and Loeb muttered something
to himself, walked several steps, nearly tripped, and
turned to study the Russian and his dog walking
away but it was as if the Russian was never there
and all Loeb could see was a stagnant stagger of
tree trunks sticking at defensively strange angles as
nothing in Quill Creek was straight.

10
City Hall

Loeb paused before entering. The twin flags, American and Alaskan, flapped idly and the twist knob door handle to City Hall was frosty cold. It was maybe forty out. City Hall was carpeted in gray and reminded Loeb of a library. Two, maybe three people milled about the back of the space but he couldn't quite make out their faces. Shelves and cabinets of books and records were interspersed among desks of old computers and their monitors and to Loeb's right, frosted glass, either someone's humorous touch or just Loeb's often sarcastic interpretation of life, subdivided the lobby with the City Council chambers.

Can a town have a City Hall? Loeb wondered. He remembered seeing the hand carved wooden sign as he pulled off the highway, *Quill Creek, pop. 240, est. 1891.*

He didn't recall it saying *Welcome…*

"Howdy stranger." A voice boomed to his left and a portly man in the uniform of a Park Ranger poking from a slick fur-collared black jacket walked down the stairs. Loeb smiled at him and his wandering vision followed the stairs back where the second story was lost in more frosted glass.

Nothing's clear in this town, nothing's out in the open.

It's a box.

The man offered his hand quickly and a grip that'd been forged by a life of hard work nearly broke Loeb's fingers.

"Randy Evans, Town Sheriff."

Loeb couldn't refuse. It was his nature, and it had landed him in trouble with teachers at school as a boy and even more trouble with his parents. Many a semantic argument had been kindled to flame by his young tongue.

"How can a City Hall have a Town Sheriff?"

Loeb could sell a lot with what many people in LA would've considered an intellectual smirk as it peeled across broad lips but in Alaska, a land of pragmatism and keeping one's self to one's self, a land of hunting and drilling for oil and snow and dangerous animals that didn't ask for a second opinion before doing whatever the hell they wanted, Loeb could tell it wasn't going to fly.

"It's simple." All courtesy kindness left the man's well-fed face and Randy Evans, stuck in his mid sixties like the Russian, wrinkled up his bushy eyebrows and pulled at the plup of his neck as gravity and good casseroles had made it waddly. "Quill Creek's just a small township and falls under County jurisdiction seeing as it sits right outside a national park, but, we're as small of a town as they get, and don't like to ruffle any feathers...or any *quills*." Sheriff Evans chuckled and a fraction of his courtesy kindness reentered. "Everyone here is a volunteer in a way, like a family, and we all have quiet little lives and don't get in anybody's way if they don't get into ours, you know." His voice had a sleepy, convincing dryness, but no real accent, other than age and the side effects of having to explain things to people. "Most are retired government workers or retired military, on pension, just living out their days in peace, but there's some that still get by on tourism and small business-like ol' Jig's Music Shop, he builds some of the best acoustic guitars in the country with Sitka spruce…Quill Creek's just that kind of place."

"It's unequivocally beautiful." Loeb said and crossed his arms thinking that might not've been the best choice of words.

"You're the one that came from Los Angeles?" The Sheriff asked, even though Loeb had already resigned to the fact that handling things through the offices of Max Rayberg, in particular Solderman and Pearle's ever-lunch-break-eager secretary Lily, for the obvious financial reasons, had caused quite a stir in the town where nothing, repeat *nothing* happened, and if it did, no newspaper or radio station needed to broadcast it.

So how would the *purpose* of his visit go down? And what would they all say about Catriona, the long lost niece of Sarah Enos? Did they know? How could they? She looked so different, didn't she?

Loeb had yet to see a human being his age and wondered about older people and their memories.

"Yes, Loeb Cohen from Los Angeles. I'm a writer. I'm actually here to write a book on the murder of Sarah Enos."

Sheriff Randy Evans was stunned and couldn't hide it. He thought about what to say and turned to walk back up the stairs before saying, almost unclearly,

"Then follow me."

They walked the first flight and Loeb's mind

began to crack and sizzle as he read the etching on the frosted glass, *Quill Creek Police Department.*

What it didn't say was, *army of one.*

They walked past it and up a second flight of stairs.

"Fiction or non?" The Sheriff asked.

Loeb felt as if he was climbing Quasimodo's clock tower.

"Non."

"Oh good." Evans said, and it became readily apparent to Loeb the third floor was reserved for storage of all kinds and seldom visited. "I've got just the ticket for you, like a, um…starter kit, if you will."

A heavy ring of keys were unearthed from his pocket and the Sheriff had a hard time in finding the small one that fit the jagged slit in the doorknob.

It had been awhile.

Once they entered, and contended with the hazardously thick mustiness of the storage room, seen floating as a haze in the shafts of light slicing through a small portal window, Sheriff Evans walked to a series of shoeboxes on metal shelves with plodding steps.

He mumbled to himself incoherent things and found a pair of them and stuffed them under his arm and then walked behind a small partition made by unshaped cardboard shipping boxes in search of a much larger box.

"This is all that's up here. Why don't you take it and I'll go and get the files."

"…Okay." Loeb said as the Sheriff plopped the old shoeboxes on top of each other and clouds of dust puffed into the writer's face. Loeb fought a cough and nearly tripped to follow the shambling Randy Evans.

"Why don't you take all that stuff down to the Council Chambers and I'll be along with the case files. You want some coffee?"

"Uh…sure."

"Black?"

"Perfect."

Loeb trod the distance with caution as though the boxes would disintegrate in his hands. They were from 1991. All Loeb remembered of '91 was the Gulf War and the fall of Communism, and that was because his parents sat in front of the TV every waking hour of the day, always news with the occasional based-on-a-true-story movie, as they wrote reams and reams of editorial columns for local publications and the odd memoir only their friends bought and their closest friends actually read.

The door to the frosted glass-ensconced Council Chambers was another knob job and Loeb was about to spill the dusty boxes and make a scene, not that anyone would've noticed, when a controlling pair of hands touched both his shoulder and the door, quick to open it.

"Allow me." The voice was smooth and articulate and did not belong to the Sheriff.

"Oh, thank you."

Across the tips of his shoebox stack Loeb saw a granite-faced man who had all the potential to look frightening and instead was quite handsome in a rugged, forty-five year old way. He had small eyes, shielded by a raptor's beak of a nose, and broad shoulders perhaps twice the span of Loeb's with a thick chest and knotty biceps to match.

The Council Chambers were an obligatory closet of pale wood and held all the cheap trappings of a small claims court and none of the prestige or authority.

"Mr. Cohen, is it?"

Loeb shook the man's hand and again was nearly bent in half by this new Alaskan tradition of handshakes.

"Yes, I guess I'm quite the subject."

The man was taller than Loeb and had a distinguished flair of silver near his ears on a thick head of hair that was otherwise reddish brown and swept back.

"No, my friend, *she* is quite the subject." Loeb noticed all too late he was talking about Sarah Enos as the man began to dismantle the boxes and deal out the contents in them like a game of poker. "So much so we don't talk about her anymore and haven't for years."

Sheriff Evans returned with two thick files.

"Oh, I see you've met Ericson West."

"Not exactly. He got the door for me, or else all this…" Loeb gestured toward a spread of 4x6 photos and dozens upon dozens of small plastic bags that held evidence samples and unclear secrets. "Would be on the ground on the count of my clumsiness."

"E's the Mayor."

"That's a fancy load of crap." The forty-five year old West said with a masculine chuckle.

"MVP of Quill Creek." Sheriff Evans added. "Most volunteerable person."

"So you help out with everything?" Loeb asked, beginning to make mental notes of all those he would encounter, with the smallest question clouding and taking bites at each of them.

Did you kill Sarah?

Did you?

"Everything and anything…" West then

changed the subject. "I handled your arrival and all with your offices. You're from LA?"

"Yes, that's right." Loeb said as a nondescript woman who'd been stuffed in the back of the lobby arrived with two coffees. She was in her late fifties.

"None for me?" West joked and she rolled her eyes at him. Loeb smirked at West's boyishness and how, in LA, Loeb could get away with what game West was cashing in on here in Quill Creek.

"Thanks, honey." Evans said and Loeb saw by her reaffirming touch on Evans' shoulder that the ordinary woman, whose haircut was bleached and mannish, was Evans' wife.

Mayor West sat down so that Loeb was flanked by the two larger men, claustrophobically so.

"Yeah, I read, um...*City of Vipers*, was it?" The Mayor said and then cleared his throat.

"Yes."

"I thought it was great, especially the action. Makes me think you know what firing a gun feels like. I used to be in the military. Lotta people around here have. We're the kind of people that know right away if someone's legit or not."

Loeb nervously took a sip of his coffee as the bluntness of West's words hung in the air and his shoulders seemed to stretch and ripple under his heavy flannel shirt as he leaned forward on the table. His hands looked as if they could split wood without an axe.

"I don't think you're gonna get very far with all this, though...you'd better make it a fiction book."

"Why's that?" Loeb was quick and inquisitive.

"A lot's gone on since then. I was twenty-two

when it happened."

Sarah's age...

The calculations of more possibilities sunk in.

Sheriff Evans let two dense file folders smack the table next to Loeb's coffee cup.

"One's the murder, the other's the robbery."

"Robbery? I didn't read anything about that in the papers."

"Well..." West sighed. "We kind of believe things went down a little differently than the investigation set in stone. You see, if Quill Creek doesn't know what happened to Sarah, then no one does, and no one ever will. So whatever you read in old papers and crap on the Internet and all that, well, it might as well be as fictitious as your *City of Vipers* and your other actionfests. All of it's right here. All of the facts. And all of the facts say that she died of a single stab wound to the stomach. It just so happened that very same night at that very same time, there was a robbery further on up the street."

Sheriff Evans wheezed as he pushed himself further from the table to drink his coffee on the count of his stomach size not being as small as it was the last time he sat at the table. Evans' eyes were droopy under his thick white brows.

"Feel free to do what you'd like, Mr. Cohen," The Sheriff said and showed his age in a squint. "But don't go poking and prying where you're not welcome."

"Just a friendly warning on a sore subject." West added with a winking smile. "Besides, there's enough here to write a damn good bestseller and Quill Creek could use the publicity. Especially if you throw in some wrinkle about Russian spies or something. After all, it was 1991."

And with that, the enigmatically handsome and charmingly intimidating Ericson West left the quiet closet of the Council Chambers and let Loeb Cohen study the evidence as Sheriff Evans failed to defeat his natural lethargy and began the dreary and irreversible process nodding off to sleep.

1 1

Lunch, with Death

Loeb's skin burned. It was just after an initial and somewhat scattered assessment of the many assorted pieces of data on the murder of Sarah Enos that he spotted her diary. It was a 5x8 book, leather bound in faded tawny calfskin with a gold inscription.

Diary.

Strange thoughts bored into his skull in that moment and in between two of Sheriff Evans' wheezing snores, Loeb stole Sarah Enos' diary, plastic bag and all and stuffed it in his waistband underneath the oversized fleece.

Sheriff Evans was still asleep when Loeb put all of the evidence back in the boxes and took one of the file folders two minute's walk along Shore Road to a café named *Logan's* where he ordered a bowl of salmon chowder from a cute red-haired waitress that flirted with heavy-handed charm. His uncomfortable wooden seat took in the sun's dismal attempt at burning off the fog's pillows and blankets of sleepiness and Loeb knew it was only a matter of time before snow would arrive and make his Alaskan experience inescapably complete.

And while his skin throbbed with the heat of

every eye in the world glaring at him for his being from LA, for his blue-haired girlfriend, and for stealing the diary of Sarah Enos from under the nose of Sheriff Evans, Loeb Cohen sat in the quaint and brightly colored restaurant the size of a postage stamp and thumbed through the police report to let his mind plagiarize a more human view of the terse and chilling font as each word stood on the page like a headstone in a haunted graveyard.

Ms. Sarah Enos was discovered deceased by Mrs. Gina Farnsworth of 2A 1212 Shore Road, and officiated by Sheriff's Deputy Royce McElroy, the cause of which being complete exsanguination from a single stab wound to the stomach at or before 8:36 PM on October 4th, 1991. She was found lying on her back, feet facing the door of her ground floor apartment, 1B, 1212 Shore Road. Her body was frozen from the twenty-degree temperatures. Her hands were frozen to the handle of the knife. The murder weapon was classified as a six-inch chef's knife and was from the butcher block in Ms. Enos' apartment. The door to her apartment was open. A further search of Ms. Enos' apartment yielded no indication of suicide, though no prints other than Ms. Enos' were found on the knife. The knife and the gash to Ms. Enos' stomach contained dish soap consistent with tepid sink water in Ms. Enos' kitchen. Found in the house was Ms. Enos' niece and legal ward, Catriona Enos, two and a half years of age. Mrs. Farnsworth said it was the child's cries that alerted her. The child had cried for at least five minutes before Mrs. Farnsworth investigated. Mrs. Farnsworth saw Ms. Enos lying in the snow from her door, immobile and bleeding and called the police at 8:41 PM. Sheriff Randall Evans was indisposed at 1081 Shore Road

investigating the suspected robbery of King Minos'
Wood Shop. Sheriff Evans suffered injuries in
pursuit of a suspect. Sheriff's Deputy McElroy was
called from City Hall to assist Sheriff Evans in
pursuit and responded to Mrs. Farnsworth's call
instead, reaching the scene at 8:43 PM. Sheriff
Evans lost contact of said pursuant and returned
from the woods north of Quill Creek. VCCSD was
then notified of the incident and arrived on the
scene at 10:01 PM. Sarah Enos was deemed to be
murdered by the findings and assessment of Valdez-
Cordova County Deputy Detective Gareth Wilson
III, who determined that critical evidence was
purposefully destroyed by an unidentified guilty
party when Ms. Enos' diary was found two days
later by Captain Walter Furo of the private fishing
vessel Windcutter in the waters near Eagle's Pointe,
two miles northwest of Quill Creek. Detective
Wilson assessed that the deposit of the diary in the
water to ruin its contents was inconsistent with
suicide as there was no note in Ms. Enos' apartment
and no signs of stress or suicidal tendencies from
eyewitness accounts of Ms. Enos the day of or days
leading up to October 4th. It was also a well-
established fact that Ms. Enos loved children and
was very fond of her niece and had recently
graduated early from the University of Alaska
Anchorage with a degree in teaching, and served as
a substitute elementary teacher ten miles away in
the town of Tamo. Detective Wilson further
speculated, and though his professional opinion of
the events leave no room for doubt considering the
circumstances, it is not of general consensus, that
Ms. Enos was well-acquainted with her killer and
had let them enter the house. It is his belief that the
stabbing occurred just inside of the doorframe in a

*quick and sudden manner, with the guilty party
retreating in a manner that left no tracks in the
snow. A thorough investigation of the town and
citizens of Quill Creek, however, have exhausted
any further means of fact-finding and the murder of
Sarah Enos has been deemed by the State of Alaska
as such and is unsolved.*

The cute redhead made the spoon clink
against the empty white bowl and saucer as she took
his soup. He hadn't touched the complimentary
crackers.

"Soup's alright?" She asked with sunniness
not found anywhere else in Quill Creek and twisted
her head. Her wavy hair was in a ponytail and
flipped catching the light with its healthy glossiness.

Loeb was distant and immersed in a pictorial
replication of October 4th, 1991 and his gaze
lethargically travelled up her body to locate eyes to
contact and speak back to out of trained courtesy,
not focusing on what was before them, and by doing
so, he had accidentally, and gratuitously, checked
her out.

"Um, yes, thank you." Loeb smiled with a
hint of self-loathing and knew that he could've
made childish monster faces at the girl and she still
would've taken it as a come on.

His head sank and his mind was riddled with
the riddle of Sarah's shocking exit stage left.

*A robbery and a murder in a town where
nothing happens. Same night, same time.*

No tracks in the snow.

Loeb looked again to the small hook of the
marina as water had carved out jagged points in the
dark green cavern of trees, *stabbed* them with hacks
and slashes.

I don't believe in coincidences. I never will.

"Oh there you are." The smoothness of a familiar voice startled him and just as Loeb was about to rise and turn to be polite the controversial diary poked him in the belly and he offered only a bent wave.

It was Ericson West.

The redhead came from the kitchen at the sound of the smooth voice, ponytail leaping, and was quick to throw a hug at West and kiss him on the cheek. It was only in their togetherness that he could see the similarity. Ericson's face was hard and distinguished, skin weather worn whereas hers was compact and girlish. Her skin freckled and her nose upturned in the slightest whereas his beaked downward with cruelty. Even their eyes were different shapes and colors but she was still his daughter, Loeb would've bet money on it.

Now for the expensive question he'd have to find a subtle way to ask, *how old was she?*

He was forty-five, Sarah's age if she were still alive...

West spotted the open file folder and Loeb didn't hide it.

"Have you read it?" He asked, sitting down and was forced to be friendly because his daughter immediately took to his lap, even though Loeb thought, if but for a moment, he'd detected a wolfish and possessive streak flash through West's small, hard eyes as he entered the café.

"What is it, Dad?" She asked with a bounce in her voice. He beheld her with a flat mouth that she found comical and she, though perhaps five foot five, about Catriona's height and much thicker than Catriona if that was a great difficulty, shrunk on his knee against the juxtaposition of his broad chest and shoulders. She looked to be twenty-two or three and she acted as if she were twelve and loving it.

"It's about Sarah. This man's going to write a bestseller about her."

"Oh?" Katie West's eyes swelled. They were a lovely shape, hazel and almost completely round with the slightest downward taper at each corner. "Are you from Hollywood?"

With the downward snip of her eyes, the upward tip of her nose, and the glossy red ponytail she had an adorable cleanliness ideal for advertising cosmetics, or even things like cereals and household products.

"Now now, Katie, don't bug him. Writers like to be alone, you know. They don't like young girls pestering them."

Katie frowned a simple thing that Loeb guessed she'd used before and had pushed Daddy's buttons with.

"But nothing happens here Dad, you know how boring it gets in the winter." Her voice warbled with an immature plea. "Just let me talk to him for a little while, like ten minutes? There's nobody here."

"Not now, Katie. Later. Daddy has to tell him something important first, okay?"

Loeb squinted at the use of the third person patronymic to keep from retching.

"Fine."

Katie slid from the strong leg she'd been perched on and stormed off to the kitchen perhaps to take nibbles at the desert tray and think youngish thoughts.

"Sweet girl." Loeb said, not meaning a word of it. "How old is she?"

Ericson West was caught in his sheer, granite-carved manliness between two choices and chose to be sycophantic, even if he didn't know what that word meant, Loeb did, and was convinced West was an expert in its art.

"Pace yourself, you've only just met." He said and in leaning across the short table slapped Loeb on the back with one had and folded up the police report with his other. Loeb, in his bent elbow lean, smiled a curious smile, and considered that the man's deftness and dexterity was something of note.

I wonder, Mr. West, if you know your way around a knife...

"It's very interesting." Loeb said as West rose to leave.

"The case? Yes, it is...*this*, by the way, must stay with all the other things at City Hall. You have as much access to all of it as you want and may do so in the Council Chambers, during City Hall hours, as long as either Sheriff Evans or myself are available."

"Oh, I'm sorry." Loeb waved his hand. "I just thought a change of scenery would be nice."

West's lips formed into a dagger, wondering what exchanges had passed between his daughter and the artist-haired writer without his knowledge.

"Don't think. Just write."

West then reached into his pocket and put a twenty on the table and left.

It was just when Loeb thought his blood pressure would never return to normal from the disease of thoughts and their curdling of his veins he rushed off, bent posture and all, after West.

West's tall stride had almost returned him to the door of City Hall when Loeb called out.

"Do you know where I can get some whiskey?"

West stopped and turned, disarmed.

"Pardon?"

"Whiskey. I ran into Ukaskaya and he said if I go see him I should bring some whiskey."

West's head became heavy and a storm caught wind behind his eyes.

He approached Loeb quickly, which was for him a matter of two or three steps.

"Take it from me, that old codger is a wash up and doesn't deserve your time. He's driftwood, just waiting to die. He's lonelier than a crippled dog in heat and'll say anything to get the stardust of your career by your coming here to write. Do us all a favor and leave him the hell alone."

"I'll tell him you said that."

West's face broke into a devious grin.

"He already knows. Why do you think he stays locked up across the county line over there in that shack of his, staring at the water pretending to write something."

"...Whiskey?"

"Fisher's Restaurant'll have some. If not, wind that toy car of yours up to Anchorage."

"Okay." Loeb pressed his hand to his stomach. The diary burned.

"You okay?" West asked, frowning down on Loeb.

"...Flour in the chowder." Loeb winced, guarding the diary, improvising. "I'm gluten sensitive."

West's hooking nose curled as if he'd smelled something offensive and his eyes said *damn Californians...who invited you? This is my town. Mine!*

He turned brusquely for the door to City Hall and the sanctuary of assumed power it was and hesitated.

"You know," He said with no small gesture of

someone trying to remember something and failing to sell it. "If there's one thing that report doesn't say, it's Mills Anderson."

"Who?"

"Mills Anderson, he lives about two miles east of you, up in the sticks. Drive around in that toy car of yours and you'll find him. He's got some vicious dogs up there, though, I'd beware."

"What about him should I know?"

"Well…" West sighed and looked to the water. "Let's just say he's a registered sex offender. He's lived in Quill Creek all his life, except for his stint in the State Pen. His sentence ended in 1991 a couple months before Sarah's murder and he's lived as a recluse ever since."

West let his words hang in the air and marched off with his loping stride to disappear into City Hall.

Loeb Cohen felt the lightning strike of a shiver again in his pathetic fleece and nearly ran back to his palatial lodge, tripping on the shore rocks and catching the diary down his left pant leg before it slipped out and hit the ground for all of Quill Creek's prying eyes to see, even though all Loeb could see staring him back in his hurried glances to safety were the quiet sentinels of the firs and pines, rough and unkempt as they grew wild and green and dense in the cruel cold and pressed him closer to the water's edge.

12
Catriona

Cat munched on a cookie. They were snicker doodle and she'd overcooked them in the slightest and though they weren't the best breakfast she'd taken a few of them up in the woods and aimlessly traipsed the trails. The scent of pine, dirt and saltwater was thick and therapeutic in her nose. The land *felt* old, untouched, unused, and she couldn't resist the sentiment of being some form of explorer as her feet carried her far and wide along the slopes behind Shore Road. It was strange being back, and when moments of stillness and peace came to her they were stolen again by accusations and fears.

And Loeb hadn't followed her into the bedroom last night. So they'd both slept alone.

If they'd slept at all.

The morning walk had cleared her head and she was convinced the longer they stayed together and Alaska slowly began to freeze around them that everything would work itself out.

It had to.

Having finished her cookies she worked her way back to their palatial residence. She'd been in the cabin for a few minutes when the shore-facing downstairs entrance near her master bedroom sucked and slammed and she left her post-walk repose in the dining room to investigate.

Loeb was nearly breathless and was quick in pulling off his oversized fleece in the sauna-like hall and mudroom and Cat silently moved to lean against the doorframe of her master bedroom with the crescent-like remains of yet another cookie in hand.

She spotted the plastic bag poking from his waistband and whatever was in it stuffed inside of it.

"I missed you." She said, and took a nibble.

Loeb looked up and rushed to her affectionatelessly. His eyes were stricken with paranoia.

"Take this." He said, and gave her Sarah's diary.

"What is it?" Cat turned it over in her hand and wondered why it was in a plastic bag. It wasn't a gift, like the many nice things he'd bought her, some of them still in bags in her room. She tried some of them on last night after rolling around and failing to sleep and was blown away by his generosity and good taste.

"It's Sarah's diary."

Cat's lack of eyebrows didn't stop surprise from swallowing her face and she dropped the moon shape of a cookie.

"How'd you..."

"Sheriff Evans was on the scene that night. I went over to City Hall and talked to him and he showed me all the evidence, the pictures, the police reports, all of it. There was a robbery, too, that night, at the *exact same time*." Loeb unleashed the flood of information as was his way and stopped himself. "...But you already know all that, don't you?"

"I know what was in the papers, and I know what I remember." Cat said, eyeing the diary as if it were a missing puzzle piece that fit a holy spot in her thin body.

She couldn't help but wonder what would happen to that empty sensation if she read the diary, if it would only further cast misunderstanding where light so desperately needed to shine, or if it would actually work the slide puzzle inside to make some sense of questions that had no answer otherwise.

"Cat, I stole it." Loeb said, grabbing her shoulders. "You've got to take it. I was thinking about you, not the investigation. I want you to have it, I don't care about them. You need it."

Cat's unicolor brown eyes were glittering with mist.

"I don't know." She said.

"It was found in the water up by Eagle's Pointe, wherever that is. The Detective on the case thought that whoever killed Sarah dumped it there."

"That's by Ukaskaya's place."

"You know him?"

"The Russian?" Cat shrugged, still dealing with the burden of the diary and if she should read it or not. "I kind of know everyone here, or at least everyone that was here when I was here in the way that I know *of them* and what I think of them, but I don't know much more than that...and no one here would recognize me as I wouldn't recognize them until they hear the name *Enos.* Then they'd recognize it as I'd recognize theirs. It's like...free association, you know? Instead of a word and a word, our names are all sealed together with October 4th."

She looked Loeb in the eye with a faltering honesty, as if she was full of insecurity and needed his help not to be.

The twenty three year old murder was a mighty sore wound to lance.

"We can do this, Cat," He said. "But we have to do it together. You're my only hope in knowing what happened because I'm getting the feeling nobody here *wants* me here, and they haven't even met you yet. If they know you're *the* Catriona Enos they might as well come and lynch us both."

"You think?" Cat frowned, and the more she thought about it the more sense it made.

If the incident with Sarah cast a shadow on Cat's life, what had it done to Quill Creek? Was that why the place looked dormant when they drove through it? Cat still had yet to meet one of the residents, and if it weren't for Loeb she'd feel helplessly alone in the large house and the cold sea-facing view of the broad dining room windows, not to mention what uneasy silence poisoned the forest.

Loeb stood up tall and sighed, running a hand through his hair, coming down from the overheating of his brain.

Cat was his pressure valve. He needed her balance, but he, in his analytical turmoil wasn't reading between the lines.

Catriona was caught in the depths of her own bitter struggle.

"They're all hiding something," Loeb said. "Every one of them...every one I've met, at least, but, I'm sure it'll be par for the course. Survivor's guilt, complicity, duplicity...I've got some ideas but we'll have to go about it *together*. I don't want us separated anymore, okay?"

Cat's face was flooded with concern.

"You don't feel safe?"

"No, I don't." Loeb said and hugged her and as her thinness was enveloped in his arms she pressed herself into him.

Damn, it feels good to hug you, she thought, *for you to hold me and touch me.*

Just hold me. Don't say anything. Just let me hear you breathe.

I don't ever want to be a part from you. I've gone through so many different foster homes, so many different last names, so many different shells to wax over a flickering pilot-light inside...I don't want to do it again.

I want to be with you.

I want you.

Loeb didn't say a word about the night before but he pecked her forehead and smiled, letting the hype of the *could be's* of the case float away like an untethered balloon in a stiff breeze.

It would all work itself out, it would all be okay.

Loeb smelled a hint of the perfume he'd found for her and bent his neck to inquire about the rest of it.

"Do like them?"

Cat looked down at the thick cowl neck cashmere sweater of creamy white, tight-fitting low-rise dark blue jeans bound with a soft leather belt and handmade light brown boots of caribou suede, capped with an off-white furry cuff. Thin sliver rectangle earrings to match her upper lip studs. Dappled and hand pounded, they caught glints and snips of light as they dangled an inch above her shoulders.

Cat's answer was a merely suggestive shrug of her shoulders.

"Everything fits alright?"

The shrug twisted and Loeb knew why. He'd never purchased women's underwear before but since a young age had been guessing and assuming strange things like what size person x was and what person y was named and if person z chose paper or plastic and whether they slept on their back, side, or stomach. At times he'd condemned himself for invading their lives with his prognostications, and his only reward for his thoughts had been headaches and eyestrains.

How good it was to be fulfilled in getting it right.

Cat was about to kiss Loeb with a heavy dose of desire when the doorbell rang.

Loeb didn't know they had a doorbell and walked past her. Catriona rolled her eyes, then smiled broadly to herself and ducked in her room for a minute before following.

13
Hospitality

The woman was beautiful. She had a healthy body, curvy and natural in that it complemented thick waves of rusty, nearly copper-toned red hair that spilled in a bell shape from the crown of a high forehead. Her skin was soft, sunned and freckled. She was in her forties but could've passed for early thirties, easily, though Loeb wondered if in her teens she'd looked much different.

Loeb swallowed hard as he stood in the doorframe.

"Hello." She said with an easy-breezy smoothness that wasn't applied like her husband's, and her beauty, unlike her daughter's cutesy freshness, was in no way a forced appliqué. She was, just as Alaska was, innately and effortlessly *perfect.*

"I think I know you." Loeb said with his most charming frown-smile and ushered her into the cavernous all-in-one of the cabin's entrance. The woman adjusted her shoulder bag and took it in, her eyes lingering on the magazine-worthy spread of the fireplace sitting area, the restaurant quality kitchen and the dining alcove, and how it was all stepped and graded to look independent but was all one happy family bound in soaring heights of warm cedar.

"Gosh, I've never been in here." She said, a little off guard and then addressed Loeb's comment. "Yes, I'm Melinda West."

Loeb shook her hand and the connection was a tight balance of grip and size, confident but not overly so, with her free hand gliding over the top of his to complete the cage of warmth. The touch of surprisingly supple skin was soothing and her thumb rubbed his adductor polliscis with the slightest hint of a circle. Her hands were scented with feeble flavors of citrus and there was a kinetic energy hidden deep within them.

A tremor of heat fluttered up his spine, reminiscent of a hot tub water jet.

The heat said *relax, stay awhile, sink in and forget.*

The longer he looked at her the more he fell apart.

He didn't want to think it but she was *sensuous.* Just standing there in a snug powder blue sweater and jeans she epitomized the hourglass. She was womanly and full and framed by the same energy he felt in her hands.

The fascinating allure of seduction.

Now'd be a good time for you to say something Cat, something like hi or hey or get away from him. You know I have a hard time not being polite. One look at your blue hair and she'll run back out the door, I'm sure.

Hurry up, Cat...

Loeb seemed to fall into her eyes as they were blue like his, but darker and colder, nearly black or violet like deep stunning lake waters under the spell of the eventide moon and she pursed her lips and let her lake water eyes wash over his and wander away.

"Oh." She said, reaching into her bag. "I brought these for you."

She produced a sausage, wrapped in reddish brown professional packaging though missing a label and a bottle of dark liquid, unmarked, but nearly identical to the same kind used by monks to make small batch beer.

"Bear sausage and homemade IPA. E's gone three months out of the year hunting for the whole town with that big rig and gun collection of his and don't worry if you don't like the beer. It's not for everyone. E brews it in some cobwebbed back corner of our property he says to get away from me but I know it's just so he can spend time with the his bosom buddy, Sheriff Randy."

Loeb took the items and wondered where the hell Cat was and why he was afraid of everything now that he'd met three men who'd been unLA to him.

It's Alaska, Loeb, chill out! Not everyone is here to kiss your ass! You said it yourself, these people are action heroes and you're some lightweight from sunshineville, so take it easy, okay? Now you've poisoned Cat into thinking everyone here is a suspect.

Does this woman look like a suspect to you?
Does she feel like a suspect?
Her husband, maybe...

But Loeb couldn't fight the darkness gilding his interpretation of life. He was a writer, after all, and a master of adrenalized action-suspense.

Is this a peace offering, Mrs. West? Did E tell you to come see me after our impromptu meeting at Logan's? Is he loading up one of those hunting rifles right now and waiting for me to come back to

City Hall for more questions?

It was then Cat made little to no sound as she came from the hall past the kitchen.

"Oh, hello." Melinda said sincerely, looking past Loeb's shoulder to the twenty-five year old's bushy spike blue hair.

"This is my girlfriend...Cat." Loeb tried not to hesitate and stared at the foodstuffs in his hands as if they'd distracted him with their promise of deliciousness even though they had no labels and there was nothing to stare at.

"Is Cat short for anything?" Melinda asked as she shook Cat's hand kindly, but quickly, not lingering as she had with Loeb. Loeb watched the woman's face intently and it didn't seem to bother the woman Cat had no eyebrows. Melinda caught Loeb's invasive study of her face and turned to meet his gaze and he looked away clumsily, to which a pleasured grin bent her red lips.

"Naw," Cat stuffed her hands in the butt pockets of her tight jeans, taking it in. "Just Cat. Meow."

"And you're from LA, then?" Melinda took it in stride as Loeb walked over to the kitchen counter to sort out thoughts he didn't want to think.

First Katie West. Now Melinda West. What's big E gonna do to you if he finds out? Just because you're from LA, he'll say, before he beats you to a pulp and leaves you for the wolves. By God Loeb Cohen, the next woman you see better be an ugly old forest hag with a cauldron and a cornhusk broom or the half the town's gonna think you're coming on to them and the other half's gonna wanna dump you in the bay and drag you behind a fishing boat!

Stop staring, stop thinking, relax!

Crack open that beer!

Loeb did so and found three glasses. It was twelvish or a little later; either way the afternoon was still fresh.

Cat and Melinda were sitting together on the black couch perpendicular to the fire and Loeb gave them their glasses. Melinda's fingers managed to brush his and again the jellied sensation of loose, wet, comfort rippled along his spine and he all but fell into the high back chair across from them.

"My husband read one of your books and loved it." She said, glowing. "*City of Vipers.* So then he got the one that came out right after it without even reading the back. He just saw your name and had a reaction and threw the book in the cart. We were up in Anchorage doing our monthly shopping and right there in the supermarket, on a table, *Fractures*. He was so happy, he was like, *look honey, Cohen's got another one out already. How cool is that? It's even World War Two!*" Melinda laughed in retrospect. "He stopped two pages into it and threw it away."

Cat's face was permeated with the humor a parent would have about something zany their child said or did, as if immaturity itself held humor.

"I picked it up out of the trash, granted I don't really care for...actiony stuff, and my God, I couldn't stop. What a book. It was such a cold winter that year, too, it really helped me through with E being gone so much, doing all the stuff he needs to do to keep this place afloat...I read it every night, some nights I'd take a hot bath and reread what I'd read the night before."

Loeb averted his gaze and filled his mouth with beer. He didn't want to think about Mrs. West reading *Fractures* in her bathtub. He couldn't.

Block it out block it out block it out…
He took another sip.

The IPA was a showcase of hops and rang with bitterness, initially far too strong for Loeb and his Californian dedication to fruity reds and dry whites, but it wasn't until the liquid had fallen to his stomach that the lingering stringers of the dark amber brew curled around his tongue and begged him for another sip.

"I love *Fractures*." Cat said and Loeb was shocked that Cat was either completely genuine or just *that good* of an actress. She seemed to be enjoying the company of Mrs. West. Had Loeb tainted her view of Quill Creek or just his own?

Stop thinking, dammit, stop it!

"And you're writing a new one?" Melinda asked.

"Yes, about Sarah Enos."

"Oh good." She said. "It's about time."

"Why's that?" Cat asked. She was such a good partner.

Keep talking, Cat, keep talking…

Melinda wiggled her hips in on the leather couch to sit up, as if she were spilling a secret.

"Because when something stays in the dark for a certain amount of time, whatever attention it gains only adds to the mystery of the original event…so, your book's already going to be a best seller. People will hunt and peck about it on the internet and find out how confusing the whole thing was and it'll make whatever result you come to in your book look like the *only* possible solution, even though whatever you publish'll be fiction. No one'll ever know what happened to her. It's a great mystery."

"So you'll buy a copy?" Loeb smirked.

"Damn right I'll buy a copy." Melinda met his smirk and raised him two evocatively, as if it would've been a brash insult to her husband to have Loeb Cohen in their house, on their dining room table or their kitchen counter.

In their bed.

"What about E?" Loeb sipped.

"Who cares?" Melinda finished her beer and did so in an unpretentious and ladylike manner, not frowning at its nasty bite like Loeb was.

Loeb's eyes were glued to her as she relaxed into the arms of the couch. Her chin was tipped upward and her moonlit lake water eyes glared at him down the bridge of her nose

"If I could add my spin on it I think that it was your fellow writer, Grigory Ukaskaya."

"Really?" Loeb moved to the edge of his chair. "Why?"

Loeb wasn't thinking about Cat now as she sat silently on the far edge of the couch. It was as if she'd disappeared from the periphery, and Melinda was a tunnel stealing his attention.

"Because," Melinda's beauty flashed with an audacious flirt. "Writers are like onions, layers upon layers upon layers. If you treat them right, you'll enjoy their sweetness. If you cut them, you'll cry…Everyone here knew the Enos's were Russian immigrants, they couldn't hide it, no matter how hard they tried. The smell of fresh baked piroshkies alone was a dead giveaway, not to mention the fact that Sarah was never bothered by the cold. The day before her death Sarah was over at Ukasakya's place for three or four hours. Then a couple of days later they found the diary over there, in the water."

Melinda West then checked her watch with a brevity too quick to ascertain the time.

"Well, I have to go." She rose. "I'll be seeing *both* of you again, I'm sure."

She waved and left, with a glance lingering on Loeb that left him staring blankly after her and when his eyes came back to Cat he saw her eyebrowless features facing his direction, frozen flat in obvious disapproval.

14
Warrant

The doorbell rang again. It rang at a moment when Loeb was about to say something apologetic to quell the chilly unhappiness emanating from Catriona and it rang again and again with an angered buzz as if the one doing the ringing was in a flustered hurry.

Loeb flinched to answer it and Cat sprung up in a flash and ran to the door on silent tiptoes before slowing to an easy walk, smoothing out her crème-colored cowl neck sweater around the hips. Her shock of blue hair was already antagonistic enough and she thought of many salty things to say to Mrs. West.

Cold air surged through the mansion's entrance. The politeness die-cast in her face fell to see the potbellied figure of Sheriff Evans instead of the redheaded cougar. His Park Ranger hat, the dull badge of which Cat couldn't quite make out, was tight on his head and his teeth ground together.

"Uh, hello, Miss…" The Sheriff removed his hat and bowed a small thing. He knew nothing of Cat and his eyes nearly crossed on the count of no one telling him the writer wasn't going to be alone, as he'd anticipated.

The Sheriff's gentlemanliness departed.

Overtime would need to be paid if it made any more appearances.

His bushy eyebrows sank as he spoke.

"Miss…may have a word with Mr. Cohen?"

"What is this about?" Cat asked quickly, with a waitresses' professional mix of emotions gilding her voice before Loeb could rush in and stumble over his own words as the perfect adjectives made Wall Street-type bids for his sentences.

Cat knew how it was in Alaska. People were simple and kept to themselves. Don't ask any questions and none will be asked of you. What you do with your time is your concern, and if you don't have anything to do when the deep freeze sets in don't go knocking on doors for a friend.

But Loeb had already blown whatever grace they had in the matter, especially being from California. Even citizens of Washington State resented SoCal transplants, and Loeb was on full boil thinking everyone in the town killed Sarah Enos when Cat was sure he was only misinterpreting their xenophobia.

And the Sheriff, he was here for the diary. He had to be, Loeb had stolen it from City Hall; the diary Cat had well hidden in her room for her own purpose.

She was running her own investigation, thinking her own thoughts. She would help Loeb as he pieced together the possibilities but when the sun left the sky, the emptiness of Cat's bed forced her to dwell on Sarah's murder, and the same thought came to her again and again.

The truth; locked deep down in her guts, forever buried in a two and a half year-old's memory.

A glance. A shape. A ghost.

A murderer.

Cat had seen the killer, that night, as Sarah begged them to come in for a cup of tea and some lemon poppy seed cake.

Amazing I can remember lemon poppy seed cake and not someone's face, Cat thought as she stared at Sheriff Evan's bushy whitish eyebrows and how they were a ridiculous contrast to her lack of them.

The very thought of it makes my mouth water. It was her recipe, not Dad's. Sarah's a better cook than I am, Dad would say. I can only make soups, Sarah can make anything. They would argue in the kitchen and throw flour at each other and I would laugh, just waiting to lick the bowl.

God I miss you, Sarah.

I love you so much.

Sarah had been lonely and sad that night, unusually so, and Cat had sensed it even though she wasn't entirely conscious of what she was sensing. She just knew mommy wanted someone to talk to, someone that could say more than a physically tiny yet linguistically precocious two and a half year old.

Cat remembered a slurred and muffled glimpse of the one who'd ended Sarah's life and was too undeveloped to comprehend exactly what she saw, too undersized and half-hidden at the foot of a loveseat near a bookshelf with a coloring book she never got the chance to finish.

Quill Creek would bring it all back.

Sheriff Evans was grave. His feet were planted firm on the stone outside the door.

"Mr. Cohen knows what it's about."

Cat cocked her head and let her posture sag as she held loosely on the doorframe.

"He's really busy." Cat was hoping Loeb

wasn't about to make a fool of her. "Can I take a message?"

The Sheriff looked her up and down more than once and swore to himself. She watched him disappear and cuss to himself again as he walked back to the rusty-bottomed snow white Jeep Cherokee that was parked what must've been half a mile away on the edge of their private drive.

Loeb was close by. The curtains were still closed along the forest facing windows, untouched since last night.

"It's about the diary, isn't it?" Cat whispered.

"It must be…what's he doing?"

"Five'll get you ten he's going for a search warrant."

Loeb's right hand ran through his hair and stopped.

"What have I done?" His pupils seemed to shrink and sink in his liquid blue irises.

"Relax." Cat said, watching the old man's stiff legs move their fastest.

Then she told Loeb where she'd hid the diary.

"You think that'll work?"

"He'll search every square inch of this place. I'm sure he'll give up. Eventually."

Evans reached his Jeep and began rummaging through the glove box.

Loeb stiffened.

"I know what's driving him, too. Ericson West is just *itching* for a reason to throw me out. He's got to be hiding something, or at least he's afraid that I'll find something he doesn't want me to."

"Stay away from him. Stay away from the evidence, too, until you absolutely have to."

Loeb stood closer.

"His wife is…"

Cat's backhand was reactionary in snapping a flat blow across his arm, though her eyes were locked on Evans and his frustrated search for his search warrant.

"Ow…" Loeb recoiled. "I was going to say, in mock surprise, with *layers* of humor, his wife is another fan of *Fractures.*"

Cat snarled a real snarl and not a smile. It was uneven and disgusted. Her thoughts nearly morphed themselves into promises.

Layers…ha! Writers are like onions…you get any lonely winter ideas Mrs. West and you'll be the one crying. Don't you try to bring any more of that homebrew around here…

"Hopefully he doesn't ask you directly if you took it, but if he asks you if you have it, you can say no."

"Right." Loeb said, nodding heavily.

"And you should go out there and talk his ear off, throw him off balance."

"Good idea." Loeb moved for the door and felt the brisk temperature in his t-shirt as Cat and her lovely warmth had been keeping him from it. "Shouldn't I get a coat, or something?"

"No no, run out there right now. I'll get your computer and act like I'm typing for you, it'll look like you've been inside for awhile."

"Good idea." Loeb smiled and began to jog with a wince, the air nipping at his skin with frosty teeth. "Get my voice recorder too, have that out. It's in my room."

Cat ran as fast as she could with light tip taps on the hardwood.

The diary would be safe.

It was about the time Sheriff Evans found the

accursed search warrant and wondered why he'd put it inside of his logbook even though that made a tremendous amount of sense when Loeb Cohen shouted a friendly greeting that caught his attention. The Sheriff turned and lost his hat on the roof edge of the Jeep and, already flustered from the whole affair of napping on the job and the red-faced ultimatum Ericson West had shouted at him in the frosted glass-ensconced closet of the Council Chambers, Sheriff Evans was about to have a heart attack.

"Mr. Evans, I heard you were looking for me?"

"Sheriff!" He barked, even though the Park Ranger attire needed some clarifying.

Whatever he was he had a .357 revolver strapped to his hip, and Loeb knew he carried authority, if just a little, because Ericson West, Mayor of Quill Creek, was beginning to feel like some sort of obsequious dictator.

"What can I do for you?"

"Where is it?"

"Where is what?"

"Sarah Enos' diary, you know damn well what I'm talking about."

Loeb frowned and let his stable, symmetrical brows slide together and become critical.

His voice was stoic and thick with clarity.

"I don't know where it is…you *lost* it?"

"You…"

"You were sleeping when I left." Loeb acted as if he was retracing his steps. "I guess your wife brews a pretty weak batch of coffee, anyway, I took her case file with me to *Logan's* and Mr. West already reprimanded me about it. It won't happen again. His daughter was there, Kim's her name? No,

Katie, *real* sweet girl…yeah, but like I said, West
was all over me for taking it…Sarah's diary,
though-gosh, that's rough…I made sure to put
everything back as carefully as possible."

At the mention of *West* and *reprimand* in the
same sentence Evans froze, and not from the cold.
His eyes were beady and indistinguishably caught
between fear and misunderstanding.

"You're welcome to come inside to look."
Loeb offered a broad gesture and ushered to the
open door of the cabin past the Prius. He leaned in
and whispered as if West was hiding behind one of
the many evergreens that surrounded them with a
sense of eternity. "If even just to get that bastard off
your back."

The Sheriff licked dry lips and held the
unwanted warrant with heaviness.

"You don't need that." Loeb assured. "Come
on. We have cookies. It's a big place, you'll need
'em."

Randy Evans' weather-beaten face and
Alaskan-aged body perked up at the idea of food.

"Well, okay."

He made it inside to find Cat at the dining
room table, typing as actors did when trying to
convince people they knew their way around a
computer, when in actuality Cat wasn't a very good
typist because she'd once had a falling out with a
set of parents that'd forced her go to another family.
The fight was about a keyboarding teacher in
middle school that hated Cat with a vengeance and
was a close friend of the parents. Cat was constantly
berated by the mother even though the teacher had
been lying about her, how she refused to type and
would always be listening to music instead when
the parents didn't realize Cat had poor motor skills

as a result of being hopscotched to different families. They cited they could *no longer guide the young woman in the ways of maturity* and threw Cat back in the system to be taken in by another family. Loeb had only assumed by her urban armor that she was adept at such things when in fact she rarely browsed the Internet and hated texting for its impersonal nature.

She didn't look at him but kept up her keyboard pounding, off in the corner by the broad window's edge. The Sheriff was lost in the expanse of the floor and boards creaked as he left the great room for the hall to Loeb's bedroom and the hall that split from that where one staircase ran up and another ran down.

Loeb came to stand behind Cat and examined her work.

"What's…*krgurzhzatchin pzozsnikksnin?*" He asked and she tried not to smile. The skin where her eyebrows should've been pinched together.

"I think it's Russian…" She half-whispered. "For what on earth is he doing?"

Loeb left her to put some cookies on an invitingly clean white plate and sensed Evans was beginning to feel not only condemned for invading their privacy but the dwarfing emptiness and untouched sparsity of the house was beginning to disorient him and whatever search procedure he was so ineffectively running.

He was about to go downstairs when Loeb caught his eye.

"Cookie?"

The Sheriff shook his head and continued, turning and slowly and descending into the windowless darkness of the bottom floor. It was then Cat shut the laptop computer and twist-flicked

the voice recorder next to it so that it whirled like
spin the bottle on the glossy table as she came to
stand close to Loeb. Her eyes were locked on the
darkened staircase as creaks and cracks became
softer and softer.

"I can only imagine his face…"

"Maybe I should go see, then?"

Cat snarled her smile and shrugged and Loeb
left with the plate of cookies, munching on one in
the hall approaching Cat's dark downstairs master
with some form of stealth.

He came to the door as Sheriff Evans, half-
bent over, stuck his hands in one of the shopping
bags and removed a silky blue nightgown that Loeb
had chosen as it sat between the color of his eyes
and the hue of her hair. Evans' bushy eyebrows
wriggled and danced and his fingers and thumbs
made small circles on the straps of the shoulders.

"You sure you don't want a cookie?" Loeb
said, and his bassy voice startled Evans, who
dropped the simple article as if *it* had been the one
to touch *him*. Redness and embarrassment came into
his face and he backhanded a dry fist across his
nose before bending down to wad and stuff the
nightgown back down in the bag as it was full of yet
more lingerie, and only lingerie.

Or so he thought.

"No." He said, gruffly, and waddled past.

He was quick and perfunctory in every room,
even going so far as to hastily lift the lid of toilets
and open cupboards and chests of drawers the
renters of the house had not yet touched.

Then he left, without a cookie, and without
the diary.

As he drove off, flicking pine needles and dirt
with the mashing of his foot on the gas, Loeb

slipped his arm around Cat.

"Do you think he'll come back?" She said.

"I hope so." Loeb nodded.

"Why's that?"

"Because we're gonna drive over to the Russian's place and you're gonna read to me on the way."

"You know I like to read."

Loeb tried to stow a smirk that was spreading across wide lips.

"I think he liked your nightgown."

Cat smiled with all of her teeth. At Loeb. At her typing. At cookies. At forty-five year old red-haired women that thought they were *the cat's meow* and the town was too small to tell them any different.

"Well then, we should swing back into Anchorage and get him one."

15

Shiva

Cat squinted as she read.

"It's ruined." She said, and Anchorage swelled around them in their insignificant Toyota Prius. The Chugach Mountains stole Loeb's vocabulary with grandeur that demanded imaginations of distant realms and heavenly kingdoms.

"I need to write a fantasy." He said to himself, staring.

"Did you hear me?" Cat thumbed through page after page.

Sarah had written in pencil.

"All of it?"

Cat shrugged and thumbed and something caught her eye.

"Hold on." Her fingers were nimble back to a spot that was done in pen and nearly sealed to the page before it. Her neck craned and hooked and she held it up to the light of the window.

It was horribly bent and jagged but as clear as day.

"Doctor's appointment…September 15th, 1991…Diagnosis, extreme anovulation…I am barren and will never be able to have children."

Loeb glanced at Cat quickly before examining

her face as the diary sank into her lap and her skin flushed of its sunny color.

Loeb parked the car near in a small shopping complex and leaned on the wheel.

"Talk to me." He said.

"It's the only thing on the page." Cat said, and slumped in the seat. "Not even what she thought about it or if she told anyone."

"What are you thinking?"

"I don't know." She said. "It might explain a few things, though…"

"What things?"

"Things we haven't yet discovered." Cat bit her lips and straightened, pulling at her cowl neck to ventilate herself. Loeb had the car far too hot.

"It's obviously a key to her soul." Loeb said thoughtfully. "Her lasting memory will be her love for children…it kind of…gives us perspective to know why she loved children so much. Starting with you."

"…Yeah…" Cat said, to herself, and closed the diary to lay a thick, mindless gaze on its gilded leather cover.

Loeb could only wonder what Cat would've been like if Sarah had raised her as her own daughter. Sarah's femininity had been captured and kept forever in the static black and white of the newspaper and Loeb's mind needed no stretching to think of what tenderness and joyful affection Cat used to receive in her arms twenty-three long years ago.

Cat was silent and stared into the road as automobile traffic, mostly rusty-bottomed trucks and sport-utilities flared past.

Sarah's love was still living inside of her.

"Let's go get some booze, before I cry." Cat

said, and smiled at him, her unicolor brown eyes comforting Loeb as to say he wasn't to blame for her years of foster care.

It was over.

Water under the bridge.

They ate fast-food burgers in the car with the shelf of a backseat and handbag of a trunk brimming with bags and it was nearly five o'clock when they arrived at Grigory Ukasaya's place.

In many ways, tucked in a tight cluster of sound-diffusing evergreens, it was the same as Loeb's rental only about a tenth of the size.

Loeb noted Ukasaya had no car and when he zipped up his jacket and walked a few feet to the small veranda guarding the home's entrance, the tall writer emerged from the darkness of his house and stood in the threshold of a half-open door.

"I don't want you here." He said, thick and blunt.

Loeb turned.

"I brought whiskey, 120 proof. Small batch, single barrel from Kentucky."

"I don't care."

"Stoli, then? I've got some of that, too. And frozen Piroshkies from a Russian bakery. Broccoli and cheddar."

"No. I don't want you here." He said, hardening with no emotion. "Leave."

"I'd really like to ask you some questions. I'd be grateful."

"No." Ukaskaya hadn't moved a muscle and Loeb was beginning to wonder about the location of the wolf-like dog he was sure was trained to kill.

Loeb had broken the writer's patience and was, for the Russian's sake, fighting a thought that said *present silence confirms past guilt.*

It was then Cat came around the hood of the car and the Russian noticed her blue hair and their eyes met.

"Who are you?" He said.

"Catriona Enos." She said.

Loeb's vision was slow and gloopy in dancing between the two of them and the twenty or thirty feet between the three of them was silent in the dense forest where only the lightest hints of the sea muddled the edges of their ears.

The Russian stepped from his dark wood bunker walked with slow, tentative steps. Shiva followed, stout and formidable. She was in tune with her master's uncertainty.

The Russian must've studied her face for ten minutes if it was ninety seconds, and Loeb was getting cold as the sun sank and sank and sank.

"Yes," He finally said. "By God, you are."

Then he shook his head.

"Forgive me for being so coarse…please come inside. We have *much* to discuss."

Ukaskaya graciously accepted the items they'd purchased for him and once whiskey was in his hand the writer failed to stop talking about his early history till nearly seven o'clock, whereupon the fast food was quickly fading from their stomachs at the smell of piroshkies baking. They weren't counting on the writer sharing. His happiest state seemed still to hold a very flat and steady gaze of dim graying eyes.

"So that's how you got the scar?" Loeb asked.

"Yes. Russians had been American's enemies for so many years, young men raised their entire lives predestined to hate a people group they'd never met individually. I foresaw the same thing happening to Vietnamese and to Arabs because I lived through it, first hand. It's not like the media helped, making every action thriller with an AK-47 and a red star-not that I blame them, but collateral damage is as true a physical principle in this life as gravity."

"Still," Cat leaned forward, not having touched the whiskey she'd been given. "Why didn't you report it? You could've died."

Grigory Ukaskaya was wistful in remembrance and in that same moment Shiva left his side, crossed the space of a carpeted living room and sat down next to Cat, whose arm was hanging over the edge of her chair so that Cat was touching the dog's fur and couldn't resist. Cat began to pet the wolf-like dog and Shiva began to pant and looked up to Cat as if to say *don't leave, we're the only girls in the house.*

"I was afraid. I though the Sheriffs would beat me too. I thought everyone in America hated Russians, my life was so closed off and secluded...I had no friends. Sarah came to try to convince me to go to the police. Everybody knew about the beating but she was the only one who cared."

"So the police knew?"

"Yes, they knew but wouldn't investigate unless I came out with accusations against specific people and pressed charges."

A few days before Sarah died, the Russian had been followed to his home by a group of masked men and severely beaten. Ukaskaya always believed it was to commemorate the collapse of the Soviet Union and didn't even know if they were Russian or American, since he was an anti-communist writer in exile, he had *two* enemies.

They were probably high school football players hopped up on adrenaline and alcohol but what difference did it make?

The scar was still on his face, regardless.

"What did you make of the diary being found in the waters out here?"

The writer sighed with lungs that sounded creased and weary.

"Eagle's Pointe is a cove and carries an odd half-whirlpool tide. I believe her diary was planted there because it would be guaranteed to float and then I would also be incriminated as the outsider that I was." The writer sat up in his heavily padded chair and poured himself more whiskey. "I wasn't even approached by the police until they found the diary. Jurisdiction of this house falls under the next County. It took them at least a week to work it all out. By then, the damage was done. I'd healed just enough to look guilty of something negligible and talk was going around town that Sarah had come and seen me but there was no evidence. The rumors were already eating away at everyone. I don't know how many times they searched this place. They even confiscated some of my writings and never gave them back…anything *romantic* in nature. I've never felt so ashamed."

The oven pinged behind a thick wall covered in cubist art paintings and Ukaskaya pressed himself up with difficulty.

"Come on Shiva, dinner time."

The sweet smell of Piroshkies permeated the drab and sullen house and the dim view of Eagle's Pointe, in which birds of prey were commonplace, was swamped in darkness.

Shiva did not move. She pretended not to hear her master.

Loeb finished his whiskey with a wince and stood. Cat still didn't touch hers and stood and

Shiva watched her intently and her throat resonated with a low-pitched whine almost too subtle to hear.

"I wish I could've known Sarah better." Ukaskaya said. "It wasn't until that day that I knew her parents were Russian and that she was a Russian Jewish immigrant. It breaks my heart. I would've been like a father to her...and to think that she'd graduated college with help from her brother's restaurant...to be a teacher...what a gift she was..." His hands went to his pockets and gravity sucked at his skin and pulled his head toward his chest. "But I was in exile and her death only made it worse. I'd cut myself off from the world and only drifted further out into space."

Loeb's posture straightened with a final question and prepared himself for the cold and dark.

"Who do *you* think it was?"

"I don't know. But I do believe they still live here, somewhere, and they've stayed in control of things, keeping a lid on their secret." Then the writer smiled with hollow bitterness to himself and turned for the oven. "If I killed someone I'd leave town as soon as possible. But that would make sense to a man who's already fled adversity..."

Shiva longingly soaked up Cat's final strokes through her hair and Loeb knew the feeling. They looked each other in the eyes, Cat and the dog, and seemed to have an unspoken understanding Loeb didn't grasp the fullness of.

Loeb zipped up his jacket and breathed in the brisk frost of the dry night. Snow had not yet made an appearance but Loeb had a feeling it was not far off.

Cat rubbed her hands together quickly to get heat in them and Loeb interrupted by grasping her left hand with his right and interlocking their fingers.

"I think it's about time I took you out to dinner for a proper date." He said.

Cat's lips curled in their pleasured snarl.

"Do you think this dump has anywhere decent? I mean…" Cat hips sunk in a lean and her right foot twisted on its toe and her right hand hung on her cowl neck. "I can cook you just about anything you want. Especially if you ask real nice."

"There'll be plenty of nights for cooking." Loeb said. "Tonight, we've got to relax. Let's not talk about the case at all."

Cat followed him to the car but had a premonition that would not be so.

16
Fisher's

The restaurant was nearly empty. It was a quaint thing that conjured up images of a time when seafaring was a means of travel, whaling was legal, and clean-shaven non-smokers were a rare and unmanly breed. Cat enjoyed the historical black and whites in black frames dotted around the place and though Loeb didn't give two thoughts about the décor, he was beginning miss the familiarity of LA's colors and man-made materials. The restaurant was named *Fisher's* and its dark wood booths, though intimidating at first, were rimmed in over-polished brass as was the bar top and ship's wheel hostess stand and the mood lighting provided the perfect environment for Cat and Loeb to sit across from each other and talk about nothing.

"What kind of first name is Loeb, anyway?" Cat asked, placing her cigarettes and lighter on the table.

"It was only a matter of time." The blue-eyed man smiled and sat back in the booth, stretching out his legs in the aisle. "I have a big family-it puts other big families to shame. They all live in San Fran and I don't see them very much, but when I was little I thought I'd never get away from them…" Loeb then poked his straw around a fizzling glass of root beer and the ice clinked. "I have a bit of a different view on that now that I know a little more about your family situation. I left them for LA because I felt trapped. Their pressures of college and career were...*outrageous.*"

"Sidetrack." Cat said, her nails rippling the tabletop. Her brown eyes were tight on her boyfriend.

"Oh yeah...Loeb is an amalgamation of my Grandparents. Lenora and Oscar Rosenthal, Mother's side, and then Esther and Bartholomew Cohen, Father's side. Some people say *lobe* like *earlobe* but Mom and Dad always said *leeb.* It kind of sounds like a last name, I know, but an actor-musician friend of mine who I see from time to time in MacArthur Park has three first names, Paul Michael James. He's going to marry someone with three as well, and she won't drop hers because she's on the rise in the biz so she's going to add a hyphen. Her name'll be Lois Anne Christopher-James."

"Okay." Cat smiled. Even Loeb's *to the point* contained sidetracks. "Now I know. What about..."

It was then a young red-haired waitress arrived with complimentary sourdough bread made from a hundred-year old starter. Cat didn't like sourdough. She only made soda bread.

"Hi again." The young girl said and Cat's levity all but vanished as the full force of the redhead's cutesy appeal centered on Loeb like a laser beam. Their previous waitress had been a decrepit 1901 model and had taken nearly ten minutes to get complimentary waters and another ten to grab Loeb's soda.

"Don't you work at *Logan's*?" Loeb asked.

"That's lunch. This is dinner. Dad owns both, so, why not?"

Katie then turned to Cat in wonder of what magical object could hold Loeb so steadily in the palm of her hand and made no attempt to hide a curling of the nostrils and hardening of the eyes she'd inherited from imitating her father. Katie's chin rose in the slightest and she turned back to Loeb.

"Mom did all the recipes way back when. Mom's quite the cook. You should see her hack through a winter squash in a minute flat. Gutted and chunked and everything. She and Dad used to work like dogs. Dad pretty much owns all of Quill Creek. He gets a lot from the mooring licenses. Quill Creek is close to one of the best salmon runs this side of the Kenai peninsula."

"King salmon?" Cat asked.

"Yeah." Katie said, passing her an immature face that said *of course King, what are you, stupid?*

"Well," Loeb took a sip of his root beer and even its cloying taste couldn't rid his mouth of the tension rising between the two women and their indelibly obvious differences. "I'll have a garden salad with thousand island to start, no croutons please, and the King Crab and Tenderloin special…can I have steamed potatoes instead of mashed?"

"You can have whatever you want." Katie eased with a touch of her mother's smoothness. Cat's fingers gripped the edges of the giant menu.

"And for you?" Katie asked.

In that moment Cat's mouth sagged open as thousands of images flashed through her mind without her expecting them to, scenes of working a twenty-four hour diner where female waitresses did gross things to offensive male diners or, in the rare case a boyfriend'd been stolen, to the women as well. She'd seen spitting in drinks, snot in soup, and even...

"I'll have an unopened bottle of beer." Cat said, tightly.

Katie shrugged and took their menus and was about to leave before facing Loeb.

"We have excellent deserts, too."

"I'll keep that in mind." He smiled and his forehead was on fire with Cat's unicolor glare.

"Why didn't you get anything?" He asked.

"I was afraid she'd spit in it. I'll share yours. Besides, I don't eat very much."

Cat then grimaced and fanned her hand before her as if she'd caught a whiff of an outhouse.

"She smells like a preteen cheerleader."

Loeb laughed to himself as she stuck the pack of Marlboro Gold to her mouth and lit the one that stuck, blowing the first puff around her through her mouth like a cleansing incense. "I hate that *disgusting* fruity smell..."

"Oh..." Loeb stopped laughing and laid his left hand on her right for a small squeeze. "You're one of a kind, Catriona."

At the mention of her given name her face remained placid but Loeb was sure he caught a glimmer in her brown eyes.

He didn't have time to pursue it. A tall man burst through the vestibule of the front door, bringing with him a frigid slap of air. Loeb turned to see the man was heavily bearded with a matted tangle years in the making and the hair of his head was buzzed down to the nubbins. He looked like a Viking warrior, the ethos of which was sealed in semi-insane hazel eyes and the odd light they possessed. His steps were announced in steel-toed weatherproof boots and everything about him resonated with *form following function*. Loeb spotted a multi-tool in a holster on one-side of his hip and a cellphone in a holster on the other.

He seemed to be looking for someone.

His eyes pinged the room like a Doppler and locked on to their target.

He was looking for Loeb Cohen.

About halfway into making it to the heavy walls of the booth Ericson West entered in a similar manner.

"Hey!" He shouted. "Get back here."

"I've got nothing to say to you." The man half-turned and continued toward Loeb, who was bending to see. Cat was wide-eyed and was shrinking into the booth at the man's tangible ferocity.

"You get out of this restaurant right now or I'm gonna get Sheriff Evans over here."

That froze the big man. He turned slowly and Loeb could sense the diners on the other side of the restaurant, though he could not see them, begin to coagulate in the stiffness of the wooden booths and low mood lighting glinting off the polished brass.

"That's your answer to everything, ain't it you big coward? I'd like to see you do something about it yourself and not hide behind your precious little town-just me and you, for once, like it always shoulda been."

The man bowed up to West and in contrast West looked about ten years older and ten pounds heavier. West said he'd been in the military but what did that matter in the face of a man with wild eyes and forest gnarled hands?

"That's what I thought." The man said. "You're a coward."

"What's this about?" Loeb said, standing.

"None of your business, Cohen." West hollered past the Viking and Katie swept in from the kitchen with a hurried shuffle, only to stop and take it in with no small horror.

"Shutup, *Mayor.*" The man said and shifted his powerful weight so that he only had to turn his head to speak and stood in a strange Mexican standoff between Loeb and Ericson West.

"You're the writer, right? The guy that wants to know the truth about Sarah?"

"Yes, that's right."

"Don't give him the time of day, Cohen." West ordered.

Loeb moved a step forward and leaned on the edge of an abutting booth. Katie inched closer and was somehow now in an alliance with Cat to see that Loeb came to no harm.

"The name's Fox." He said. "I'm a Bounty Hunter. I run a company called FoxHunt International, it's based in Tamo."

"Pleased to meet you." Loeb said.

"Word travels fast around here and I wanted to talk to you." Fox disregarded Loeb's politeness and turned to West and his granite face for emphasis. "*In private.*"

"You can come to my cabin tomorrow." Loeb said. "We have cookies."

It didn't dispel the bloody tension between the two men and Loeb could only guess what ancient rift was about to drive them to fists.

The novelist's mind zipped with possibilities, but he'd been wrong before and stood his ground like a statue.

"Whatever he says is a lie." West nearly growled without breaking eye contact with the Bounty Hunter.

"You said Ukaskaya was a liar too." Loeb was quick, failing to keep his mouth from staying shut like Cat's was. "And he didn't trust the cops enough to tell them he got beat up."

"The Russian's still here?" Fox's mean face twisted and turned to Loeb. "I'm surprised these bigots haven't shamed him to death, yet."

"You shut your damn mouth, white trash." West raised his finger and Cat turned to Katie who was beginning to get upset. Part of Cat was urged to comfort her, the other part wanted to swat her away like a fly.

"Or what?"

"Just because you've got a concealed weapons permit doesn't mean you can carry in here. The laws of this town are very *very* clear and I've told you once if I've told you a hundred times, you're not welcome in Quill Creek and if you don't leave *right now*," West worked into full shout, "then I will throw you in jail myself!"

Ears rang in the subsequent silence before Fox's strange hazel eyes glimmered with simmering intensity. He pulled his hands up across the breadth of his chest.

"It's okay. I'm just passing through, like I said. I'm in the area looking for somebody and I just wanted to have a few words with the guy while I waited. I'll spend the night across the county line to show what a gentleman I am but tomorrow, I'm going to see Mr. Cohen, okay? And there's not a damn thing you can do about it. I'm not breaking any laws talking to somebody and if you want to sit and wait outside his door to bust me for carrying a concealed weapon when you have some hokey township constitution against it, written in parchment and signed with a quill, just try and see how that would fly in court. I dare you. Keep in mind," The Bounty Hunter named Fox was doing everything in his power not to get physical with West. "That *I* put criminals *back* in jail for a living. What the hell do you do? Huh? You're a fake, West, you always have been. Your town's a fake and I won't even talk about your wife in the presence of your daughter but you know damn well what I'd say if she weren't here, and it's not her fault, okay? It's yours."

With that, Fox left, and brushed the edge of a well-muscled shoulder against West's shoulder for antagonism's sake.

West stared into the floor, breathing as if he'd run a mile. Purple tinted the edges of his face and his large hands were vibrating, squeezing themselves bloodless in fists. Loeb turned when West wasn't going to speak and saw Katie was crying with soundless sobs and Cat had her arm around her.

They were both seated in the booth.

West left in the bluster he'd came with and Loeb informed Katie they'd have two King Crab specials as he was sure Katie was well over the thought of spitting in Cat's food.

Loeb finished his root beer as Katie returned with his salad, having put the order in like a wilted flower. Her makeup was streaked and she was still cute but her falling apart like a house of cards had drastically aged her and her cuteness was obviously that of a simple young girl's, locked in a certain space and time.

"It's okay." Loeb said.

Katie sniffed, tissue in hand, which made Loeb glance sideways at the plate of salad.

"You don't understand."

Cat surprised Loeb yet again but Loeb was finding out that Cat was nothing but one surprise after another.

"If you want you can spend the night at our place. We've got rooms available...I know what it's like when parents fight. It won't go away with you sitting in your room with your knees to your chest rocking back and forth and praying. Not even loud music'll help. Only time and distance."

Before Loeb could protest under the strange possibilities Katie's shoulder slumped and her chin pushed forward.

"Omigosh, are you serious?" Her eyebrows rippled. "That's so sweet of you, God...I'm such a wreck."

Cat offered Katie her napkin and the girl blew her nose. Loeb saw Cat's maturity and it made him a bit proud. Cat wasn't taking the high road, she *was* the high road.

In that moment it also occurred to him that she knew a hell of a lot more about people than he did and in all of his writerly observations of humanity he'd been lying to himself that he knew what they said and did and why.

He'd made it all up.

He'd guessed right as much as a racehorse gambler but at the end of the day his batting average was less than average and he'd lost money on the whole thing.

Time was money, and unlike money, time was something one could *never* recuperate.

Cat, on the other hand, had no choice but to learn, to adapt, to make new friends, to trust and to read people in the blink of an eye in hopes of finding out who was a friend and who was an enemy. Her ability to do so had been honed by years of failure, pain, and suffering.

It blessed Loeb all the more than she'd chosen to bet on him and put her trust in him, to believe that he loved her and to trust in that love.

Katie sniffled and used up all of the tissue's edges and corners before stuffing it down the front of her apron.

"I couldn't. Dad would throw a fit."

Cat's sunny skinned-face was radiant.

"Tell him I invited you because we're the only three non AARP members in this dump. Tell him we played cribbage all night and I force fed you hot chocolate and we talked about girl stuff."

Katie took a good sigh.

"You'd do that?"

"Yeah." Cat smiled. "Like I said, I know how hard it can be."

Katie nodded her head several times and smiled.

"Okay…thank you very much."

"Don't mention it." Cat winked. "Just remember that mine's well done and his is rare."

Katie laughed as she left with a bit of a bounce and it was Loeb whose eyes were hard on Cat, if a bit confused.

Cat shrugged, making her bony shoulders wiggle in the crème-colored sweater.

"It's a waitress thing, I guess."

Loeb chuckled to himself as she took a drag of the cigarette time had nearly nibbled to the filter.

It was more than that.

17
Gunshots

Katie wouldn't stop talking. At first Loeb wasn't fond of the idea of the twenty-two year old spending the night or the thought of Ericson West banging down his door for some possessive reason but the quieter Loeb became, poorly tending a crackling fire, the more Cat was able to glean from the young redhead.

"So that Bounty Hunter is only a year younger than your Dad?" She asked, and they were exchanging back and forth as if Loeb wasn't there.

"Yeah." Katie picked at a bowl of mixed nuts while re-arranging her cards. They were playing cribbage at the dining room table while Loeb was pretending to write masterful fiction by the fire, which had tested his limits of patience in trying to light, but was easy to keep going from a woodpile on the side of the house, even if he had no idea what he was doing. "From talking to Mom and sneaking peeks at her old year book-they all went to the same high school in Tamo. Sarah, Dad, and Mom were all the same age. Fox was a year younger. Sarah was going out with Dad and Fox was going out with Mom, when in actuality, Mom wanted Dad and Fox wanted Sarah."

Loeb took notes on all of it and cards made

light smacking noises on the table.

"Were all of them aware of that?"

"Yeah, I guess. Here's the thing though, and I know this because I heard them arguing about it one time Fox came back to Quill Creek after he'd been gone for like, seven years and Mom...you know." Katie was not ashamed, as if it was an unwritten rule that infidelity in Alaskan winter was permissible. "It gets so lonely here, and Dad was gone, as usual. I was at a Girl Scout camp down in Juneau; anyway, Mom said it was just like a one-night stand...more like a one-week stand. They shouted at each other for a month solid after that."

"How old were you?"

"I don't remember, just a kid...long time ago."

Loeb wrote.

"Fifteen two, fifteen four, fifteen six, fifteen eight." Cat said and leaned to move her peg and sat back down in her seat to dunk a cookie in some coffee. "That means Fox left Quill Creek right after Sarah died."

"Yes. When he left he was kind of skin and bones, not much to look at, but when he came back he'd seen a lot, you know. He was super hard and tough." Katie didn't get any points and looked to her crib for help. "He'd done tons of crazy jobs and stuff. But that's not what I was going to say about their argument, anyway, the fact was that Sarah was a prude and wouldn't let Dad touch her. She was a virgin and wasn't going to move forward with him unless he married her and he wasn't *that* committed. He was with her just because she was the prettiest girl, like *ever*. I don't know if he really saw much beyond that. She was fond of Dad, though-you should see pictures of them. There's some real sweet ones. What a couple. He was a three-sport varsity letterman since freshman year...and Sarah was so beautiful..." Katie got five in her crib and swallowed, dry-mouthed from talking so much. "So Fox got Mom pregnant senior year and she had an abortion...it kind of blackballed her to the community here. Most of them are really conservative. Fox wanted to do the right thing and marry her and the thought of having a baby and starting a family made him get over Sarah really fast. Besides, Mom was still really pretty, but I guess she still wanted to be with Dad...I think that's why she had the abortion. Fox didn't want her to. Sarah left for college and Mom worked all day with Dad in City Hall while Fox took a job with the fishermen in the Gulf. Sarah's brother was married and had a café in Anchorage and she got extra money working there, but when her brother and his wife died, strangely in 1991 as well, she worked something out with the board, something about the restaurant I think, maybe they bought it from her, anyway, the school gave her an early out with a full degree so she came back to Quill Creek and was substituting in Tamo till a full-time spot opened up. I kind of wonder what it would've been like with her here. She would've been my school teacher, you know? She could've even been *my* Mom."

Cat nodded deeply and shuffled the cards like a Las Vegas dealer, with deft fingers. She seemed to gaze past Katie into the murky middle distance where the fingers of firelight danced against the glare of the window.

"When did Melinda and Ericson get married?"

"A couple of years after they had me. I was born in April 14th, 1992. Dad volunteered with the Army in about...August and spent most of it in

Fairbanks and Delta Junction…he came back for a
hasty ceremony and left again…so Mom raised me
almost by herself for about six years or something,
until he got discharged."

Loeb made some scribbles in bubbles, writing
names and connecting the dots.

Honorably or dishonorably discharged?
There's records of such things…

Pieces were falling into place. Loeb wrote and
wrote.

Now he *really* wanted to hear what Fox had to
say, and it seemed the Bounty Hunter had a habit of
coming back to Quill Creek when the West's least
expected it.

"How will your Mom take it that Fox's back
in town, if just for a little while?" Cat asked, dealing
the cards. "I'm sure you're Dad'll mention seeing
him."

"Catch 22." She said. "If he doesn't it'll come
around eventually." Kaite ran curled fingers through
the glossiness of her healthy red hair and its slight
waves and Cat could hear the scrapes of fingernails
on scalp as the girl stared at a spot in the table.

"Mom's cheated on him like…four or five
times, though. She's got him by the nuts, you
know?"

"Why?" Cat pegged two by playing a five
after Katie's ten.

"Mom and Dad basically the own town. They
can't divorce. They fight like attorneys but they
both knew if they divorced and split it up the town
would fail. Dad really built this place into what it is,
not that it is much, but it wasn't much more than a
boat launch and a couple of restaurants until he
came back from the Army and sunk every penny
he'd saved into it. About ten years ago it was quite a

place. We're kind of still living off the kickbacks."

Loeb frowned and wondered if Cat was thinking it too. If Melinda wanted Ericson so badly, how come she cheated on him once they were married?

There had to be more to it than their daughter could understand.

Loeb made a note of it.

But the light of the fire was dimming and he was still adjusting to firelight, feeling a bit of a old-west re-enactor for doing so and left to get more wood.

"Fifteen two, fifteen four and a double run makes a dozen." Cat yawned as she pegged and arched her back for a stretch. "What time is it?"

Katie's words were sealed in an open mouth, stolen by the staccato report of gunfire's thunder.

The rippling boom echoed through Cat's spine and wrung her stomach like wet laundry.

One shot, then a heartbeat's wait for better aim, and two more shots, close enough to hear cackle and snap across the beleaguered limbs of the forest trees.

Cat pounced to height and knocked her chair on the wood floor where it clattered and added unnecessary clangor.

Loeb was out there, in the dark.

Cat fought panic as it gripped her and clawed at her throat and lungs to make her breath tight and compressed.

Katie was stricken with worry and tensed into a frozen ball, as if speaking buried secrets about torn relationships and infidelities had prophesied something horrid into existence.

"Stay here." Cat said and began to run with tiptoes to the front door.

"Do you have a gun?" Katie called across the great room.

"No."

"What? You came to Alaska without a gun? Everybody here has a gun."

"We're not gun people." Cat said, kneeling at the window to peel back the shade and her voice rasped in a harsh whisper. "I can't see. Kill the lights!"

Katie rushed to do so and Cat's words lingered in her mouth with bad taste.

Kill? Why'd you have to say kill?

When all the lights were out Katie ran to kneel next to Cat and lifted up her own section of curtains for a view of darkness and nothing.

"Where the hell is Loeb?" She said.

"I don't know but I've gotta go out there." Cat strained to see *anything* other than black, dense tree trunks. Even the Prius was just a dark shape.

"No," Katie clamped a cautionary hand on Cat's bony shoulder. "Just wait."

Cat couldn't.

She bolted out the door against Katie's pleading whispers and wasn't more than a foot from it when she collided with Loeb who dropped an armful of fir logs and after the hollow knocking of heads they fell into each other's arms, stunned and disoriented.

Loeb braced himself to sit up and Alaska was spinning and spinning and wouldn't stop. The trees were sliding up and down like plastic carousel horses and the space between his ears buzzed as if he'd been gnawing on power lines.

Cat swore and rubbed her forehead. They groped each other for solidity and stood up with loose knees. Katie was hunched over as her dark shape pressed through the doorway.

"Guys, get back in here, quick!"

Loeb dashed to the wooden cave's entrance with Cat in his arms.

"What?"

"I heard something down below."

"Like what?"

"Glass breaking, I think."

Loeb stood in the precipice of the doorway, rigid. His teeth were clamped together and his forehead prickly with sweat even in the chill.

The three of them flinched and shrank in their skin at a second smashing and crushing of glass down by Cat's master.

The darkness of night was never ending and thousands of scenarios rushed his head. The vast expanse of the forest seemed to shrink and swirl and suck his feet to the ground. The women were looking to him for guidance and even though Loeb Cohen was stuck in a land where men fearlessly stood toe to toe with eight-foot brown bears and shot them as if swatting a fly, he grabbed each woman by the hand and bolted for the Toyota Prius.

18

Reload, Reloaded

The car ride was taut and silent.

Loeb had dropped Katie off at her parents place two miles behind Shore Road. It was a spread of small buildings dominated by a giant split-level home and the lot was fenced and littered with snowmobiles.

Loeb then drove ten miles northwest into Tamo, a city of about two or three and a half thousand inhabitants and up to five in the daytime with influx from smaller coastal communities like Quill Creek. Tamo had a bush airstrip and a high school and a string of fast food restaurants and small businesses all caught up in a tight fist on an exposed plateau below the soaring shoulders of a gray razorback mountain.

Cat was puffing on a cigarette when the driving finally stopped at the foot of an hourly motel, the sign of which was burned out so only the *m* and the *o* were lit.

The room smelled of cigarette smoke and reminded Cat of her own bedroom in its equality of heartlessness and necessity.

Cat sat on the edge of the stiff bed with her head heavy in her hands and it wasn't until Loeb pulled himself away from nervous glances through spread blinds to hold her hand that she shook her head and sighed.

"You okay?" He said.

"Yeah."

"I'm not just talking about your head."

"I know." She squeezed his hand and pressed herself up for the wet bar and dropped into a quick crouch to hunt for something sleepy.

"I thought you were just paranoid." She said, selecting a 550ml of tequila and twisted the top and knocked it back as if it were cough syrup before padding to back to the creaky twin bed, covered in a floral-print duvet. "I guess I was wrong."

"It's my fault," Loeb tiredly took to the edge of the bed and Cat shifted her legs so he could sit at her feet. She kicked off the caribou-skin boots and they slid to the floor. "I just wouldn't stop asking questions."

"There's nothing wrong with asking questions." Cat corrected. "It's *who* you're asking. Ukaskaya's right. Whoever killed Sarah is still there and our presence has gotten to them. It means we're closer, but it also means we've cornered them."

"Yeah," Loeb turned to her. "I just...I don't know. I mean, someone fired three shots out in the woods so someone else could break in. Same person, a team? They could've tried to kill us...what scares me is its similarity to the murder and robbery. Maybe we shouldn't be looking for just one person."

"We should go to the cops."

"Yeah."

"And get your buddies involved."

"Sods and Pearle?"

"Yeah."

Loeb was about to say something and yawned.

"Come here." Cat said and pulled him to lie down, shifting her frame across the bed. "We'll figure it out. Just not tonight."

Cat didn't even bother pulling back the duvet and began to run her fingers through Loeb's dark hair as he faced the door and let the distant *m* and *o* lighting up the road seep through his sore bones. He was asleep within minutes, guided by the warmth of her nearness and her dispelling touch.

An hour later, at nearly three o'clock in the morning, Cat took another 550 of tequila to the bathroom and sat in the bathtub to drink and think.

Who had it in them? If Ericson West didn't kill Sarah he's still guilty of something...and what about Fox? Was Sarah the byproduct of their feud? Why'd he leave after she died?

Cat then remembered Ukaskaya's words.

If I killed someone I'd leave town as soon as possible. But that would make sense to a man who's already fled adversity...

Even Ukaskaya himself wasn't out of the clear, yet. And what about that sex offender who lived in the woods, Mills Anderson? He sat heavy and dark in the periphery of Cat's thoughts like an old twisted up tree in a field off the highway.

Bitter. Alone. Waiting.

Cat downed the tequila and was too tired to reach the bed and crashed in the bathtub till the sunlight woke her and she hurriedly pushed herself back up and took to the bed where Loeb was on his stomach as if he'd lost a fight. His head was uncomfortably crooked and his face was a smush of fabric, hair and skin. Arms helplessly pinned beneath his one hundred and sixty pounds, he was a captive to REM sleep.

Cat rolled him into her arms and hung on to

him, her cheek against the back of his neck, lungs against his back.

I love you. I love just being with you. The thought of losing you is killing me but death is out of my control, it always has been and always will be. Mom and Dad...Sarah...we'll find the truth about Sarah, but she's still dead, and we're alive. There's nothing wrong with living and not knowing the truth.

Life is living and alive, breathing and beating...death is dead and gone.

It's the living that are important, not the dead. People let the dead eat them up and hold onto them and keep the dead alive when they should let them go.

I could've died, but I kept fighting. I knew I'd make it back to what Sarah and Mom and Dad had. I knew I'd make it back to stability, back to home, back to love.

To you.

Loeb twisted awake in her grip with the searing shafts of sunlight hitting his face and once he realized he was buckled in by Cat's embrace he chuckled and turned to face her.

"There you are." He said and his right hand was on her back, rubbing circles and slid up to her neck to massage the base of her skull.

"We've got a lot to do today."

"Shh..." Was all Loeb said. "Just let me get used to this."

Cat snarled and leaned forward to kiss him and his hand halted her lips.

"Hold on," He said with a wry grin. "We've got a lot to do today."

Cat's free hand pinched him on the ear and he recoiled and sat up, ready to play fight but something stole his levity.

Thoughts.

Murder.

"How do you think we should do this?"

"How much do you have left in that expense account? We'll have to start over. Alaska's far too big for us, I'm afraid we'll get lost if we go back there like we are now with the same damn fool questions and wait like sitting ducks in that big house."

Cat's lips were pouting thinking about the blue nightgown.

"Okay then." Loeb said.

They checked out and drove the Prius one hundred some miles back to Anchorage where they exchanged it for a red Ford F-150. Snow was just beginning to float from the clouds and Cat held her hand out the window to catch a flake and watch it melt in the palm of her hand. Loeb found a hotel across the street from the police precinct in a broad block near the city center and Cat shopped with the credit card and came back for a shower while Loeb took a few hours in a scantily clad office of oatmeal walls and walnut trim with a Police Sergeant and Solderman on speaker. He was greatly concerned by the ordeal and offered to fly up though all parties involved knew there was no point. The Sergeant, a stocky Hispanic woman named Julia Villa-Hernandez, who listened intently to Loeb's every word with kind black eyes and a wide, if a bit sorrowfully featured-face. Her fuzzy eyebrows ended in sharp downward slashes and it seemed with every nod of her head, she was mercifully receiving bad news and Loeb felt she was sharing his plight. Between her computer and Loeb's incredible memory of the police report, she was well informed of the situation.

"Did you see who broke into your home or who fired the shots?" She asked and had a notepad at hand.

"No. I got out of there when the shooting started. I was concerned about the girls."

"Have you been back?"

"No. I don't want to. If you could send someone to check it out, I'd be grateful. I've taken a hotel room across the street from you here in Anchorage, I'll give you the address. I'm not going back there, I don't care about my stuff. Any damages will be paid for by my offices."

Sergeant Hernandez pulled her chair closer to an immaculately clean desk and used its free space to twist and lean an elbow on. All of the nuts and bolts had been dealt with and she was eager to ascertain what a man who'd spent less than a week in Quill Creek had done to shake so much dust from such an old case.

"What do you think happened?"

"I suspect Ericson West killed Sarah."

Hernandez nodded on the count of the love quadrangle, not asking why. He'd informed her of all he was conscious of and Detective Wilson's notes were on order from the neighboring county's archives.

"What about the robbery?"

"That's what bugs me. It seems like it happened at the exact same time to distract Sheriff Evans. It makes me think Sarah could've made it if there was no robbery."

"Do you think the murderer was in on the robbery?"

"It seems to me like a perfect distraction, like the robbery was instigated by the murderer, or they at least knew about it and waited for it to go down. Especially if it was murder one, planned to the last detail, almost rehearsed so that no one would ever know. What time was the robbery?"

Hernandez crossed her eyes above her nose to think.

"About ten to fifteen minutes before the body was discovered. Evans was slow to respond but adamantly defended the fact that he was observing the thieves from outside the building, yet didn't call for backup until he was already in pursuit. McElroy, by the way, was relieved of his duties after the guilt trip Evans dumped on him. I believe he moved to Ketchikan shortly after."

Loeb shrugged, and was thankful to be speaking to someone who was on the same wavelength *away* from the creepy stagnancy of a town overrun by a micromanaging has-been with a cheating wife and his bosom buddy of a Sheriff whose skill at police work was ruined by the fact he was a Park Ranger assigned with managing the shores and trails of Quill Creek and wasn't really a real cop.

Loeb was growing angry over the fact that Quill Creek was a sham too petty for anyone to change, and over time those who knew it as such had chosen to ignore it and let it die while the one in charge scrambled to keep it together.

"How could we go about proving anything, though?" Loeb asked. "It's been so long, I'm sure the original investigation covered all of this."

"No." Hernandez shook her head. "Those people wouldn't say a word. It was a dead end and there was no reason to continue. No evidence, no case. It's actually believed by those who study it, since it's like a Detective's lecture piece now, that

Enos committed suicide."

"Why?"

"It's a retrograde analysis, so I don't buy it, but it's the West's child, Katie Lynn. Her conception would put their relations around July or August of 1991 at the latest. Logically they began when Sarah was in still in school, probably in the winter. The tragic death of Sarah's brother and his wife in April of '91 sent Sarah back to the only stability she had left, and looking for a husband, she found that Ericson West was no longer interested in her but he had yet to marry Melinda. He was keeping his options open, I guess. Again, retrograde analysis. From eyewitness accounts she loved her niece and had no problem raising her on her own *as* her own. But then again the whole town could be lying and there's nothing to call them to the carpet. Ericson West built that town into a real tourist trap when he returned from his time in Fairbanks and they could be covering for him because if he goes their whole town goes. It's human nature to protect one egg even if someone else has a hundred and someone else has a thousand. I don't know anyone that goes there by choice, anymore. It's a place for people who don't know any better."

Loeb hugged himself and his head sagged.

"So we need a confession?"

"I don't know how you'd get one, but that'd be the only way. You'd be speaking to him at your own risk and I'd advise you against it."

"There was no DNA?"

Hernandez shook her head and reached in the desk for a candy bar, peeling the rapper as an unspoken gesture their time together was coming to a close.

"It was either a tragic suicide or a perfectly

premeditated murder. Those are the only two options and though they both rule each other out they're both impossible to prove."

Loeb agreed, silently, and stood to get Hernandez' various phone numbers. He left the precinct with the picture of her eating a chewy chocolate-coated peanut butter candy bar and it stirred within him hunger he'd ignored. The thought of Cat cooking up a storm in their hotel room on the third floor of the clean city block as powder snow began to pull on the levers of winter warmed his bones and he nearly ran across the street.

19

Sunshine

Cat was chopping in the kitchenette. Loeb entered quietly and let the smell of her cooking wash over him. It was something he could get used to. His family had never been able to cook and so much of his life of observation had been spent in restaurants.

Sad but true.

"Is this lunch or dinner?" Loeb said, getting a glass of tap water just to whet his mouth. The hotel room was an *I* shape of two bedrooms connected and/or separated by a living and dining space.

"Both." Cat said and ducked toward the refrigerator for a turkey sandwich and a cold root beer. "Eat and talk." She said. "I don't mind if you have food in your mouth. It's not like I haven't seen it before."

Loeb smirked at her as he moved one of the chairs from the table to the mid-waist countertop to watch her cook.

To be close to her.

His eyes lingered on her, climbing up her thin and tightly clothed body, now in black jeans and a midnight blue Henley top she'd scrunched up the sleeves of. She turned her back to him and occupied herself with the catharsis of soup making.

Then he noticed.

"What did you do to your hair?" Loeb couldn't hide his surprise.

"You like it?" She asked with a half turn and a crooked smile. "I did it myself."

What had once been an unruly hedgehog of blue was shorn to not more than two inches, bleached blonde, and formed to a stiff and subtle peak that wonderfully complimented her sunny skin and facial structure.

"I love it." Loeb said as her eyes appeared to be bigger and brighter, their singular tone of brown warm and alive.

"Eat and talk." She said.

"The cops know. Sods too." He took a sip of the root beer and lifted the turkey on white, light mayo, extra lettuce and thin tomatoes from the plate to see there was a yellow sticky note below it.

I ♥ U.

"I wouldn't want you to be without your regular." Cat said, showing stamina by stirring the roux she was making. "Just think what we'd be doing back in LA right now."

"Ha!" Loeb said, and the note went in his hip pocket as the sandwich went in his stomach.

"So…how are we going to go about it now? The police know but they're not investigating, right?"

"Correct, they've nothing to investigate. Hernandez, that's the cop I spoke to, she said…"

Cat spun with a cold face.

"Is she pretty?"

Loeb frowned and thought of her fuzzy brows and the candy bar but Cat said she was kidding before Loeb could answer.

"It's only those West girls that are after

you…"

"Like I'd ever want to be with anyone but you."

Cat shrugged and stood on one foot, with her hips cocked. It was a waitressing habit.

Loeb hadn't yet reciprocated her desire and she didn't want to admit to herself that until he did, she felt more of an accessory or coworker than a partner.

A lover.

Even though every time she was close to him affection gushed within her like a bubbling geyser or a juicy, ripe piece of fruit just plucked from the tree.

"When you're done with your sandwich, there's something for you in your bedroom." Cat snarled with pleasure and hid her face in her shoulder, taking peeks at him. "I'm sorry I didn't get to fully enjoy what you got me, considering the circumstances…"

Loeb finished the sandwich and the walk to his bedroom was punctuated by the hollow rattle of the empty soda can hitting the garbage bin in the bathroom.

Cat couldn't quite hear over the sound of cooking and her face, even with its lack of eyebrows, was a picture of satisfaction as Loeb entered the room with his new guitar.

"God, Cat, where'd you get this?"

"I saw it in a pawnshop next to the grocery store…I remember you saying you played a bit in college, and I figured, since we might be stuck here for the winter…"

She didn't even get to mention how much she loved music, her body was crushed in his arms until he rushed back and the bar to fiddle around and tune it up.

It was an old Guild twelve string acoustic, the finish of it mottled and aged. The notes fell from the guitar in a soft, nearly spongy way.

He played bits of bluesy tunes and fiddly fragments of things, but no real cohesive pieces and Cat stowed her disappointments that he wouldn't sing her a song.

After lunch, Loeb called Pearle to tell him everything was okay and it took him nearly three hours to do so. Pearle kept interrupting about how it'd make a great movie and he needed to take notes but Lily was at lunch and he had no idea how to work the computer.

Over a dinner of clam chowder and soda bread, Loeb discussed with Cat the best plan of attack to shake Quill Creek of its demons and secrets. They'd leave Anchorage early morning and only stay till early afternoon, taking their time and strategically poking and prodding whatever subject would occupy the crosshairs of their queries after pouring over Loeb's notes, the writing of which he had yet to put paper and ink to since he'd left the mansion under the threat of gunfire and had forgotten to take his original notes.

So it was nearly eleven o'clock when Loeb had finished scribbling and scrawling who did what when, wracking his brain for dates and trying to remember what all had been in those dusty shoeboxes of evidence.

By midnight he was trying to write the book, falling into the tempting crevasse that had made him a drugstore writer; in the hands of near genius one minute, in the trash the next. He was forcing a reconfiguration of the machine that had formed and shaped his career, trying to blend the inspiration of his experience with *Fractures* with the repetitious weight lifting of writing bang bangs.

They wouldn't mix and his engine was ceasing as a result.

Outside, Anchorage was dreary and peaceful, sealed and silent under a heavy dusting of fresh snow. He looked for the northern lights and saw nothing but the reflection of his own futility in the mirrored glare of the window. Nevertheless, he sat in his uncomfortable hotel chair and gazed into the blankness of a white tablet till one o'clock in the morning.

He was dry, bone dry and stuck with nowhere to go. There were no words, no million-dollar bestseller opening lines.

Nothing.

He scrutinized the darkness of the window and the yellowy orb of the desk lamp as it cast an indistinguishable glare. Anchorage slept soundly, not giving a damn about him or Cat or Sarah Enos and the man woman or child who may or may not have murdered her. Anchorage was home to Athabaskan Indians before the railroaders and shipwrights took over. 50 years ago it survived one hell of an earthquake.

It was there before them, and it would be there after them.

And the white frost blanketing Anchorage with the untouchable harmony only new snow could give the eye made Loeb feel small and insignificant in comparison. The Chugach Mountains behind the city echoed with their immense silence and the waters of Cook Inlet reflected it all with the impartiality of a beautiful mirror.

What am I? He thought. *Just a dust mote in the universe...*

The acoustic was resting in its case. Lonely and untouched since lunch and for however many years it had been neglected and forgotten about in the back corner of the pawnshop. He switched off the light and his eyes thanked him for it, so damn tired of being red-rimmed and run down.

Loeb thought of the horizon, in its dark mystery, and how beautiful and simple life could be when he wasn't trying so hard and getting in the way.

Loeb thought of her.

Then he liberated the acoustic and strummed a simple pattern, singing with resonance.

"I just want you to know...I love the way you look at me. Makes me feel like everything's gonna be okay."

Down the length of the connecting room in her own bed, Cat was sleepless and was struggling to tell herself how much he loved her because he hadn't touched her and was hell bent on solving the murder of Sarah Enos. So she'd kicked out of bed to stare at herself in the mirror.

There was only one way to find out.

She'd made it all the way it all to the edge of the kitchen counter with an intimate idea welling up inside before cursing herself and had turned back to throw herself under the covers and cry when the music began to thrum and cascade through the dead carpet and wallpaper of the hotel room. His voice rang through her ears as if she were plugged into studio headphones. Every other sound disappeared, including the jostling thumps of her heart.

"I just want you to know...I love the way you look at me. Makes me feel like everything's gonna be okay."

The music wrapped tender arms around her

thinness and drew her near.

"*I just want you to know...I love the way you look at me. Makes me feel like everything's gonna be okay.*"

Cat began to walk, bare feet silent until she could see the faintest outline of his shape in the armless chair pushed back from the writing desk at which he did no such thing.

"*I just want you to know...I love the way you look at me. Makes me feel like everything's gonna be okay.*"

Cat listened as the chords changed and she reached within her shirt to hold the gold pendant necklace she never took off and rubbed it unconsciously between her thumb and forefinger.

"*And if the darkness surrounds you, don't let it confound you oh don't let it drown you...just keep your head up high. If the darkness surrounds you, don't let it confound you oh don't let it drown you...just think of me.*"

The chords changed again and Catriona was adorned only by his song for her and Sarah's gold Star of David pendant around her neck. Every other thought of rejection and excommunication from the seasons of foster care past had been lost and forgotten under a blanket of pure white snow.

"*The wind the storm blew in...will blow them clouds away again, you'll be lookin' at blue skies.*"

Cat stepped into the room, leaning against the doorframe.

"*The wind the storm blew in...will blow them clouds away again, you'll be lookin' at sunshine.*"

Silence burned their ears for different reasons and it wasn't until the music stopped and the guitar replaced in its case that Loeb felt the heat of her presence and turned.

"That was beautiful." She said.

"It pales in comparison to the one I sung it for."

"Not from where I'm standing."

Loeb chuckled at her.

"You know, I was trying so hard to make sense of everything and write it out and the more I thought the cloudier everything became." His thumb jerked toward the guitar. "Then I just picked that old thing up, stared out the window, and turned those thoughts toward you. I've never sung that song before. It just...came out."

"Did you know," Cat's right foot arced on its toes. "That I love music more than anything else in life."

Loeb shook his head, his mouth twisted in the joy of knowing their love would never stop growing, and that he could always communicate the passion of his love to her through creative expression, albeit a book, a song, or some other medium yet to be discovered.

"Or at least I *used* to."

Sarah's golden pendant jingled as Cat leaned down and kissed him on the lips and it was as if their first kiss on that sidewalk in LA had been tasted, seasoned, reduced, seasoned again and served with love.

Loeb stood and Cat was buried in his arms as they crushed her and she squeezed him back with all her thinness had to offer, unconscious of all thoughts except the one that mattered.

I love you, I love you, I love you.

The embrace ended with their heads bowed together, forehead to forehead, and Cat began humming the tune she'd heard Loeb sing only moments ago as if it had lived inside of her all of her life. Loeb took her left hand in his right and his left kept her close as they slow danced in front of the snow-white window.

"I don't want to stop." Cat said, when the tune had unwound itself and there were no more words to say.

"I know."

"And I don't want to go back to that old dump. I want to stay here with you."

"I know." Loeb squeezed her tight and pushed his chin toward her bed in the next room. "But we're going to have a long day tomorrow, and I don't want to leave this place till we know the truth. I want to spend the rest of my life with you and I don't want a moment of it wasted looking back on what could've been."

Cat smiled at his wisdom and pecked his lips before her right hand slid down his arm with a lingering grasp at his left hand, where she wished his wedding ring was and was overwhelmed in her content to wait. For the man that had written *Fractures* for her and had sung her a love song in the spur of the moment had far more to offer than physical affection and their union, when it came, would only begin a lifetime of companionship and the communication of its growth.

Cat whispered her goodnight, turned her back and shut the door between them with a heat blooming in her belly strong enough to melt snow and ease her to sleep.

All of her life, Catriona had only wanted to love and be loved.

And the reality of day had finally come.

20

The Minotaur

The sun was cold and bright.

Loeb stirred under its influence and sat up against the headboard, fighting every urge to sleep the winter straight through. He waited to gain clarity as a runner sought to catch his breath and it occurred to him that the murder was as far from his mind as LAX was from Anchorage.

He visited the bathroom and brushed his teeth and blinked puffy eyes as he made coffee and shuffled to the unlocked door of Cat's room.

Cat was lifeless, her breath too shallow to hear, and he peeled back the covers as she lie on her stomach to run his fingertips along her back.

She woke with pained blinks, her face creased from the fabric of the pillow and seeing his smile with the sunlight over his shoulder she wriggled closer and braced herself on bent elbows.

"What time is it?" Her voice was a mumble, barely audible.

"I don't know." His hand came from her back to gently touch the gold Star of David pendant around her neck, having sat *outside* of her shirt since last night.

"You never take it off, do you?"

"No, I don't..." Cat yawned. "It's because it

was Sarah's. I was always obsessed with it as a baby, grabbing at it. I think I made a fuss for it when she died, I still don't know how I got it."

Loeb sat on the edge of the bed and pulled Cat across him and kissed the stalking tiger tattoo on her left forearm. Then he kissed the gold pendant and finally her lips.

"I love you." He said, hugging her with the crown of her head stuffed beneath his chin. "*All* of you. And when we get back to LA we're gonna have the biggest wedding of all time."

"Really?"

"Yeah, and I'm gonna tell Solderman and Pearle to shove it and I'm gonna self-publish young adult fantasy books with a zany blue-haired heroine who kicks ass and has a talking pet tiger that takes her from adventure to adventure."

Cat's lips wiggled and her hand ran along his arm.

"Not mysteries about a slightly...*pedantic* dark-haired former writer turned detective?"

"Nah...who would read that?"

"I would."

"We all know you don't have very good taste in books."

Loeb caught her lips before she could speak and it was nearly nine o'clock when they finally left for the hundred-some odd mile drive to Quill Creek. Cat spent most of it gazing out the window at what the snow had done to the landscape.

"...Yeah." She said, after the mountains had taken her breath away too many times to count. "You should write fantasies."

She held his hand most of the way there, her left in his right, and Loeb was determined to get her a ring sooner rather than later.

They were bundled up in different shades of identical garb and Cat had cubic zirconia studs in her ears and her upper lip piercings were gone.

Cat passed him a look on the way, a brown-eyed beam of contentment.

King Minos' Wood Shop had been chosen by Loeb after much dinner conversation the night before as the best place to begin the investigation's second leg.

This time, Loeb promised himself, he would be subtle, like Cat was, and they would work together to find the answers they sought, keeping an eye out for each other as Quill Creek held no love in its heart for either of them.

"What a strange place." Loeb grimaced as they pulled off the highway and rattled through the snow, passing the Quill Creek sign. They soaked in the poverty-stricken lethargy. The town could no longer hide it from their eyes and it was a lesson in judgment. Loeb couldn't believe his initial reactions to the place now that he'd come back to it after a reprieve and a heavy dose of secrets. What had he seen in it on their first pass through that he enjoyed so much?

It was a dump; the festering grave of one man's dream and it had all gone sour and stolid under his tight-fisted regime.

"You talking about the town or the Wood Shop?" Cat asked. Her face was twisted at the garish display of men and animals and their artistic state of oddity that lined the door of a long barn-like structure with no particular care.

They were just there, saluting the fisherman as they returned to Quill Creek empty handed, standing there to say, *ha!*

Loeb parked near the dock and Cat linked her

arm in his as they walked. They were both prepared for the weather and were snug in gray stocking caps and snow jackets; Cat's was dark blue, Loeb's was black.

"Remember, just the robbery, okay?" Loeb said.

Cat nodded.

Once inside, King Minos' Wood Shop proved to be an even stranger display of wares and hand-crafted one-of-a-kind's no one would want, and it instantly occurred to Loeb and Cat that the only things relating to Alaska had been placed outside the store for obvious reasons.

All of the pieces were taken from Greek mythology. It was a subject that gave Loeb a headache even though it was sewn into the framework of western civilization and the large barn amplified their steps with its warehouse-like stacks of figures and sculptures. Some leaned against the wall, their crazed or attemptedly beautiful expressions staring off into the rafters, and in the woodcarver's peculiar manner of half-painting everything, Loeb felt as if he was lost in some madman's dream of catharsis.

"Find anything you like?" A gruff voice rolled through the broad space of the room made maze-like by the endless inventory of carvings. It was strange how their pilings made walls and pathways in the otherwise cavernous space.

There were just so many of them.

Thousands.

Cat looked left and right and saw no one. Loeb held her hand as it began to squeeze his. He could tell she was not at ease, not that it took a scientist to do so.

"No, we're just looking." Loeb called out and

it was when he did so that a short man with a shaggy black beard limped from a tangle of Titans to stand close to him.

His eyes were almost closed by the purses of flesh that sat beneath them and his face was wide and flat and he used a walking stick fashioned from exquisitely patterned wood, perhaps curly maple, clear coated to perfection to make it appear like waves of water rushing across sand and light or blonde hair in the sunshine.

"See anything you like?" He said.

"Well, I'm Jewish." Loeb said. "I don't care much for the Greek stuff. Dolmades, though, I like dolmades. And a good plate of falafel with tzatziki, I'll take that any day of the week."

The man's face was emotionless and he bent a bit to ask Cat the same thing with the hardness of his squinting inquisition.

"I'm Jewish, too."

"...Well I do custom pieces. This is just my passion. I wanted to have an exhibit in the forest, not far from here. Up that way." He pointed to the back of the room, the direction of the highway. "I wanted to set the world record for the largest wooden mythology park."

"What happened?" Cat beat Loeb to the punch and he was again struck by how genuine she sounded.

Waitress practice.

"Oh, I couldn't work it out with the Mayor." He croaked. "I wanted to do a big outdoor event at the end of every summer, like my own version of the Eleusenian Mysteries. It's an ancient Greek festival that used to be held near Athens, where my grandfather is from. I even worked something out with a few of the local musicians Jig works for. Jig owns a music shop down Shore Road, can't miss it. Do you play?"

Loeb could feel the man's loneliness.

Aphrodite was no comfort to him.

Loeb wanted to ask about the robbery and get the hell out of Quill Creek for another evening with Cat but Cat broke away from her snug hold on his arm.

"Who's this?" Cat pointed to a prancing horse.

"Interesting you should say who instead of what." The woodcutter's walk was painful to watch and as he passed by Loeb smelling of naphthalene and wood glue Loeb caught Cat's glimmer, saying, *it's alright. I got this. Go sniff around, I hope you find something. Just don't take too long, okay?*

So Loeb left to hunt for something of note.

The place was bigger than he thought and he carefully took mental pictures of everything as Cat's conversation with the woodcutter became faint.

"It's a god?"

"Demeter."

"Who's he?"

"She. Her daughter was kidnapped by Hades."

"Who's Hades?"

Loeb made it to the back where the woodcutter's office door was left open and he poked his head inside. The office was only a small elbow that connected his workshop to the warehouse floor and Loeb gawked back to the creepy wooden cave and all the eyes staring back at him and rushed into the shop, feeling every bit the voyeur and even more, just like one of the robbers of twenty-three years ago.

It was only when he sighed and slowed his

pace and began to look around that he quelled the blood pumping through his body.

His eyes drifted past a giant wooden-handled knife collection on the far wall as it blended into antique woodworking tools, hung as a hunter would mount his kills. Odors of thinners and solvents mixed and mingled with the soapy spices of wood shavings and human sweat.

He didn't know what to look for and managed to find it anyway.

Stashed in a dark, musty back corner of the shop and nearly hidden behind a stack of rusty circular saw blades of various sizes, three fully formed and finished human-sized sculptures stood forever frozen in a life-like action scene.

Loeb shoved his hand in his pocket for his notebook and pen, writing quickly.

The tallest figure was a fierce and well-muscled, broad chested man with the head of an evil-bull. Its eyes were more yellow than red and its body was flexed and tense, bearing savage strength against the figure that dared to stand and oppose the creature. The detail and motion captured in the piece astounded Loeb and it was raging with lust and vengeance.

The target of its desire was a slim blonde, clothed in a rippling white gown, like a bride's, blown by the wind. Her face was pure and her eyes were the most dominant feature on an otherwise heart-shaped face. Loeb wrote and wrote and then the truth of it smacked him across the bridge of his nose.

Sarah.

Loeb scampered forward and tilted the figure to see her eyes. Sure enough, they were as Cat had described them. Black pupils were swallowed in an amorphous swirl of green and gold, rimmed by a darkened edge of blue that made the swollen body of green and gold pop with a piercing electricity.

So then who was the third figure?

He was a man not much taller than Sarah, outmatched in strength and stature by the fearsome Minotaur. But who was he? The face gave Loeb no clues.

The man had no face. He had no sword, no shield, nothing.

Loeb even wondered if it *was* a man. It was more of a human figure than a man, and nothing on or about it clearly stated that it was either.

It was only in the way, holding some opposition to the Minotaur in his posture but physics would dictate that unless the figure had other powers, it would not last the battle, and the battle would be little more than one swipe of the power-hungry creature's knotty fists or a brutal gore of sharp horns.

Loeb was about to wonder if the statue was unfinished even though the carving looked as perfectly done as the other two pieces and some inner clock told him to get the out of there.

His heart was ramping up as he forced himself away. There was more to it, there had to be. He wanted to sit down on the workbench and figure it all out, piece by piece.

Who are you? Talk to me? Show me your face! Why are you trying to save Sarah? Who are you saving her from?

Cat was keeping pace with the woodcutter's slow stride, talking up a storm.

"I bet you do a lot of eagles."

"Yeah, all kinds. Mid flight, perched, catching salmon...all different kinds of wood. I've got a photo album in my office."

Loeb had his hands firmly in his pockets and pretended to be lost in study of some far off wooden deity he didn't know and didn't care the name or backstory of.

"Hey…" Loeb said, insecurely, as he wasn't very good at hiding the directness of his intentions and he began walking toward them as to seem like he was browsing and not loitering; not snooping and invading the man's hiding of his only three finished sculptures in the whole place.

"I don't see anything from Minos."

The man stopped and a funny twinkle flashed from the slits of his eyes.

"You're looking at him. My name's Minos Dimitropolous. This is my kingdom…my labyrinth."

"Oh," Loeb smiled. "I get it…hey, what about that creature, though…the one in the maze?"

"The Minotaur?" Dimitropolous leaned heavily on his walking stick. "Oh he's here."

"Really? I didn't see him." Loeb looked to Cat. "Did you see him, honey?"

"No."

"Try City Hall." The woodcutter had a grunting, animalistic laugh, and began to walk for his photo album.

Cat beamed Loeb a *get me out of here* face as Loeb was buried in undeniable thoughts.

"Well…" Loeb cleared his throat and stood tall, rubbing his hands together. "We really should be getting back to Juneau, shouldn't we?"

Cat's eyes swelled.

Juneau?

"…Yes, it's a really long drive to the ferry."

Dimitropolous turned slowly.

"You came all the way from Juneau to see me?"

The man who must've been in his sixties though he hadn't a gray hair on his head was stuck between smiling and weeping.

"Have a good day, Sir." Loeb waved and his hand was on Cat's back, ushering her away from the wooden maze of mythology.

Their steps to the F-150 were quick and crunched snow.

"Dear God..." Cat rubbed her forehead with a vice-like hand before pushing her hands in her mittens. Loeb squinted in the brightness.

"You'll never believe what I found."

"Rosemary Crane, goddess of diners?"

Loeb told her about the life-sized figurines and Cat took the disconcerting news well.

"I don't know what to make of it." She said, running her bottom lip over her top in thought. It was a gesture of habit, and her studs were not there to provide slick friction and she stopped, as it didn't feel right.

"What did you learn about the robbery?"

"Not much. Just that he'd done a giant commission piece for a resort in Ketchikan and the thieves hit him the day he got the payment for it, like they knew about it before hand. I wondered about who was working for him at the time, like maybe that was the person who killed Sarah because they would've told the thieves about the money, but, he said he's always worked alone. He's the King. It was twenty-five thousand dollars cash. It doesn't sound like a lot, but up here that could be life or death."

"I got thirty for *Fractures*."

Cat rolled her eyes and then smiled at him.

"*Fractures* is priceless."

Loeb laughed until he pulled off of Shore Road to reconnect with the highway. Cat snagged his elbow with a tight grip as two County Sheriff's Jeeps tore past them, taking the turn for Eagle's Pointe and the residence of Grigory Ukaskaya.

21

Murder One

Loeb stepped on the gas.

"I hope he's okay." Cat tensed in her seat as the F-150 bounded through the snow. A heavy system had gone steady through the night and Loeb had forgotten to get chains for the F-150.

"Yeah..."

Loeb drove as fast as he could while staying safe. The pines thinned out as he approached Eagle's Pointe and Loeb parked at the edge of Ukasakya's property to stay out of the Deputy's way.

On their approach, they could both see Ukaskaya's plight was contained to the small space of his veranda and neither gained any details to hush their racing thoughts. Loeb glanced at Cat to see her face twist with uncontrollable emotions.

Two Deputies were huddled around the porch in thick coats and hats and another was on the radio, tall against the open door of his Jeep. The Deputy, a thick man with a cleft chin, spotted Cat and Loeb and held the radio to his chest with a flat palm advising them to keep their distance.

Loeb stopped and tried to gawk past the girth of the Sheriff. He couldn't see Ukaskaya. The front door was open but the Deputies were static and stoic, as if there was nothing to be done, and studying what *had been done* with the flatness only misunderstanding could provide.

The thick Deputy finished his radio message and his face was unkind.

"You're going to have to keep back."

"We're friends."

"I'm sorry."

"Please, tell Mr. Ukaskaya that Catriona Enos needs to speak to him." Cat surged forward, seeing Loeb was spinning his wheels with the Deputy.

The name captured his attention as if his neck was collared and she'd grabbed the leash.

"What did you say your name was?"

"Catriona Enos."

The Deputy knocked his hat higher on his head.

"Are you related to Sarah?"

"I'm her niece." Cat said, and the Deputy shook his head.

"You're...*the niece?* Sorry, I didn't know."

"This is Loeb Cohen." Cat said with even more boldness. "We're writing a book on Sarah."

The Deputy did a double take and offered his hand.

"Oh, really? Pleasure to meet you! Gosh, I love your books...helped me through some winters here, you know, especially that one...I forget the name of it." Then he leaned in, still gripping Loeb's hand. "But that last one, that wasn't really my speed."

Loeb smirked and bowed a tight thing.

"You can't please everyone."

The Deputy's name was Nathason and he was twenty-nine years old, originally from Seward.

"You guys gonna stay the winter?" He asked

as they walked.

Cat said *yes* in the same moment Loeb said *I hope not.*

"Well, I'm sure you guys'll work it out." The loose triangle of bodies approached the scene munching and hard packing snow with each step and the two Deputies were still obscuring what details had transpired behind the shoulders and elbows of their jackets. Nathason had put them at ease with his affable nature but waves of trepidation sloshed inside of Cat's stomach with the nearness Ukaskaya's porch.

"Frank, Jamie, this is Loeb Cohen and Catriona Enos."

The Deputies parted and Loeb was stone cold through his core. Cat's face was glazed with horror and she covered her eyes from the hideous sight before they slid down to cover her mouth.

Shiva was frozen on the cold slats of the porch, eyes open and forever hunting the one who'd ended her life with a limp tongue dangling through sharp white teeth. A 15-inch bowie knife protruded from the her ribs at a nasty angle, eviscerating the dog and spilling her guts on the deck. Blood was crystallized on the knife nearly to the handle. The force of the wound was the result of a violent, arcing slash and the hand that'd killed the dog had been possessed with the murderous anger only found in the most brutal of hatreds. Shiva's blood was a solid lake on the slats and had pooled. Icicles dripped and hung from the steps with morbid artistry.

"Oh my God…" Cat whispered.

"Where is Ukaskaya?" Loeb asked weakly, knowing what a diabolical blow had been dealt to the writer with the slaying of his canine. Shiva seemed to be his only friend in the world and Ukasakaya's life of isolation was a cruel and unusual punishment that may or may not've been self-inflicted, considering his escape from Russia and her politics to a land where he'd been unwanted and ridiculed for his heritage, his accent, and his beliefs.

His entire existence took on a very pale cast in that chilly moment and Loeb considered the inhumanity of the crime.

Someone had known just where to stick the knife, metaphorically and physically, and Loeb's blood bubbled within his veins, loathing the fact that one of Quill Creek's very own had performed the disemboweling to get back at him. Not the Russian.

Him. Loeb Cohen.

Stay away from us, the protuberant sword of a knife screamed in the hush of the snow and the forest. *Or it's your blood in the snow next time!*

Sarah died twenty-three years ago.

Don't try to resurrect her.

"He's inside but he's in no shape to talk." Nathason said. "We've called an ambulance."

Cat cursed under her breath and looked away. Her hand was trembling.

"What do you make of the knife?" Loeb asked, crouching to get eye level with the dead dog.

"It's a hunting knife, but not the kind a hunter would use, seeing as something that large is hard to manage."

"The suspect'd have to be a big son of a bitch to be used to that kind of weapon." The Deputy named Jamie said. He must've been twenty-three.

"Not necessarily." Nathason said as he was the biggest man there and was dubious of handling the knife. "Someone very skilled with knives or someone with very strong hands could manage. Skill makes up for size, always."

Nathason's smile was wry at the double entendre but Loeb saw no humor in the sight before him. Cat was waxing paler by the second.

"Do you think it could've been like a souvenir, then? A collectible?" Loeb was thinking of the woodcutter's tremendous assortment of knives and how he'd come from some strange side entrance through his maze of wood and myth to greet them. They hadn't shaken hands but the woodcutter had lived a lifetime of hand carving and Loeb could only imagine how many times the Greek had performed the hacking slash, and how being surrounded with deities and gods could mess with the human psyche.

But what about that walking stick? A limp was easily faked, wasn't it?

No, stop putting two and two together and getting five! That's not logical!

But what about Sarah? The Minotaur? The knife collection?

And who's the faceless figure? The woodcutter? Someone else? Who would come between Sarah and The Minotaur, assuming the Minotaur is Ericson West. He's at City Hall, who else is at City Hall...

But why would someone kill Shiva? Why? Why? Why? None of it makes sense! People have reasons for doing what they do!

Whoever killed Sarah had a reason, and whoever killed Shiva had a reason!

Didn't they?

Maybe Sarah committed suicide but Shiva sure as hell didn't. Whoever gutted her like a

rainbow trout and stuck the knife back in her ribs
knew they were getting two birds with one stone.
    Is that murder two or murder one?
    Can you murder a dog?
    "It could be a collectible but it's tough to say
right now, we'd have to test it and find out if
anyone's lost or *misplaced* the knife." Nathason sat
down on his haunches next to Loeb and pointed a
finger. "But you can tell that it hasn't been
sharpened by someone who didn't know what they
were doing or there would be cross-grain scratches
and marks. It looks pretty much new, like it was
recently polished. Blood would get into the cracks
and scratches but there isn't any."
    The blood only exemplified the facts, sealed
to the blade like some darkened strawberry syrup.
    "What about the angle?"
    "Two hits for sure. The first was pretty strong,
puncture and pull towards the body, probably with a
hand holding down the neck. It gutted the dog like a
fish. We'll check the neck area for cloth fibers and
skin, all that, since some considerable force
would've been placed on the dog. We'll also check
the blood for some kind of sedative. Dogs like these
have great instincts or else they wouldn't be alive,
and he had this dog for maybe about nine or ten
years, I'd say. The second hit was a sportsman's
touch, like sticking the knife in the cutting board or
sticking it in the dirt."
    Loeb stood and shook his head.
    God, it was so hideous...
    "I'd like to talk to Ukaskaya if I could."
    "It have to be at the hospital if you did. I can
leave your name and number but I don't know if
he'd be up for it. I think he had some kind of
nervous breakdown and his general health isn't that

great as it is. Sometimes people take deaths to their animals harder than deaths to relatives, crazy as it sounds."

"It's horrible." Loeb said and was about to turn to locate Cat and comfort her when the Deputy named Frank, who was in his mid fifties and was quietly observant behind sharp features reached inside the dog's ear with latex-gloved fingers for a rolled up piece of paper.

"Got something Nate." He said as he came down the steps. Jamie crunched snow back to his Jeep for an evidence bag.

The Deputy unrolled the paper while the others looked on with bent necks and squints. Each man read the note silently before three pairs of eyes landed on Loeb Cohen's sickened and flushed face.

The pines were shrinking around him.

Ghostly voices were mocking him from the forest.

Loeb re-read the note and felt worse for doing so.

The dog's your fault Cohen. You stuck your nose where it didn't belong. Alaska is a dangerous place and if you don't leave by tomorrow night you just might have a little accident.

The worst of it was, the note was signed. Not with a signature or something intended to throw the finders of the note off track, but with a sinister and macabre sense of iconism.

The signature was a knife, a small blade that sat somewhere between the one that'd killed Sarah and the one that'd killed Shiva. It was an open mockery of everyone and everything in Quill Creek; the professionals investigators, the book-writing sleuths, even truth, justice, and the American way.

It was like a middle finger to the sanctity of

life itself.

Loeb swallowed with difficulty and Jamie gave his partner the evidence bag before lurching back to his Jeep for the radio.

"…If you could, I'd like you to come back to the station with me, considering that note." Nathason said.

Loeb only nodded. His lips were a taut line covering a choked throat and he glanced over his shoulder to find Cat.

She was nowhere to be seen.

22
Snowblind

Catriona was crying in the truck. Loeb's hands were heavy on his arms as he opened the door and bunched in the cab. Her makeup of brown mascara was stained and sandy nude eye shadow smeared and she reached across the console to hug him and hold on.

"I'm sorry, baby." He said. "God knows…"

"Why do people have to be such bastards?" She sniffed. "I mean…it's just a dog…"

Loeb rubbed her back as her body shook. The gruesome image wouldn't leave her mind.

"We're going to follow Deputy Nathason to the station."

He told her why and what the note'd said verbatim.

Cat's eyes were swollen on him.

"My God, that's awful…" Her voice wasn't much more than a squeak. Whoever had killed Shiva had done so in a declaration of war and the note in the dog's ear was a brazen threat.

Stay away from Sarah, stay away from Quill Creek!

Or the next knife's in your gut, or across your throat, or jabbed in the spine of your little girlfriend.

Loeb studied her state of despair but was quite a mess himself. He had to be strong for her.

"I can drive you back to Anchorage if you want."

"No, no." Her fingers were white-knuckled, gripping each other. "I'm staying with you. I'll be okay."

Cat sniffed away her fears and slouched in her seat. She toughed it out, swallowing several thoughts as Loeb followed Nathason to the highway where they passed the ambulance.

Loeb hoped Ukaskaya would pull through. But who would be there for him? What would he live for?

It was about one o'clock when they reached the County station, a plain brown and gray structure bristling with antennas. It was stuck in a strip mall with a bait and tackle shop, sub shop, and drug store spilling out beside it. Cat spent a few moments next door, ordering sandwiches for the three of them as Loeb sat down with Nathason for a repeat of his episode with Sergeant Herndandez.

Nathason was a blunt yet easy-going man and his surroundings reflected such. His office was a forgettable construction of pale wallpaper and waist high paneling and tin foil was pulled over each window, clamped into the molding. He took it all in with a quizzical and sometimes skeptical face but made careful notes about what Loeb had said, fact and conjecture, and called Hernandez while Loeb stepped out to find Cat.

She was smoking beneath an awning as new snow fell to the ground.

"He warned me not to pursue it." Loeb said and stood next to her, his breath coming out as a cloud of a different kind. "The police doesn't take kindly to death threats. They'll investigate, but I'm not sure there's much they can do. Whoever's against our inquiries is good at hiding it and the only information they can get is from forensic processing, which takes a really long time."

She blew smoke out of her nostrils, mad as hell. Small veins made a v in her forehead as the smoke opposed it to form an x.

"I'm beginning to think the one who killed Sarah hated her." She said, staring at her cigarette before flicking it into the snow where it fizzled to death. "And I'm beginning to hate them."

"Don't Cat."

"I can't stop it."

"Don't." Loeb caught her in his arms and squeezed. "Don't." He whispered as snow fell.

Cat liked being hugged and held and being close to him steadied her breathing. She'd gotten herself worked up as she smoked, thinking terrible thoughts of vengeance and retribution if she could get her hands on the one that killed Sarah.

Moments later a faded gold Ford Explorer peeled from the road and carved a rickety approach to the County station. Loeb noticed rosary beads hanging from the rear-view mirror, jangling in the uneven terrain.

It wasn't until the driver threw himself from the car in a red-faced whirlwind that Loeb's stomach cursed him for not chewing the cheap sub-sandwich while he talked things over with Nathason.

"Cat, it's Fox."

He looked down into her eyes and they had lost what hardness they'd tried to have a moment ago.

"We need to talk to him."

She only nodded, fighting tears.

Fox was in a logger's flannel shirt, thick and leather collared, and probably had a weatherproof jacket in the car. Without a hat and gloves Loeb surmised he'd been in his car for some time.

"I've got him." Fox said to Nathason, with a sneer, as Loeb returned to Nathason's office with Cat a pace behind. Fox turned to them with some sixth sense. "Oh, there you are."

Cat felt Loeb flinch in the slightest as the fearsome Bounty Hunter who looked as if he could snap any minute and kill all of them with his bare hands smiled and had two missing teeth on the left side of his mouth; one top, one bottom, misaligned and crooked.

Cat squinted. There was something about his eyes that were familiar, how they were nearly perfectly round and were snipped downward at the corners.

"Virgil Fox." He said and offered his hand. Loeb had to shake it and closed his eyes as Fox crushed his bones. "But just call me Fox…I tried your place, you were gone."

"Excuse me," Nathason stood up. "Fox, will you bring him in so we can process him? Then you guys can talk. We're burning daylight."

"Yeah, sure." Fox bumped into Loeb as he moved past and offered no excusatory remarks.

Cat followed Loeb to a claustrophobic waiting room which reminded Cat of a cheap clinic and they both sat in card table chairs with the brightness of the snowblind window behind them.

Fox reentered the hallway outside the space minutes later with a haggard man who looked as if he weighed less than Cat. Blue eyes were bleary and beat, blond hair was a dirty and disheveled mullet and his clothes, clothes that hung on his narrow shoulders and reeked of body odor were dappled and spotted with paint. His second-hand basketball shoes were a size too big and half tied.

"Tweaker." Fox said as he escorted the man back for processing. He returned in less than ten minutes and stood near the doorframe to block its exit, elbows crossed. There was no hiding his power and his beard alone looked as if it were fashioned from tree moss it was so thick and gnarled.

"I went to talk to you last night and I heard gunshots."

"That wasn't you?" Loeb said, his face wry. "Shooting at West?"

"Hell no." Fox chuckled as if that were beneath him. "Just because I carry doesn't mean I use it. The rule of a gun is that you gotta be *prepared* to use it but mine's more for show, just to make sure some of the guys that want to get rough don't. If I pull mine before they can get to theirs, which is either hidden under their mattress or in their glove box, everyone'll sleep better. People with guns are usually cowards, anyway, I just reinforce the fact if I draw on them. They're more worried about dying than I'm worried about the mess they'll make when I shoot them and as long as I stare at them down the barrel of a Glock 40 thinking thoughts like that they just as soon put their hands up."

"Well, I didn't do much sleeping that night." Loeb said. "Someone broke in."

"I know. I heard about that. Where you staying now?"

Loeb didn't answer and Cat was glad. She didn't trust Fox having learned from young Katie West that Fox really wanted to date Sarah instead of

Melinda. Fox was as wild and unpredictable as Alaska itself.

A suspect.

Loeb changed the subject, unable to quell his boldness.

"Do you own any bowie knives?"

The bearded man's head snapped back and his round eyes grew just a bit larger to show more whites.

"I own one, why?"

One? Just one?

"Was it recently stolen?"

The Bounty Hunter uncrossed his arms and they locked on his hips, sitting above the belt of holsters his untucked flannel shirt made lumps of.

"Why?"

"Ukaskaya's dog was murdered with a 15 inch bowie knife, completely gutted."

"What kind of handle?"

"Deer or Elk antler."

A shudder ran through Cat and her hand slowly clamped around Loeb's as the burly man's eyes dimmed until they appeared to be truly dead and cold like the current running through Eagle's Pointe.

"When?"

"Nathason has all the details. Ukaskaya had a nervous breakdown. You should see it, it's horrible."

"I've seen a hell of a lot worse." The Bounty Hunter sneered and wiped at his beard pensively, while hoping the white blankets beyond the windows would give him guidance.

"Like October 4th." He said, taking a step closer. His back bent in the slightest and his voice was a cracked whisper. "I was mending nets all day, hating life and I got stone blind drunk at *Logan's*. Walking back to my boat I saw Ericson West standing outside of Sarah's door, and they're talking. It was quiet out, nice and peaceful, 'bout five o'clock and I felt pretty good. But then I saw Sarah. I'd never seen her sad, my whole life. Never. Not once. She was like a sunbeam but not October 4th. She was pleading with him, pulling at his shirt sleeve, and he wouldn't move. He wouldn't go inside. They both saw me and I just stood there and wobbled around like the drunk idiot I was, and they paid me no attention. It was a miracle I got back to my ship and I slept and slept and slept while someone murdered the girl that I'd dreamed about marrying since the day I met her."

"Did you tell the police?" Loeb asked.

Fox stood up and swore, shaking his head.

"I was drunk. Besides, I was a suspect. That's why I left. Nome was where I started and things just unraveled from there once the police cleared me. The whole thing turned me into a drifter. There was no proof of anything from anyone. I had to leave. But I knew what I saw. West knows. It was just me and him and Sarah, staring at each other for that brief moment in time. I should've kicked his ass when I had the chance." Fox took a full lung of stuffy air and sighed. "Well, now you know...just another man's version of the truth. Do whatever you want with it. You're the only one who's cared about her since Detective Wilson and I think he died of a heart attack last year."

Fox gave Loeb a nervous nod and left for his SUV.

Loeb would've bet all the money left in the expense account the bowie knife belonged to Virgil Fox.

He had the power to do it, but then so did West. Fox drove in from where? When did he pick up meth tweaker and where? Fox has a job where he's supposed to be invisible. Unaccountability for whereabouts is an MO.

But was the knife stolen? He was away, wasn't he? Where does he live? Was the knife at his home, or in his car? Why had he reacted that way?

Too many questions, no answers. If I stay, something'll go wrong, I'm sure.

I can't risk it.

Loeb stood and Cat tugged at his arm. Her face was ashen and pale as the Bounty Hunter opened the hatchback of his SUV and began to fiddle with long coils of rope.

"What, what?"

"Ericson West is not Katie's father." Cat said, nearly apologetically, as if preparing herself to see Katie's face when the news would come to her.

"Whoa, what?"

"Look at his eyes, Loeb, and his build. Ericson West doesn't look anything like Katie. Their only similarity is in shared mannerisms, nothing physical...Virgil Fox is her dad."

Loeb turned his head left and right and stood in a half-crouch to look down the hallway and make sure no one was listening.

"Do you know what that means?" He whispered, his face stretched, but then the gist of it hit him in the stomach. No wonder Ericson West had stayed in the Army and let Melinda raise Katie on her own.

Loeb then bolted for the door.

"No, don't!" Cat called after him but it was too late. Loeb's cerulean blue eyes were locked on a thread too vital to gloss over. The questions surrounding it would eat him up when the sun went down and if he was risking his neck for the truth then he wanted to *know the truth*.

Loeb crunched snow and Fox stood tall, coiling rope around his elbow at the back of his SUV.

"Did you have a one week stand with Melinda in the mid-nineties?"

Fox was staring at the ground, coiling unconsciously and the coiling stopped.

"What?"

"Did you…"

"That's none of your damn business."

"Yes it is!" Loeb nearly shouted. "Because someone's trying to kill me!"

"Then get your ass back to the airport and forget all about it." Fox's voice was a mock whine. "Go away and don't ever come back."

Loeb rushed him and didn't know what his hands were doing as they grabbed Fox's leather collar.

"Tell me the truth!"

"Get away from me." Fox tapped Loeb on the shoulder and he fell back in the snow.

"Katie's your kid, isn't she?" Loeb said, his fists clenched, as he crab-crawled for balance.

Again, Fox's perfectly round hazel eyes, snipped down in the corners, became dead with a swirl of cold water.

"Get the hell away from me." He growled and the rope dropped to the snow, making no sound.

"She's your kid," Loeb stood and pointed with an accusatory finger. "And Melinda never had an abortion like she told you she did, did she? She only told you she did because she knew you wanted a family and tried to crush you because she wanted

West. And she told you that since you're Catholic
and she knew that'd kill you. After Sarah died you
left and when you finally came back seven years
later she laid the whole trip on you, telling you how
you had a kid and how she wanted to leave with you
and she tried to seduce you."

"I said shut up!" Fox tore at Loeb's jacket and
hoisted him off the ground. His hazel eyes were
streaked with insanity.

"Katie's your daughter!" Loeb choked.
"Melinda only used her to get West to marry her!
West knows it! Why do you think he calls himself
Daddy?"

Fox reared back and smacked Loeb across the
face and he collapsed to the snow. Tremors ran
between his eyes as the tree line shook and he
searched for equilibrium, the frozen wet piercing his
Los Angelean skin with icicle knives. Then the
earth soared underneath his stomach as Fox grabbed
him by the collar and the waistband and launched
him further into the snow. Loeb landed head first
and tumbled to lay spread eagle on his back.

Footsteps were furious in the snow and Cat's
voice sounded like a stretched rubber band just
about to snap.

"Stop it, damn you! Stop it!"

She rushed to his side, nearly jumping to her
knees and Loeb saw her wonderful faces, all three
of them, phasing in and out and becoming one only
to separate again. He thought he was going to be
sick. Cat moaned and ran a hand down his cheek
and pressed herself up to face the Bounty Hunter.

"Do you know who I am?" She said, bearing
teeth.

Fox was caught in the fury of life, how it'd
lied to him, raked him over the coals, taken his

dreams and desires and scattered them to the four winds at the claws of a woman who never wanted him and had only used him as a means to an end to get to someone else.

Fox just stared at Cat. He wasn't going to hit her, but she stood between Loeb and the Bounty Hunter as the faceless man stood between Sarah and The Minotaur.

Cat clawed inside of her coat for her necklace, the golden Star of David pendant she never showed anybody and the only reason Loeb had seen it was because she was his fiancée.

It was Cat's one connection to love; in a life of going from home to home, to new rules and new laws, it was Cat's one connection to her heritage, to her history.

To family.

"I'm Catriona Enos!" Her breath was a puff of white. "I'm Sarah's niece!" She shook the necklace and Fox's hard face immediately flushed and he staggered back. A weather-scarred hand came to his mouth and his feet wobbled beneath his muscular weight. Cat pressed on, as if showing a cross to a vampire.

"My God…" He said, softly, his hazel eyes streaked with some form of nostalgia long forgotten.

Smothered.

Buried.

Cat took soundless steps in the snow till she was standing near him.

Her voice had lost its fangs, seeing the change in his hazel eyes.

"You were the one who bought this for her, weren't you?" She asked, gently. "Only someone who really loves someone buys a Russian Jewish girl a Star of David pendant as an American Catholic boy. It must've taken you years to save up for this, it's solid 14K gold."

Loeb pressed himself up, finally catching his gyro. The tree line past the road wasn't moving *all* that much and his legs were ready to hold his weight without pitching back down to the snow. Was his nose still on his face? He wiped it to find what felt like runny snot was blood and what confused him even more than that was the sight of Cat, ten feet away, standing on her tiptoes to hug Virgil Fox as the Bounty Hunter's body shook with heavy sobs and he leaned on the hundred and ten pound twenty-five year old for support.

23

Arctic Fox

Fox had a place in Tamo. He had a plane
there, too, a four-seater Cessna 170 and Cat
shivered entering his one bedroom rambler near the
high school because it was void of color and life;
new in that it was unlived in and used up in that its
antiquated seventies construction hadn't dated well.
Tin foil had been crimped to all of the windows. He
offered Loeb and Cat a beer, which they both
declined and he drank three himself as they talked
into the early evening.

"So you refused her?" Loeb said, speaking of
Melinda.

"Yes. I'd changed so much those seven years.
I'd lived a hard life. It seemed to be the worst
temptation a man could deal with. But you see,"
Fox sipped his beer and took nearly all the space in
a loveseat. "I was raised Catholic, I was raised to be
moral. I wanted family and I fell into Melinda's
scheme to get Ericson. I must've been the dumbest
box of rocks in Quill Creek. Ericson and Melinda
built that town into what it is and Sarah even went
off to college but I was going to be an elbows and
knuckles laborer all my life. I knew Melinda wanted
more than that, I always knew. Just the way she
used to look at him, she never looked at me that

way. I was what I was but Ericson West was always her dream of what could've been."

Cat frowned and toyed with her stocking cap, unconsciously crimping it in her fingertips as if it were a Piroshky. She was seated next to him, Loeb opposite them on a milk crate near the front door.

"There's no delicate way to say this." She said.

"It's okay. Whatever's left of me is used to run around this place getting bail jumpers, meth tweakers and the like. Sarah deserves the truth. If there's anything I can do to help, I'll do it. Especially because you're Sarah's niece. I remember wanting to hold you but never having the guts to ask Sarah. Plenty of other people did, and they always made such a big deal about you. It made me think even more about kids."

The Bounty Hunter finished his beer and tossed it toward a plastic bag on the floor. If he'd known Cat was Sarah's niece back at the station he wouldnt've hit Loeb and hadn't apologized for it and more than likely wouldn't, though Loeb gained a few points in Fox's book for not running in the station and telling Nathason the Bounty Hunter'd struck him like a piñata.

"If Melinda wanted Ericson so bad, then why'd she cheat on him so many times after she finally got him?"

Loeb gently touched his nose to see if it was still tender and was content to let Cat carry the questioning. Her methodology had gotten them both a lot further in Alaska than his. He'd never thought of himself as abrasive or pushy. Maybe it was just because Cat was from Alaska, she was one of them.

Or not.

She just had a way with people, in the same

token Loeb had a way with words.

Fox coughed a grumbling thing.

"Revenge, I guess. She was obviously unhappy with him when she tried to get me to take her up north, so, whatever problems between them had only gotten worse. Only *they* know why they can't get along. I don't know but I'd say she didn't start cheating on him till she knew she couldn't get me to take her."

"That makes sense." Cat said, and seemed to gain more sensitivity. "What's the story with the knife?"

"The knife was a gift from Minos Dimitropolous, more of a prize."

Loeb tensed in his seat as Fox moved to a galley kitchen to rattle drawers and then cursed because he couldn't find what he was looking for.

"Prize?" Loeb said, biting his tongue as the words flew out. Cat seemed not to notice but Loeb's skin blushed because he was trying not to talk and couldn't help it.

"Yes, Tamo had an outdoor festival, before Dimitropolous got into all that Greek stuff and kind of became a hermit, he used to help sponsor this outdoor festival at the end of summer. Anyway, he built this crazy obstacle course for our high school. The winner got that bowie knife. He's got quite the collection, and it was really sweet of him to give it up like that for a prize…especially since it the only piece he'd ever done with elk antlers." Fox thumped the floor to sit back down and Cat had to stand up to sit on the arm of the loveseat and did so in a sculpted thinker pose. "I think, because he had no children, he wanted to give one of the men something manly that would carry them on through life after they graduated. Ericson was so furious that

I beat him, I mean, I was pretty wiry, and he was so big and athletic. But I wanted to beat him, I wanted to impress Sarah. I knew Melinda wanted to see him kick all of our asses, every boy in a ten mile radius, but I won fair and square, and Ericson resented me for it."

"Were you friends before then?"

"Not great friends but we didn't hate each other. It just really…slid downhill after that…" Fox chuckled and stared at the shag carpet, colored, as it was, the most unfortunate shade of puce. "It's funny how you remember stuff like that. I've done so much in my life, so much more than him-I've rough necked the pipeline, been on crab boats in the Bering Strait, learned to fly and solo canoed around Kodiak Island…but I remember that day like it was yesterday. I've never wanted anything so bad. I wanted to win more than I wanted to be with Sarah, more than I wanted to wake up the next day. It was all I thought about that summer. I had to win. The knife was just a symbol of what I'd done. I never used it. I carried it everywhere but I wouldn't even sharpen it. It was almost like a tattoo, or like a ceremonial sword."

Virgil Fox's hazel eyes held Cat's unblinking gaze.

"I don't know how any of that helps you." He said.

"It does." Cat said, moving on. "How'd Dimitropolous get his limp?"

"Hell," Fox held a thick fist to his mouth to stifle a belch. "He's had it as long as I've known him. The guy's like, seventy something. You know those Greek genes. Ageless…"

Cat nodded and her posture stiffened.

"Well, we were with Dimitropolous earlier

this morning in his wood shop. What can you tell us about the Minotaur?"

"The what?" Fox frowned.

"The man with a bull's head?"

The burly man's pensive face deepened and froze, either trying to remember something or completely ignorant of what someone wanted him to remember.

"Beats me." He stroked his beard with his bear paw. "...How'd what I say help you?"

"Whoever got your knife to kill Shiva practically sunk the town." Cat began. "Ukaskaya was eager to help us and now he's in the hospital, shattered. Dimitropolous is implicated because he's got a giant knife collection, it was originally his, and he's also got a statue of a mythical monster trying to get at a statue of Sarah. He could've done it if he drove and his hands are strong enough but why? Whoever did it's just trying to throw the cops off their trail and knock another lonely old guy who can't take the rejection. When asked where the Minotaur is, he said City Hall, but he never said outright *who* it is. It's got to be Ericson West. They've had disagreements in the past. Also the Minotaur and Sarah are the only *finished* pieces left in his shop. Everything else is a graveyard. Even the faceless figure isn't done yet. I would venture a guess that he's waiting to put is own face on it before he dies. I don't know if he knows the truth about Sarah or if he's just suspected Ericson West killed her but he's obviously carried a torch for *her* and carried a grudge against *him*. You're implicated because it's your knife and you're strong enough to perform such a violent procedure. Also, you're naturally unaccounted for, coming in and out when you please with no one keeping tabs on you."

Fox sighed, the weight of his lungs catching the hairs of his beard and rippling them.

"God, you're right."

Loeb stood.

"So we've got to get a confession from West."

Cat held up a hand, her eyebrow skin pinched together.

"When did you lose the knife?"

Fox's hazel eyes held a glimmer, complimenting Cat's investigative mind, her intuition, her easiness with tough questions in contrast to Loeb's pushiness.

"That week I spent with Melinda. At first I thought she was just being kind letting me stay at their place, they've got this…maze of a ranch, some kind of weird farm with tons of sheds and outbuildings and guest cottages. Anyway, she tried to come on to me once in the shower and I ran away in the forest buck naked. That was the end of it for me. I must've left it there but I never knew until it resurfaced in that dog. You know how you try to retrace your steps and it makes you forget all the more? Well…"

Cat laid her hand on Fox's shoulder.

"Katie said they argued for a month after that. Ericson must've found it and thought you'd been there."

"Well I had!"

"No, I mean that you slept with Melinda when you didn't."

"Why would she say that he did when he didn't?" Loeb interrupted, his lower back aching from his time on the crate.

"Because she wanted to leave him, yes, but she wanted him to have a reason to divorce her. It was her last play. Then she'd take half of what they had, *including* shared or maybe even full custody of Katie and she'd make her final offer to Fox, only with the goods in hand instead of just empty promises."

Fox's teeth came together in a moment of rage and then he pushed himself back in the sofa, his bowling ball of a skull clunking against the drywall, covered as it was by cheap, lead-filled paint, eggshell in color.

Cat sighed on the arm of the loveseat and let the words sink in.

"We should go." She said, standing. Loeb thought he caught a flash of sadness in Fox's round hazel eyes and as he saw them he saw Katie. They were exactly the same, God knew how he missed it.

Sometimes, Lobster, Loeb heard Pearle's wisdom rattling around the back of his mind, *you can look for something so hard you'll never find it.*

Fox stood with his hands aimlessly at his sides.

"Well, it was good to talk to someone." He said, roughly. "Like confession. I haven't been in so long."

"Yes it was." Cat said and gave him a hug, which he reciprocated and tried not to squeeze too hard for fear of breaking her.

Loeb just waved, wondering if his hands were in any shape to write after all of the handshakes they'd been through.

They crunched snow to their truck and the elevated plateau of Tamo with the razorback granite mountain behind a jagged line of firs and pines was a haunting, monolithic sight. It was as if Sarah's killer was looking down from its peak, saying *come and get me. I'm still here. You know where to find me. What are you waiting for? Bring the cops, I don't care! I'll kill you all!*

Loeb clasped Cat's hand for a squeeze.

"What a sad guy." Cat said, shoving her stocking cap back on her head, adjusting it to show her cubic zirconia studs. Her breath was white and she dug into her coat for cigarettes.

"Yeah…"

"I mean, he's done the right thing all of his life and always got the wrong end of the stick for it." Cat lit one up and her face wrinkled against the dark harshness of the cold and the bitter fog hanging in her lungs.

"We've got to go back to the cops." Loeb said, opening the door to the truck and letting the granite-faced mountain steal his attention in the falling dark. "I still want to know who was shooting at who and who broke into our place."

Cat nodded, smoke rushing from her nose.

"Maybe we should swing by there and see if they took anything or they left any clues."

Loeb twisted his head at the ornery gleam in Cat's unicolor eyes.

"You're on."

24

Labyrinth

Cat rolled down the window. The air was a frigid knife and she was quick in flicking her cigarette into the woods. Each of the blackened tree trunks and limbs glowered back at them as the diamondbacks of poker cards dared a gambler to cast his bets.

"Are you ever going to quit?" Loeb asked.

"No." Cat said, and she reached out to tap his shoulder, her hand falling to cup and squeeze the back of his arm. "We should be getting back to Anchorage. We can check the place out tomorrow, in the daylight."

The savagery of Shiva's demise had taken every bravery she'd left to offer and what she'd thought she'd be able to handle back in the broad plateau of Tamo suddenly made no sense in the clutching and unendingly tangled limbs of the dense forest.

"We'll be quick." Loeb smiled. "Besides, it's your idea."

Cat chuckled.

The snow had disoriented Loeb in the slightest and just when he'd nearly lost his way he found the arcing Y that passed the old mine and followed its curled and twisted path to their once idyllic private cabin.

The mansion sat on the slope to the water like a cursed and haunted house and the forest was eerie in its lack of sound.

It was quiet.

"You know, I haven't seen any moose yet." Loeb said, as he got out of the truck. "Or bears or anything. Not even an eagle. I must not've been paying attention."

Cat disregarded him as her thoughts were buzzing with possibilities. Her hope was that whoever'd broken in had left some indication of their purpose in doing so, or even better, their identity.

At the creak of every floorboard her posture stiffened and Cat took in the breadth of the great room. The sight of Loeb walking to the fireplace to find his notes had been destroyed in the fire they'd left burning at their escape comforted her, if only faintly. It also struck her that the intruder could've burned the place down and Loeb would've taken the blame. It would've kicked them out of Quill Creek for good, and as callous of a thought as it was, Cat wondered why the intruder hadn't done so.

She was getting the creeps, there was no stopping it now.

Her first destination was her downstairs master. She couldn't refuse the spookiness of the mansion's sheer square footage, even when she'd thrown a few lights on she still felt as if eyes were watching her. Her clothes had been spread out across the room as if the bags they'd slept in were simply upended and shaken and then ripped apart in fury.

Sarah's diary was gone.

Cat then checked the shorefront door of the

hall near her master, the one Loeb'd entered in a winded stagger when he'd stolen the diary. Its window was a jagged mess of glass and glass was shattered outside of the door on the hard gray rocks but not inside in the hallway. Not the dark sparkle of a single shard.

The discovery frightened Cat. Whoever'd broken the glass had been *inside* the house. Their breaking of it had been an alert or a scare, or even a response to the gunshots.

Cat froze as her senses zipped along her spine, flaring with the possibility that they were being hunted by a skilled predator, fearless of the cops.

How long had they been inside? Had they been listening? It was so dark, with only the firelight and the light from the kitchen, we would've never seen them! They could've killed us!

They heard what Katie said, they knew Loeb was writing it down!

After all, who was the foolish one? The one who broke the law or the one who refused to leave when the law was being broken? The cops' only advice, their *only protection* was an order to leave.

To walk away.

To forget.

The diary was gone, what else? Loeb was on the ground floor, looking for his laptop and his voice recorder. Cat nearly rushed up the stairs but then stopped herself and snuck back to her room.

She needed a weapon, something for at least one strike so she could run away, just in case someone was camped in the palatial estate, waiting for their foolish return.

No. Don't go back up. Go outside. Look around some more. Her mind was riddled with options and her heart began to race. She wanted to call out to Loeb and run up to the truck and strap herself in as he drove like a madman back to Anchorage where he could hold her till it all went away for the night.

She needed a cigarette and searched for her pack.

She was out.

Cat told herself to stop being a baby and rolled her favorite clothes in a wad with trembling fingers and stuffed them in her jacket, down by the belly. She thought of what a dream her first time in the blue nightgown would be. She'd never felt anything as soft and silky in her whole cotton-bound life. Then she removed her belt, which was for fashion as her pants were so tight they weren't falling off her any time soon, and cinched up the jacket so they wouldn't fall out. Cat then went outside to carefully look along the shore.

Futility struck her within minutes. Other than a few razors of glass she was faced with a long line of rocks and round pebbles that would've been difficult to find a scrap of evidence in even with the noonday sun high overhead.

Cat put her hand to the broken door's knob when the sound of the truck gunning its engine in neutral stole her breath. She twisted, as a still and stoic statue, to stare out into the freezing waters of the frosty fjords for an answer.

Was Loeb leaving?

Without her?

The truck growled and was thrown in gear, its motor winding to kick snow with a low moan.

It was surreal, *unreal* in that she couldn't believe it and she flew to the far side of the house to scamper up the snow-covered hill on all fours. The slick instability of pine needles hidden beneath the snow mocked her scuttles and scrapes.

Her boots slipped against their resistance and when she reached the woodpile to crouch against its rough bulk as it stretched from the stone façade, her forehead was prickled with sweat under her stocking cap.

The red F-150 was wheeling slowly around the circular drive.

Driving.

Leaving.

Red brake lights were shrinking in the heavy-handed dark, stealing all reason and logic with them.

Cat squinted and strained to see a second passenger and could not.

It was too dark.

The fear of being left alone in the forest snuck up behind her and shocked her to life.

Cat bolted after the truck.

25
Fallen

The truck ambled through the woods. It was as if the driver was being held hostage, told to turn where he was turning, ordered not to drive too fast or too slow and it took all Cat had in her tank to keep up. A few times the harsh, dry air cut through her lungs to force and involuntary cough and she wiped a knitted mitten over her face and pressed on. Her smoking of seven cigarettes a day was in no way helping her pursue the hijacked red truck. After ten minutes of ducking low branches and high stepping thicker patches of new snow she thought would suck her down like quick sand, the red truck eased to a halt and Cat's nearly expressionless face was wracked with pain at the sight.

It was the old mine.

Why the old mine? It's been condemned for years? Whoever's forcing Loeb to drive there can't put him down there, he'll die! There's no way out of there.

Cat caught her breath in heavy heaves and took to a squat with the support of a crooked fir branch she held onto like a handle. The headlights were impartial in the cold white, stretching into the selfsame woodland fairy tale only to end abruptly in the void, thus making the beyond that much darker.

The driver door opened first. She could hear it
above the low grumble of the F-150. The passenger
door remained shut. The passenger in the seat,
anonymous. Loeb was out and walked with a limp
pace and a darting glance before sprinting into the
woods. Cat wanted to scream his name at the top of
her lungs but the stony figure of Ericson West
pressing from the truck with a shotgun in hand
made any attempt at rescue stillborn and vain. Her
heart squeezed in her chest to think of Loeb taking
one to the back and she'd never felt so helpless in
her entire twenty-five years of life. Ericson West
stood tall and cocked the shotgun and its telltale
declaration of imminent pain and anguish stopped
Loeb in his tracks.

He turned slowly.

The truck was maybe a football field away
and Cat ran in a hunch past several old tree trunks
to get a better view. She wondered if Loeb saw her.
His blue eyes were extremely light sensitive and the
pale wash of the headlamps had more than likely
shrunk his pupils to see only the barrel of the
shotgun as it held its defiant angle over the empty
truck bed toward his chest.

"Let's talk about this." Loeb said, his resonant
voice rolling to her ears.

"There's nothing to talk about." West slurred,
and though he was a tall and solid figure against the
red truck, Cat got the feeling he was drunk. It made
her loathe the shotgun in his hands even more.
Drunks were unpredictable, like mountain weather,
clear and calm one minute, erupting into a deadly
storm the next.

"I'm sorry the County's going to annex Quill
Creek, but there's nothing you can do about it."
Loeb said. "And even if you could that's still no

reason to go kill your wife."

"My wife's got nothing t'do with you!" West roared, staggering as he walked around the headlamps. Cat advanced like a commando from tree to tree till she was only ten feet from the truck. Her slight frame was well hidden but the ten feet between her and the truck were bare and exposed to the free white snow of the seldom-used road.

"Then why do you have to kill her?" Loeb said, nearly begging, perhaps on his own behalf because he was going to be first; target practice to make sure the shotgun was properly functioning and all. "Think about it, you don't want to kill Melinda, please leave her alone."

"You have no idea what it's like!" West raised the shotgun, passing around the hood. The chance to run to the truck seized Cat but she stayed put. The truck was between her and West, but what could she do?

I have to help him, how can I help?

Loeb, please for Christ's sake don't say anything foolish! Please Loeb, I love you, don't do anything stupid, just let me think of something!

"For twenty-three years everyone n'their mother wouldn't come right out'n say it but they all thought I killed Sssarah, every damn one of them..." West stopped three feet from Loeb, who was stuck on a small slope, off balance, caught in his half-baked attempt to escape by running up a hill. "I gave m'whole life to this dump and they knew it. I made this place into what it is n'the County's jusss' gonna take it away from me? It was our silent contract...I, I gave them a better way of life, more revenues n'better wages and they kept their mouth shut about Sssarah. That's the way it is here. If they'd all said I killed her and I didn't, I'd be in jail. But what does that matter now when they're gonna take my town away from me, from all of us? Huh?"

Loeb didn't know what to say, what to do. An irrational man was caught in an irrational situation.

"Let me drive you back and we'll talk to Katie about it."

West cursed as if he'd been shot in the kidney and dropped the gun, his grip having slackened beyond the point of recovery. He stared at Loeb as if he had holes in his body and all of his vital fluids were rushing out.

"You're a ssstupid bassstard, aren't you?" West staggered where he stood. "Don't you know Katie's not mine?"

Cat could nearly feel Loeb swallowing awkwardly and repeatedly and it was then Cat took to the ground to belly crawl toward the truck, inching every so slowly forward in the snow, afraid of what her footsteps would sound like, even with the idling truck between them. The sliding of the snow against her jacket and jeans crackled so loudly in her ears she thought each inch would be her last and she'd be discovered by the drunken man with the gun but she pressed on. The heat of being caught was pouring sweat down the back of her neck and she shoved and rustled, not knowing what she'd do once she got close enough, just that she had to get there. She had to get close to Loeb, she had to save him.

"Are you going to kill her too?" Loeb asked, his eyes darting to the shotgun on the ground as West leaned against the truck for stability. The Mayor's head reeled and tottered on his shoulders and he tried to stand tall but the weight of life's muddle was making it hard to stand at all.

Cat hit the back right tire and sat against it in a crouch, straining to hear their voices as Loeb was attempting reason.

"I know she's cheated on you, but she's still your wife. Can't you work it out?"

"You don't understand, she never wanted me, she wanted the town, she only wanted me because I wanted the town, it's Quill Creek she's after, all of the money. We've only got forty-five thousand in our bank account but my assets in city property and private property like that cabin you rented are worth nearly twenty-eight million. I'm in charge of it but Quill Creek owns it-even though it wouldn't be here without me! None of it!"

West was caught in the middle of his conniving ways. He'd manipulated the monies of Quill Creek with his winsome and assertive nature, pouring what money he had into it, constantly reinvesting what monies and revenues they'd gained in their heyday, all the while growing into some possessive dictator unable to detach himself from the fact that he didn't own what he felt he owned and his wife was some strange business partner, just as much his rival and competitor as she was the mother of a child who had the same last name as the Mayor of Quill Creek but carried no DNA relation. Yet that very same girl had no idea the man she'd called *Daddy*, the man who she was raised to believe had formed Quill Creek from the sweat of his brow and the ostentations of his sycophantic smiles and handshakes, was not her *Daddy*.

"If Melinda wants the assets of Quill Creek so badly, what is she going to do now that the County's going to annex it?"

Annex? Cat searched her mind for the definition. She'd lived in Los Angeles most of her

life, a place that was miasmic and zoo-like long
before her birth. If anyone wanted to hold on to
their own little slice of it they were criminally
insane and LA had a way of breaking everyone and
making them all retreat back to their dens, hovels,
and bunny trails. But here, it made perfect sense.
Ericson West had sunk all of his money into making
something out of nothing and now, apparently, the
County was going to take it, perhaps develop it,
change its dynamic, twist its demographics, its rites
and its rules and he wouldn't get a nickel. Taxes
and values would be reassessed and shuffled and
everything would be made, in some ways, brand
new.

Everything West had so tediously worked for,
all made worthless and vain in one moment.

"Ssshe won't even divorce me once the
County comes in, she'll just leave. I can't handle
the shame. I've had everyone thinking I killed
Sssarah for twenty-three years'n I can't take
anymore."

"But you did kill Sarah. Fox saw you talking
to her that night. She wanted you to marry her but
you wouldn't. You'd already dumped her for
Melinda."

"That'sss a lie!" West bellowed and lurched
for the gun from his steadying lean on the truck bed,
falling over as he did so, scraping for it.

Cat raced around the side of the truck. Loeb
gasped to see her and was frozen solid by her
movement as she rushed past him and kicked
Ericson West across the face as hard as she could.
The tall man wailed and rolled over, clutching at his
rock hard features. The dull amplification of pain
was disorienting and sickening in his drunkenness
and he couldn't tell the difference in his cataclysmic

state between having lost a tooth and having lost his wife, his job, or his life.

It was all the same, all a downward free-fall into darkness and snow.

"Quick, Loeb, in the car!" Cat yelled, bunching up into the passenger seat of the F-150.

Loeb didn't even think of taking the shotgun as his only experience with guns was his writing about them. He knew the make and model of the shotgun and how it fired slugs and could blow apart a giant pumpkin with one shot but didn't even think of throwing it in the back of the truck to keep it from West.

Loeb ran past the Mayor of Quill Creek but West threw his leg out and Loeb caught air before falling ungracefully to the snow in a mess of shoulders and elbows.

West eschewed the shotgun, his drunkenness demanding visceral punishment. Cat threw herself from the passenger seat and slipped in running around the bed of the truck for the shotgun. West buffeted Loeb with arcing blows, wailing on him as if he were a beanbag and it was all a big joke.

But it wasn't.

West's fists were stones and anger was his master. Loeb was breathless and West wouldn't stop.

Not ever.

He would beat the colored lump of jacket and flesh before him till it melted in the white snow.

The shotgun was hefty in Cat's hands and she held it stiffly as the barrel tipped to the sky.

The blast was deafening in her ears. Dead and heavy snow shook from the spread of low-hanging limbs surrounding the road.

"Next shot's to your back!" Cat screamed, her

entire body trembling as if frostbitten.

Ericson West stopped and stood tall, wobbling. He glared at Cat in the way she'd seen so many drunks glare at her in her life of being a foster child in LA, being a waitress in a twenty-four hour diner, being a girl with blue hair.

Like they wanted to rape her.

An animalistic wrath, wild and untamed, exploded in her stomach. It begged for retribution, for reaction.

For finality and judgment.

This is the man who killed Sarah. Shoot him! Nobody wants him, nobody needs him, everybody knows he's a murderer! You know it!

You're justified! You're Sarah's niece!

Do it, damn it, just squeeze the trigger, what are you waiting for?

The shotgun was heavier in her hands and West was unmissable, perhaps seven or eight feet from her. He knew if he made a lunge for her he'd be screwing himself and the ball was in her court. His life was in her hands. A slug center mass would shove him against the red truck and he'd fall to the snow and bleed out or die of hypothermia, whichever came first.

"Whattare you gonna do, little lady?" West growled, his small eyes hardened by his years of playing an act and whatever liquor he'd gotten his hands on had stripped the veneer covering his charade with sixty grit sandpaper.

The hideous glimmer hidden deep in his eyes begged Cat to pull the trigger, to make it easier on him and the mess he'd become when he could've had it all. He was like a feral forest animal whose foot'd been caught in a trap and had struggled with the train wreck of destiny for long enough and wanted to be, not redeemed or restored from his plight, but just plain flat put out of his misery.

"We're going to go back to your place and talk it over." Cat said. "All of us." Then she closed her eyes and fired three more shells into the air and threw the gun end over end into the woods where it stuck in the snow like a spear. "No one's going to die, no one's going to kill anybody else, no one's going to lie anymore, you got it?"

Ericson West wobbled and his head dipped, dragging down his shoulders and statuesque posture as whatever softness was left inside of him proved that it once did exist, squeaking with a beleaguered and broken voice.

"Good luck with that."

26
The Aurora

Wisdom prevailed. Cat's decision not to fight fire with fire had broken alcohol's demonic grip in Ericson West and he passed out when Loeb tried to wrangle him in the passenger seat.

"Gosh he's heavy." Loeb said and Cat reached over the driver's seat to help. Loeb eyed her nervously. "We should call the police."

"Why?" Cat said, moving around the lights to stand next to Loeb. "We're going to go talk to Melinda and hash it out."

"Is that a good idea?" Loeb whispered and a quick glance to West told him there was no need for tact. The large man had drunken his fill and was apt to sleep the rest off.

"If Ericson West is truly guilty of Sarah's murder there'd be some way she'd know, either something at the house or something he said or did, she must've had a record of it and was just waiting till he divorced her to come out with it."

"That doesn't make sense, Cat. If she wanted to force his hand, wouldn't she threaten him? I mean, if she really had evidence? She supposedly couldn't stand the guy."

Cat was lost in a swirl of thoughts and pawed at her nose and sniffed against the frost.

"I don't know…obviously she wanted the town but there was a reason they stayed together, and we won't know why standing out here in the cold."

Loeb grimaced as he rubbed his stomach where West'd let him have it. His voice was nearly a plea. He wanted at least a good night's sleep before anyone else decided to hit him.

"But we can call the cops and they'll take him in for aggravated assault. Maybe he'll confess to it under the lights."

Cat squinted at Loeb in the icy night and the breath clouding in front of his face.

"Under the lights? You've seen too many movies. If we charge him with assault we're going to have to talk the whole thing out for official record and say how I kicked him and held him at gunpoint and just like he said, this place is some strange court of public opinion, just as long as nobody messes with anybody else. It'd be our word against the Mayor of Quill Creek. I don't like our odds, especially after the police told us to leave. Nobody wants us here, but Melinda will be at least grateful we saved her life and gave her a chance to deal with it gracefully, not having to have her name smeared all over the news with her husband."

"What about Shiva?" Loeb leaned in. "What about the gunshots and the break in? He had to be involved in at least one of those…he was here when we came, waiting upstairs. I can't believe you didn't hear him come down, all drunk. He had a shotgun in one hand and a bottle of Crown Royal in the other…I don't know which scared me more."

Cat flinched and wiped a mitten across her nose again, sniffing. The possibility of what could've been spread around the eerie quiet of the dim forest. She was still freaked out, frayed at the edges but holding together.

"I was outside, on the shore."

It didn't matter, Cat, the glass and the window. You should've been inside, you could've stopped all this. Stop doing your own thing. You're not going to find anything. Just go to the cops, let them deal with it. You're not doing any good.

Loeb touched her shoulders with steadying hands and kissed her forehead, at least what was available of it with the stocking cap's snug fit.

"It's okay, we're here now, and we'll be there then. Let's take E home to mommy and hopefully Katie's there, okay? Melinda will know what to do with him, especially if we find anything linking him to Sarah's murder, anything prosecutable."

Cat only nodded and pressed into the small space behind the driver's seat, cinching West's seatbelt as tight as possible.

Once the dome light clicked off, Cat slipped her hand to Loeb's chest and she stared daggers at West as the rocking of the snow knocked the limp lump of his head back and forth. He was deplorable, spineless and weak. He was selfish and he was finally going to get what he had coming to him all these years.

Justice.

Loeb drove carefully as new snow fell. Once he joined up to Shore Road and the calming flatness of the waters, the northern lights stole his focus.

"Look, Cat, have you ever seen anything like it?"

She had, a lifetime ago. Sarah had bobbed her in her arms, she was only months old. Cat remembered only dusty neon greenish gold and the warmth of Sarah's body, her heartbeat.

It was in that moment Sarah had passed on to Catriona the love of music, as Sarah had sung an old Russian Jewish folksong, weaving the melody between the sky, the color, and a young child's impressionable ears.

"It's beautiful, isn't it?" Cat said, snapping from her flashback. Neon green waves broke and fluttered in the yawning breadth of the sky above the black teeth of evergreen treetops. The rippled glass of the water caught the tint of it and the living beauty of the strange phenomenon held no comfort to Cat; she couldn't share Loeb's joy as he kept dipping his head for a peek as he drove.

Something was wrong.

What am I missing? What am I not getting?

Cat's hand left Loeb's chest as he drove past Quill Creek's sleeping village of brightly colored facades and what lies they protected.

Someone had been misplaced in her mind, a key player had been somewhere or done something her assumption of Ericson West's guilt had overlooked. Of course, if he was guilty, then proof of such would only be a matter of magnification, ripping apart every fragment of his life to find the connecting thread.

But what if Ericson West wasn't guilty?

What if he was a victim?

The victim?

The thought ran a shudder through Cat, a tremor that cursed her subjectivity.

What if's crushed her and she felt claustrophobic in the false bench seat of the F-150 as the truck pulled toward the highway where Loeb would take the hill rising behind Quill Creek to the expansive property owned by the incredibly strained though outwardly idyllic West family. All three of them. Katie had a part in it too, even if she didn't know. Her birth was a bargaining chip, giving to one by robbing another.

The tangle of it all, like an old sea dredge-crusted fishing net.

Cat was struggling to breathe. Was it her smoking? No, it was the truck, and the twister of new questions that had no answers, no rhyme or reason.

"Loeb, stop the truck." She said.

"What?"

"Stop the truck, let me out."

Loeb did so and said nothing but was noticeably confused. When he stepped from his seat to let her brush past he saw the paleness of her sunned skin in the snow's refraction of green light.

"Cat, what is it?"

"I can't." She said, walking, walking away from the red truck and the liquored smells of Ericson West.

She had to think, alone.

This was her struggle, *her* mystery. Only Catriona Enos knew the truth.

Loeb had shaken the snow globe but whenever he got involved he had a way of convincing her of his truth and editing her sorting of what lie *beyond* the facts, what the snow had swallowed up as beautiful auntie Sarah had bled out twenty-three years ago.

Cat needed a moment of distance and time to figure out what she was overlooking.

She wanted to hear Sarah's voice and stopped in the middle of the road with her brown eyes on the sky. It was as if Sarah was speaking to her through the northern lights, the otherworldly glow, a vibrant verdant voice in the dull darkness of the heavy forest, beckoning for her to look up, to get up above the snow and see the secrets for what they were.

"Are you okay, Cat? Talk to me…" Loeb slipped his arm around her and she turned to squeeze him tight.

God, I love you. But I need to think this out alone. I hope you understand.

I saved the blue nightgown, by the way. I know it'll be a nice surprise for you, like that Guild twelve string.

I like surprising you. I like it when you look at me like you don't know who I am for that split second and then realize I'm more than you thought.

Cat nuzzled her head against his neck and squeezed harder.

You've people-watched all of your life and assumed things and put people in boxes, well, that's what everyone's done to me my whole life. Judged me with one look. Nobody knows that I read people in a flash and remember their names the first time I hear them or that I've adapted myself to survive so well I can say ten conversational phrases in thirteen languages.

You know me, Loeb, and you love me. But it'll take the rest of your life for you to really know me, and I look forward to that.

But this walk I have to be by myself. I can't talk to you. I can't look at you. I can't think about wanting to be in love with you.

Sarah's killer is on the tip of my tongue and I know it.

I know it.

"Drive him up there and tell Melinda what happened. Lay it out for her and spare no detail, she'll understand."

"What about you?"

"I'll be along, I've got to walk it out." Cat frowned, her eyebrow skin pinching together and stifling a long-diseased ache of pain. "This's been a lifetime process for me. I've just got to take a moment of silence."

Loeb pulled back from her and studied her face before nodding.

"I understand."

He didn't.

Loeb bunched in the truck and the red F-150 ambled up the incline veering sharply from the highway. Cat lost the truck's brake lights in the gloom of the foresty murk.

Cat gazed into the lights. Alaska was so different than LA, and with snow on the ground, it was some kind of dream. People came to Alaska to leave what they were knee-deep in; maybe persecution, maybe climate, maybe jobs or bad relationships, Alaska had the guts to make one forget.

It was a mile to the West's place, and Cat stuffed her mittened hands in her thick jacket and began walking, grounding her molars together at a new set of suspects.

Motive.

There were only two reasons anybody did anything in life, and it was a rule which had no caveat.

Money.

Love.

Money couldn't buy love and lust never, at any stage of its existence, could evolve into love like a Pokémon.

Cat's footfall munched snow and she'd thrown out any and all random fisherman or highway travellers, any citizens with whom some strange infatuation with Sarah had caused a criminal outcome. Ukaskaya was right, the killer had stayed in Quill Creek, either as a monitor or a captive, time would tell. If the killer had been some random person the community would've known. The indexing of random civilians was their business, their livelihood. And there's no way it was someone from college, some possessive jilted wannabe lover. Sarah's wholesome purity was undesirable to the dirty of mind, to the party people, to the promiscuous and loose. She was the meek, bookish, *quiet* kind they thought an instant fantasy about as she walked to her seat in class but ultimately the immoral would know was pre-domesticated, already spoken for, and not worth the effort.

She knew her killer, had lunch with them, spoke with them, laughed at their jokes and probably let them hold little old me.

The one who killed Sarah knew me, said how cute I was, told Sarah how lucky she was.

They never knew I'd come back.

Well I'm back.

Cat's molars increased their grinding as the field narrowed to October 4th and October 4th only.

Virgil Fox.
Sleeping.
Ericson West.
Wouldn't go in.
Sheriff Evans.
Tied up with robbery.
Sarah Enos.
Alone with child.
Grigory Ukaskaya.
Recovering from beating.
Minos Dimitropolous.
Lost in art.

Mills Anderson.
Sex offender?
Isolationist.
Red herring.
That left Melinda…what was her maiden name?

The air left Cat's lungs with a sharp puncture. Her mouth was frozen open in the arid frost.

Melinda, smoky delicious Melinda'd never given her maiden name, never talked about what she'd done the night of the murder, where she'd been or who she'd been with.

Her name wasn't in the police report, her name wasn't anywhere.

It was as if she didn't exist to a certain degree, why was that? For all intents and purposes she was the catalyst of the love quandrangle.

And her visit, her lightning strike of an appearance, well she had been so gracious and charming it hurt. She'd spoken of reading *Fractures* in the tub which may or may not've been true and brought gifts of IPA and bear sausage but after that, she'd stirred Ericson into a right bloody frenzy, the Sheriff too.

She was a ghost, a manipulator of manipulators all the while working her own twisted scheme to gain control of millions of dollars of property.

Back in the day she'd used Virgil Fox as the stud horse and Ericson West as the plow horse and had ridden them both till she was on top of everything Quill Creek had to offer, hiding it with the wavy tresses of her hair and the sweet poison of her lips.

Cheated, four times? Five times? With whom? With whomever she needed to.

She was a trap door spider, an expert fisherman, a skilled hunter of the woods.

Now she was so close with Ericson at the brink of wanting to kill her and the always impressionable Loeb Cohen becoming the delivery boy, the writer who she'd buttered up like a dinner roll her very first opportunity.

Oh my God...

No, Loeb, no...

Cat broke into a dead sprint.

27

The Ice Queen

The West's owned a large spread. The lot
was nearly fifteen acres total, fenced by a traditional
farm's double line of black wood slats though Loeb
strained to imagine what farming could be done in
the snow. In some ways the lot looked fictitious,
nearly Rockwellesque, and the green smears of the
borealis on the quiet hush of the staggered
smattering of outbuildings and the treeless snow of
the rolling acreage only added an unnecessary
stroke of beauty.

Loeb sighed and looked over to West, how he
slept and how his throat gurgled as he choked on his
own half-snores and drunken hibernations.

Take it easy, buddy, I got this.

Loeb took the keys and couldn't deny the odd
peace of the split-level home before him, how it was
long and dark and set back from the road.

He left the truck and began to walk.

The light glowed orange and cozy in a bay
window to the right of the front door and its inviting
alcove in which one could stand outside in the
threshold of the door and feel the yin-yang energies
of Alaska; brutal frostbitten artic cold on one half of
the body and spine-tingling hearth-crackling
warmth running up the other.

Maybe it was bull, maybe just a writer's thought; a wish of the sublime in a world where no such thing existed. It held the guise of such, and Loeb was a man who lived on the hope of images, and taking a picture of one thing to assume it was another was an assassin of unforeseen consequences.

Loeb marched to the alcove and knocked on the door, looking back behind him to the dormancy of the red truck as it slept like some old-fashioned paddy wagon a safe distance away while he, the agent of reason, attempted to right the wrong.

The smell of citrus was first to his nose and Loeb turned to see Melinda West. She was barefoot, wearing dark blue jeans and a man's brown, green and yellow flannel shirt, the heaviness of which bunched and fanned as the buttons were only done up halfway to reveal the ribbed texture of a white cotton tank top. Her sensual shape was accentuated in mystery in that the essential parts of it were smoothed over and hidden, giving the eye no place to fall but back to her own deep dark lake water eyes.

Her eyebrows flinched in surprise and then twisted together.

"Hey, what are you doing here?"

She reached out to hug him and Loeb was born and raised to be polite and embraced her back. He couldn't avoid the huggability of her body and the smell of her copper-toned hair as it spilled free and careless in the throes of fallen night.

It was intoxicating.

"Ooh." Melinda pulled away and Loeb's eyes went to her milky bare feet as they'd stepped on the small concrete slab outside the door.

"Careful," he said. "It's like a freezer out

here."

She stood on one leg without wobbling and rubbed her left foot against her right calf, to rid it of its chill.

"Well come on inside, then." Melinda said, stepping back into the heat of her home, which was somehow dim and intimate. The lights were soft and the neutral colors his eyes had forgotten existed while traipsing around the colorblind display of Quill Creek's buildings along Shore Road had been spilled across Melinda's home as if pitchers of coffee, caramel, and barbecue sauce the ones were responsible.

"Are you hungry?" She said, with the slightest bounce in her head, and the youthful twinkle her daughter couldn't suppress was alive in her dark blue lake water eyes as if she'd pushed a button inside of her soul to make them seem so.

Loeb shut the door behind him and unbuttoned his jacket. The coat rack was next to him and he placed it there.

"No."

"Howbout a beer, then? Maybe not E's IPA but I'm sure I've got a brand or two you might like."

Loeb didn't want to be standoffish and hard. He had to be delicate about Ericson West, he had to be delicate about knowing that Katie was not his child.

"I…"

"No wait," Melinda said, backing up and turning into the kitchen, which was just down the twist of the hall and her feet made small sucking noises on the hardwood. "You're from California, you're a wine guy."

Loeb shrugged.

There was no fighting it.

"I wouldn't mind a glass."

Melinda clapped her hands together and held them.

"Red or white?"

Loeb shrugged again. It would only be an accessory, after all, just something to hold while he searched for the right words.

"You pick."

Loeb could hear clinking though saw no light in the kitchen and was drawn in by the invitation of the bay-windowed room. A small, crescent shaped fireplace of cream bricks, the simple focal of which was an oversized keystone, shaped much like a King or Queen's crown, sat opposite a large leather sectional. Nondescript bookshelves lined either side of the fire and the subdued lick of flames dancing around the room made it hard to read the various titles, but a spark of satisfaction wove through the young writer to know his beloved books were among the collection. A stubby upright piano of tawny wood sat at the bay window for melancholy inspiration and Loeb sat down on the sectional, relinquishing the clenching of his ribs and his teeth.

He was afraid of Ericson West and his rage, but in his home, not his home, *Melinda's home*, he felt welcome and free to let go what trauma, physical or mental, the intimidating giant had inflicted upon him with his whirlwind of rage and misunderstanding.

Melinda returned, her feet again making sucking noises on the floor of the kitchen and the hall till she reached the carpet of the living room and Loeb took the half-empty glass of red, already smelling its spicy-sweet bouquet as it mingled with the citrus scent on Melinda's hands.

"Don't be shy." She said, as he'd politely taken it by the stem and avoided her hands as they cupped the goblet and begged for a connection.

She had a glass of red, too, and sat on the same angle of the sectional as he did, facing the fire, back to the door, a cushion away, one leg crossed underneath to dangle bare and free in the air.

"Mmm, that's nice." Loeb said as the intangibly complex combination of vinegar and sugar passed over his tongue.

"Vineyard of the year, I think, but I forgot the name. It's a Cab from Sonoma. You like Cabs?"

"Yeah."

"I thought you were maybe a Merlot guy, but I had to take a guess."

"You were right."

"Why don't you guess what year it is?"

"2007?"

"Yeah, how'd you know?"

Loeb shrugged.

"Some things you just know, some things you don't."

Melinda sipped, cherished the taste, and then licked her top lip.

"So why are you here?" She asked, leaning her head against her hand as her elbow crested the crown of the couch and she brushed back her ribbons of copper red hair. The dance of firelight rippled across the waves and hints of curls. "I mean, not that I'm not glad to see you, because I am, let me tell you, I've hoped to get a chance to talk to you ever since I found out you were in town, just us, you know, it's just that…so late, I don't know, I think you would've had a reason."

"It's about Ericson." Loeb said, gaining tightness in his neck and shoulders, not on her behalf but on his own and how it would make him feel down in the pit of his stomach to relate to her the truth about Ericson.

There was no delicate way to say it, and he was cursing himself already. Cat had been so good with Virgil Fox and if it weren't for Cat he wouldnt've been able to speak with Ukaskaya, or the cops.

Where was Cat?

That's right, walking it off. Probably smoking and staring at the lights dancing across the sky.

Loeb turned inward without her.

I've been just about useless this whole time; wasting money, barking up the wrong tree...I don't even know what I'm doing, why aren't I sitting in MacArthur Park writing bang bangs? They're so easy. This is crazy, this is all craziness, I have no control here, what am I doing in these people's lives, in their homes?

"What about Ericson?"

Suddenly Loeb changed the subject, not ready to drop the bombs on her about the savage passed out in the red truck hundreds of feet away. He couldn't fight the fact that she may've been thinking about cheating on him again, it seemed that was a chronic trait of the things he'd done to her. He could only imagine what it was like to be married to such a hard man, a man that everyone was sure had killed a young woman.

The detour of words flew out clumsily and laid in his lap.

"I'd like to put you in a new book."

"Oh?" Melinda's lips twisted. "You don't want to talk about E?"

"I'll get to that." Loeb took a sip. "I want to put you in one of my action books."

Melinda chuckled and sipped, curling the
glass away from her face to lick her lips as a frown
spread across her timeless features. Nothing about
her was harsh, angular, pointed or severe. She was
like her home, neutral, balanced.

Beautiful.

"Love interest?"

"Too obvious."

"Villain?"

"Too obvious."

"Too obvious?"

"Yeah, you're speaking in archetypes, flat
one-dimensional yawners. It'd be an immediate
failure if I made you simple and boring and
predictable. That's not you, is it? Or is my guess
wrong."

"Oh…well, when you put it like that."

"Come on, guess."

"Hero?"

"Too obvious."

"What then?"

Loeb stood to finish his glass of wine and set
it on top of the upright piano as it mocked him with
its sense of right and wrong.

*White, black, white, black, white, black, white,
white…*

A great piece of music wasn't one or the
other, but the right combination of both.

It was the best opportunity he was going to
get.

"A victim…a captive."

The woman's deep dark eyes fell to the
leather of the couch and searched around its comfort
to find none.

She knocked back the rest of her wine and
winced, crossing the distance to set her glass next to

Loeb's.

She sat down at the upright piano with a demure sense of composure, trying not to cry. She ran hands slowly down her thighs to smooth jeans that needed no such smoothing and stared at the linear checkerboard of the upright. It was as if she wanted to be able to play but could not.

When she did speak, her voice was coated in the dusky heat of ruby wine and firelight, barely audible.

"So you know, then."

"...I went back to the cabin to get something and he was waiting for me with a shotgun..."

"And a bottle of Crown Royal?" She finished the sentence, her dark eyes darting up at him and falling again to the keys of the piano. "Welcome to my life."

"Why haven't you come forward?" Loeb knelt, his symmetrical brows scrunched together. "Katie's twenty-two, she can handle it."

Melinda shook her head in tight, shivering shakes. Her best efforts to hold back tears were vain.

"It'll rip this place apart."

Loeb tentatively put his hand on hers.

"You've got to go to the cops."

The shakes of her head elongated and exaggerated. Her eyes were glossy with tears, but they wouldn't yet fall down her cheeks.

"He'll take everything and everyone down with him, he'll ruin everything I've ever wanted. He'll ruin *everyone's* life, I can't handle the burden of that! There's hundreds of lives at stake, I can't be so selfish..."

Loeb squeezed her hand.

"Melinda, it's not like that...I know that

Katie's not his daughter, and I know why you've cheated on him…I know he's abused you."

Her face, lovely in that it was clean became hard as she refused to cry, but it would never match the natural granite-carved features of her husband's stoniness.

She was being tough, and failing.

Gravity pulled at her tears and they marbled her skin.

Loeb pulled the woman to him and stood tall, letting her cry against his shoulder.

Her body was soft and begged indulgence. He was a statue against her sobs, staring off into the odd brightness through the bay window of night snow.

Loeb moved her to the sectional and she slouched, staring at the ceiling as if spent.

"You have no idea what it's like."

Loeb said nothing as she wiped her eyes on her sleeve and seemed to regain her composure. Color re-entered her face and she sighed away her thoughts.

"He beat me, Melinda. He was drunk. I thought he was going to kill me. I don't know how many times he punched me but it was like getting attacked by a bear. I know he's got murder inside of him, I know it."

Melinda's face was cut by a grimace as she listened. Her murky blue eyes held an odd light from the fire.

"He's outside, in the truck, passed out." Loeb turned to her, imploring. "Now's the time, if you know anything about Sarah's murder you've got to come out with it, anything at all."

"You came here?" She squinted. "You came here before going to the police?"

"Yes." Loeb nodded. "It's such a terrible situation I wanted to give you the option to handle it gracefully."

Melinda's face flashed with a throb of overwhelming gratitude, and held a striking stillness as her eyes skipped around Loeb's face.

Then she surged toward him to bridge the inches that separated them, grasping him with a strong grip.

She hesitated as Loeb's pounding heart raced to his throat, slowly rising in her seat as if pulling a turboprop from stall.

Her chest swelled and brushed his. Her mouth was open and longed for his.

She wiggled her hips to hold her posture as if averting the edge of a cliff and using every muscle in her curvy body to stop some inhuman urge to dive off.

Loeb's body zipped and buzzed. She didn't know what she was doing, what was happening, what swirl of emotions she was caught in the undertow of and he couldn't stop the inevitability of her lips pressing against his but was trying to.

He pitied her, lost in her horrid relationship, and though he was cornered with nowhere to go he couldn't push her away.

He wanted to but he was too weak. His muscles were not themselves. Drowsiness crept along the edges of his vision with spidery legs. He was glued to his spot in the dense corner of the heavy leather couch, eyes syrupy and transfixed as they fell into hers.

She kissed him fervently, an unending stream of puckers like gunfire as Loeb's one hundred and sixty pounds were swallowed in the force of her clasp and her lips wouldn't break their magnetic seal.

She smothered him, stealing his breath with each kiss and blood fluttered in his body.

Her lips spread his and her tongue was warm with firelight and sweet with red wine, sour in that it was forbidden but the pulses of her tongue spread within him the incapacitating heat that'd jellied his spine the very first time they met.

His mind rippled with images as if Melinda had telepathically planted them there.

The static pictures became slides and the slides sped quicker and quicker into movies crying out for perverted pleasures under the dark sky of the first snow.

Her tongue was a knife, jabbing him, *stabbing* her will into him and he was powerless to resist.

No!

No!

No!

*Please, don't! Don't do this...*Loeb thought and she felt his resistance as he attempted to weather the storm of her desire.

She broke her kiss and her cheek was hot against his and her lips were at his ear, unearthing a low, breathy moan from deep within that prickled the skin covering his spine with warm shivers.

Her hands symmetrically squeezed up his thighs in a slow and careful vice, catching his gracilus muscles to send a rippling message along his legs.

Loeb swallowed with difficulty as the sensations she'd sparked were undeniably visceral.

His body was unduly awakened and he fought the ridiculous temptation to press into her.

It was not his, not from his heart, it was as if it was a burden that crushed him, a tempest of peer pressure beyond anything he'd ever felt before.

He loved Cat with all of his heart but Melinda was sheer magnetism, like a moth to a candle. His brain was becoming thoughtless as the moment consumed it. His blood was making the decisions now.

And he didn't know it was all a ruse, all a sick game of practiced technique to whip his blood into a froth as it raced up and down his spine to his brain to spread the liquid ecstasy date rape drug she'd slipped into his wine.

She was like a puffy white summer cloud in which lightning deceitfully slept, or a bed of pillows that promised the sweetest night's sleep.

Loeb stood, unevenly, and she let him. The damage had been done, like a perfectly executed surgical procedure. All of his blood rushed to his head and flew right back down to his feet and he wobbled and tottered and sunk to the couch.

He frowned as he tried to focus and forced his eyelids to blink the fog away but they would not.

The faster he blinked the less he could see, and his skin burned and flushed that he'd aggravated the fact, destroying what precious seconds of lucidity he had left.

The orange tongues of the fire flicked across the glossiness of his eyes.

In his mind the fire spoke of the confident strength Melinda's arms, her honeyed lips, the skin of her thighs, the promise of her heat and nearness.

No! No! No!

I don't want that, stop it! Get away from me! Please, no, I can't, I won't!

What's happening to me? What's wrong with me?

Loeb stood boldly with his last rush of

conscious will and fell sideways at her feet in a clump.

His brain was being squeezed and twisted and his watery blue eyes searched for the glass of red wine that sat empty on the piano as things that had only moments before been so definite and mundane became unshapely and diseased with ever-dimming hallucinations.

What...have you done...to me?

Melinda West only twisted her head, tipping it to stare down at the weak man, the writer, the dreamer who lived so far in the caverns of his imagination he failed to see what sat directly in front of him.

Men were disgusting, hideous creatures, so weak and easy to manipulate.

She said nothing as his eyes flickered their final pulses of clarity.

They were drowning in their own color, pupils dilating and swelling till his eyes were nearly as dark and lifeless as hers.

28

In Low Places

Catriona was going to die. What had begun in a sprint fell quickly to a mushy jog and for what seemed like an hour but was closer to forty-five minutes she'd kept herself upright with a spent stagger of hacks and wheezes. The dry air and her habit of cigarettes had worked in perfect harmony with the snow and the steady incline to make her heart feel like it would explode in torn wet shards within her chest any second. The darkness was lonely and each stinging squeeze of her eyes flushed away confused and contorted imaginations of Melinda West, the wicked witch of Quill Creek. God only knew what she was doing, what she was capable of, and Catriona was conscious that every second she stayed in the snow, struggling to lift her foot for even another step, Melinda West was working her black magic.

Cat's thoughts were caught in white clouds of sticky air. *Why'd I tell you not to get those cell phones, Loeb, why? She's guilty Loeb, she's guilty! You have to see that! Don't let her touch you!* Her nose had started bleeding halfway up the mile long trek and the careless streaks of it gave her a vampire's red goatee.

Her head bobbled on her neck with weariness

and it wasn't until the hill evened out and the terrain began to make sense that Cat saw the edge of the black fence surrounding the West's compound.

Where's the truck? Why isn't the truck out in the road?

Where's Ericson? Are they in on it together? Were they always? The both of them?

Oh God...

Cat picked up the pace with snowbound scuffs and stumbling kicks. Her eyes were plastered to a point on the congestion of the horizon, cluttered and cut by the black fingers of snow-dusted pines. Her mind resolved to make it to that singular point or die trying, not giving her body permission to give up until she'd made it.

Damn you Melinda, Cat thought, *if you so much as touch him I'm going to kill you.*

Her lungs fired puffs of hot breath like a steam engine rushing down the tracks.

First Sarah, now Loeb...

Cat made it past the first stretches of the fence and couldn't stop. Her legs were jelly and her arms were numb. She couldn't feel her nose or any other part of her face and it wasn't until she reached the tire tracks of the missing truck that she fell to all fours.

She would've tossed her cookies but they'd frozen down inside of her stomach and her eyes tracked the dual grooves rutting the fine white snow as her lungs squeezed and screamed for help. Her throat was nearly raw and her mouth was dry.

Cat pushed herself up and lurched to the black of the fence, squinting throbbing eyes toward the front door and the inviting glow of orange light cascading from the bay window.

There were two ways to do it.

Cat decided that her feet had chosen for her and she removed her mittens. She stuffed them in her jacket pockets and lunged forward. Her point of focus had changed but the ultimatum to reach it or die had not. The door and the cozy awning covering it swelled as one foot followed the other and it was two feet from the door Cat caught her heavy steps on a snow-hidden root, stumbling clumsily into the frozen white blanket.

It took everything within her to press herself up, and before she did, her eyes seized up at the orange light washing across the snow.

"Hello." Melinda said, with the smoothness of leather, cognac, and coffee with cream. Her hands were behind her back and her powerful figure was subdued in the man's flannel shirt that stopped near the top of her thigh. "You look terrible."

Cat pawed to her knees and Melinda put a finger to her lips, pulling a .22 caliber marksman pistol from behind her back. It was semi-automatic and was the size of a drug-store cell phone.

"What are you doing?" Cat said, her lack of eyebrows not necessary to convey what desperation possessed her face.

"It's okay, you don't have to lie to me." Melinda West soothed. "I thought you knew the moment you saw me. *Catriona.*"

Melinda stepped from the house, bare feet and all across the snow, using the threat of the pistol keep Cat motionless on all fours as she scratched at Cat's coat for the necklace.

Melinda held it in her hand, white fangs of teeth sliding over the fullness of her lips.

"So you did come back."

Melinda didn't wait for an answer and clubbed the gun across Cat's forehead and Cat fell with a whimper to a heap.

The woman wasted no time and snagged the collar of Cat's jacket and drug her, as if she were a sack of potatoes, across the snow and the rough concrete patio to the slick wood floor of the hall that lead to the kitchen and shut the door.

The blow'd disoriented Cat and a jagged swathe of pain throbbed through the side of her head as sticky red blood laboriously dripped to the floor.

Melinda rolled her over with an unfeeling bare foot, twisting her head inquisitively to look down the barrel of the gun.

"So how do you wanna do this?" She asked.

Cat squinted and winced, still not having caught her breath and was spent far beyond a point of returning to comfort.

"Where's Loeb?"

"Somewhere cozy."

"What have you done with him?"

"Drugged him with cherry meth. GHB." Melinda West's beautiful face simpered with an incredulous grin, hideous in its pride and revelling glory. "Date rape."

Cat swallowed. She looked immortal, unchangeable, as much a witch as any fairy tale could provide, beckoning her prey with one hand and only to draw the knife with the other.

But she wasn't.

She had no special powers.

She nothing more than a murderous bitch who'd stop at nothing to get what she wanted, in any way, whether in a conversation, a relationship, or the course of an entire town's destiny.

She was pure poison, unfiltered in its potency but carefully secured and packaged in a honeyed box that smelled of citrus Christmas spice.

"Is that what you did to Ericson, October 4th?"

Melinda frowned and the pistol sagged in her hand.

"You still care, don't you? I'm going to shoot you and leave you for the wolves to use as a chew toy and you still care?" Melinda shrugged, casual and without remorse. "Yeah, that's what I did. I did the same to Fox to get the kid."

Cat winced when she said *the kid*. It was as if she'd stuck a knife in Cat's ribs.

How many times had *she* been called *the kid*, how many different parents had treated her like an object.

The remote. The car. The bed.
The kid.

Adrenaline zipped tracers of rage down Cat's arms as she lay on her back, vulnerable and exhausted.

"You see, I don't like sex." Melinda crossed her arms and the gun whirled on her index finger once and hung limply. "I hate it. I hate men, I hate everything about them. I hate the way they think, the way they talk, the way they look at me, I've hated it all my life. And you know what's the worst part," she kneeled down and whipped the gun back into her hand, sitting at Cat's feet, begging Cat to kick her. "They have no idea I'm date raping. I've never been with a guy where I didn't." Her face livened with the confession, the dark eyes gaining a flicker of unnatural light. "They're *my* conquest. I'm not theirs. I own them. I could castrate them if I wanted to, but I don't. You wouldn't believe that feeling of power. That's what turns me on."

Cat swallowed again but her Adam's apple refused. She choked on the blood in her mouth and

twisted on her side to cough it up and spat on the
floor. Melinda stood, her mouth a flat line and
walked a pace to Cat and kicked her hard in the ribs
and stepped over the blood to pad to the kitchen.

"Why...why..." It took all of Cat's energy to
roll onto her stomach and Melinda spun in her view
as if defying gravity. She was swallowed in the
darkness of the kitchen and Cat roughed up her
throat to call after the killer. "Why Sarah?"

Melinda West returned from the kitchen with
a six-inch grocery store chef's knife, not unlike the
one that'd been used to end Sarah's life. The .22
was stuffed in her right hip pocket, handle out, and
the fabric had been bunched around it to make its
access easy.

If only I could reach it...

Cat's monochrome brown eyes darted
between black and silver, between the chef's knife
and the handle of the gun.

Where is the truck? Where is Ericson West?
Where's Loeb?
Where's Katie?

"Why?" Melinda asked. Her lips pursed.
"That's a good question." Melinda eyed the knife
and tested the blade's sharpness on her fingernail.
Cat could hear the grating of the scrapes. It was
sickening and made her shiver.

"Let's just say I hated her too. She was
beyond my control, someone who wouldn't play by
the rules. She wouldn't hate me back, there was
nothing I could do to get her away from Ericson.
One time I yelled at her and called her horrible
names and she refused to hold it over me. She was
like, this unbearably perfect little angel and she
wanted the man I wanted. That's why I had to get a
kid, because she had one. But for Ericson it wasn't

about the kid. He was like a dog in heat, and that's where I had an edge on her, in a way. She may've been saving herself for marriage but I just plain flat hated sex and always will. It's disgusting. So how do two girls who won't have sex fight for a man who wants nothing more? Idealism. I wasn't born in Quill Creek, you know, I chose it. I was the one who fed all the ideas into E's head to make it such a grand attraction, only, just like every foolhardy man before him, he was blinded by the fact that no amount of blood, sweat, and tears could've made this place last. I knew it'd all fizzle out. That's what I wanted."

"You wanted a dead town?" Cat nearly squealed. One of her ribs was almost broken.

"No, no, no...the money. I wanted this place to rise and fall so I could sell the rise again. How do you think the County got the idea to annex it? Who do you think supplied them with the votes? When my poor little husband found out you know what he did? Took one of his man guns out from his man gun collection in his man den and walked in the woods to kill himself. Can you believe it?"

Cat couldn't. Melinda laughed as she padded past Cat for the front door.

"Those...gunshots?"

"That was him." Her face stretched with laughter. "He tried three times! What a baby! How can anyone who's trying to kill themselves miss *three times?*"

"And you were in...our house?"

"Yup. I heard every word you said. You've gotta watch those youngsters, always running their mouths. It was funny seeing you guys run off with your tails between your legs. I burned Sarah's diary, by the way. I guess that's the third time I've touched it. That's how I got her, you know. I stole her diary and then that night I returned it to give myself an excuse to be in her apartment. The knife was in the sink. I knew those boys who beat up the Russian were going to rob the wood shop, I'd overheard them talking about it at *Logan's*. I got lucky, I guess, after all these years. I had already drugged E at dinner and left the door unlocked so when the police came to question us they found us sleeping naked in bed. Would you believe that no one *ever* suspected me? They never even questioned me a second time. Again, men are something, aren't they? You see, every time they looked me in the eye and asked me a question they immediately looked away because they remember me unclothed. Their impartiality was completely gone from that moment…it was flawless."

The coldness in which she'd spoken of *the kid* and *youngsters* deeply troubled Cat, but whatever emotionlessness lie beyond that shadowed her face when speaking of killing Sarah Enos and how conceited she was to have planned the crime *and* the getaway.

Lucky?

"So, you stab me or shoot me and leave me for the wolves, but what do you do with Ericson?"

"He's in the truck, in the garage. In about…" Melinda's head bobbled and one eye squinted. "Five or ten minutes he'll be dead from carbon monoxide poisoning."

"Just like that?"

"Just like that."

Cat strained to raise her torso with bent elbows.

"What about Loeb?"

"I'll put him out there too…after I…" Her lips

pursed and her eyes rolled to rest under a crown of arched eyebrows. "Pay him a visit."

Cat rose to sit, bunching up her knees.

"And Katie," she winced. "You're going to kill her too?"

"She's going with you. You both are going to get," Melinda used air quotes, which looked strange with the kitchen knife in one hand, "*lost* in the woods with a few *broken down* snowmobiles. What coroner around here can tell the difference between a stab wound and bite marks when there's not much left of the carcass but bits and pieces."

Cat shook her head. Her features were bent with dismay, unadulterated in their shock of such a hideous creature.

"All for a couple of million?"

"Not a couple, I'd guarantee over a hundred when it's all said and done. This time next year there'll be no evidence that I was ever here. This whole place'll be developed beyond belief. Rumor is they want to make Seward look like a joke. Big spenders from Vancouver are looking for the next hoity toity hotspot and who better to spin a lie about this crappy little place than me? They have a saying that goes like, you can catch more flies with honey than you can with vinegar, but I guess the modern interpretation of that is, you can get whatever you want if you make the right man thinking that you've slept together and he had such a great time he can't remember a lick of it. Like your poor boy toy. He was trying so hard to stop me but I was just running the usual procedure to get the soap through his system as fast as possible."

Cat ground her molars to think of what she'd done and let any callousness fall to a sardonic statement about the dog.

"Nice touch with Fox's bowie knife in Shiva."

"Thanks. That was an all in one I couldn't refuse. The old man was still sleeping and Shiva thought I was bringing her bear sausage like I do all the time but they won't find any bear sausage in her system. It's easy to pick out because dog's don't swallow what they eat. They're a bit like men. Or...is it vice versa?"

Cat was continually baffled by Melinda's *layers* of psychopathy.

Endless.

The darker her actions the more she enjoyed them, reveling in the power of getting away with it all.

"You really don't care about Katie, after all these years of raising her?"

"Katie's a spoiled brat." Melinda shook her head. "I thought *you* would've known better."

Cat finally caught her breath and her eyes rolled around the room, gauging its size.

Her heart clenched in her chest as her fists did the same with a bend of bony elbows.

"Some people just never learn."

Cat sprang to height, lunging for the gun.

Melinda was deft and focused, her deep lake water eyes streaked with insanity.

The slick silver of the razor-sharp knife glinted in the dancing firelight from the living room and slashed, with the low arc of a brutal uppercut, into the depths of Cat's belly.

29
Endings

Catriona doubled in half. The gun was in her hand. She staggered back with choppy steps and air whooshed from her mouth. The distance between her and Melinda swelled until Cat planted her feet in the floor and grit her teeth.

Her brown eyes danced around the floor and she snorted hard with flared nostrils and raised the gun.

Melinda's features rippled with shock. The knife was buried in the stomach of Cat's jacket, nearly to the handle.

Cat reached into her jacket pocket for a mitten and made a C-shape of the mitten to remove the knife and set it on the floor.

Melinda was lost between the jolting blow of Cat not being dead and what to do about it.

Cat removed the belt and unzipped her jacket. A thick wad of clothes fell to the floor, dotted and dappled with blood. Cat winced as she pulled up her shirt. The knife had made a two-inch incision just to the left of her belly button.

Painful, but not fatal.

"My turn." Cat hissed.

Melinda's mouth began to flatten and stretch. Her dark blue eyes were watery and flooded with a whirlpool of emotions.

"No, please, don't send me to jail."

"Shut up and get on you knees." Cat jabbed the gun forward, bending to let her free hand scratch for the blue nightgown only to bunch it up to press it to her wound.

Melinda sunk and her body began to heave with sobs.

"I can't go! Shoot me, please, take your revenge for Sarah, I can't go to jail. I can't."

"Take the belt and tie it around your feet." Cat said, fighting everything inside of her not to squeeze the trigger till the gun was freed of its bullets.

Melinda was a storm of fictional tears. Her wails were overdramatized and she began to walk forward on her knees and fell to all fours.

"No, please, I'll do anything. Shoot me, please."

Melinda wouldn't stop crawling forward and it wasn't until too late that Cat saw the near-feline shape of her hips as she crept forward.

The tears were dry in her eyes as they locked on to Cat's.

Cat squeezed the trigger and the click of the bolt mocked her. Its hollow clack echoed through the wooden hall.

Melinda lunged for the knife and scraped to her full height as Cat threw the gun at her and ran off into the darkness of the kitchen with syrupy steps. The pistol smacked Melinda's knee and she shrugged it off as if it never happened. A streak of lunacy ripped across the redhead's face with a tangible hunger and her lake water eyes had been stirred with a primal and savage current.

Cat was her prey.

The smell of her fear was heavy in the air.

The knife was sweat-sealed to Melinda's hand and she stopped and listened for her quarry, standing equidistant in the hall between the kitchen and the door and the nearby living room entrance. If Cat was going to come back to the living room she'd have to rumble around in the dark and find the pass through in the dining room, but the stairs were nearby, at the end of the kitchen. Had she taken them?

Clomps of Cat's snow boots rolled in the darkness and Melinda sneered as she spoke.

"You won't get away from me. This is my house! This is my land!"

Cat's breath was hot and congested in the darkness and the whiteness of the snow still dotted in her eyes like sunspots. She hadn't thought about it trudging through the snow on hell's treadmill to reach the house but the lack of light in the kitchen exemplified it. She blinked at it but it wouldn't leave. It was some strange side effect in her near drugged out state of exhaustion. The distortion of time and distance worked within her, the thought of all thoughts ever creeping behind her.

Melinda.

Death.

A phone to call the cops? A weapon, like a knife? A rolling pin? What was the answer?

Escape?

Oh God, what do I do? I can't get away from her!

Cat couldn't run. Her knees were limp noodles, wet down her legs with sweat that made her shiver.

Where's Loeb? Where are the stairs?

Cat tensed. Melinda, barefoot Melinda was

padding toward her. From the right or left? Up the darkness or around through the living room? God knew. She could feel it. The nape of her neck prickled with fright.

Hell had no fury like a woman from hell.

Cat backed up, facing the darkness of the hall running toward the kitchen. Overhead shelving and low countertops bumped out to block the light of the fire in the living room and the kitchen angled to break her focus of the hall as it ran to the door. She bent to spot Melinda, flaring the pain near her belly button. The blue nightgown was warm and wet and she dropped it, turning to grope in the darkness. Her hand pressed to the gash to stop the red ooze. She was light headed and worn out, as if she'd smoked a thousand cigarettes back to back and had abstained from water for three years.

Her guts were glue. Glue was tightening her body.

The madness had to stop.

Cat pressed forward in the lightless space and after three steps the sensation of falling off a cliff preceded the hollow hardness of a closet door smacking her in the face. Stunned, Cat wriggled away a halo of disorientation and latched onto the bulbous end of a stair rail.

Her vim leaked from her and the snow boots were unreasonable burdens. The cut wasn't that bad, was it? Where was her energy? Even her coat hung on her as if dumbbells were jammed down her pockets. Cat's forehead was a slick glaze of sweat.

She groped for the rail and the thumping rush of bare feet snaked behind her.

Cat ducked with a yelp as the kitchen knife sliced through the air and bit into the carpet of the stairs.

Cat's hands were rigid claws, gripping the black and shapeless air for leverage. She bounded up the stairs but her left ankle was in Melinda's cunning grip. It was like a robot's, unfeeling and tempered by careful practice. Her hands were long and strong. Of all things it had gripped in its days, from the knife handle's that killed Sarah Enos and gutted Shiva or even the organs of the men she'd raped, Cat's ankle was the most profound.

Waves of numbness, inane and irrational in their limitless flood of helplessness possessed her body.

Melinda had touched her there before. It must've been when Cat was little, just a baby. Melinda had touched her there with the sincere affection of a young adult beholding a new life, and even through the anchors of snow boots Melinda's touch had a paralytic effect, reminding her of what it was like to be an unthinking, codependent infant that captured the heart of everyone she saw. All had been right in the world as the center of attention, all had been bathed in the warm syrup of undeveloped eyes that knew no falsehoods and a newly formed heart that believed in love's tactile sensation with irrational faith.

The knife wiggled in the carpet of the stairs and Melinda grunted to dig it out.

Cat flipped on her side.

She had one chance.

Melinda's hand tensed around Cat's ankle and anger fluttered through it as the knife broke free. Cat saw nothing, and the sound of the metal pinging the air was barely audible above the thumping pulse of her own blood rushing from her heart to her head and its diversion to the gash in her stomach.

Cat's right foot pulled into her chest,

squishing blood onto her hand and she let it fly.
Twenty-two years of resenting the faceless killer
who'd ruined her life engulfed her body and zipped
through the heavy boot.

She didn't want to kill Melinda.

She didn't want revenge.

She just wanted to wad the whole thing up
and drop kick it into outer space.

Melinda shrieked as Cat's heavy snow boot
thwapped her face, catching her left eye and her ear
near the temple, grinding cold plastic teeth against
her skin to leave her with the sickness of a narrowly
averted concussion.

Melinda held her position, her deceptive
strength heavy on the stairs. She searched to regain
composure.

But her grip slackened.

Cat squeezed her eyes and pulled her leg back
again to kick her troubles down to the darkness of
hell from which they spawned.

Her leg snapped into the nothingness of air
and she didn't care.

Cat kicked again and caught Melinda in the
throat.

The redhead's grip departed, snatched away to
tend to her stifling pains and Cat nearly tripped in
rushing back into the darkness of the kitchen where
her hands were steady in front of her to guide her.

The edge of a low-lying quartz countertop
gershed her wound, jabbing its blunt edge into her
stomach.

Cat stumbled and fell to her knees and scraped
to height, rushing with a ragged limp for the door.

Faster, Cat, faster!

Her blood ran cold as Melinda unearthed a
hideous shriek from the cavernous depths of her

bewitching soul.

Faster!

Cat ran and ran, and the snow boots mocked her equilibrium. She cursed herself for snickering to the other waitresses about drunks filing in and out of the diner at three and four in the morning, how they couldn't get a hold of themselves, how their faces were always frozen in the never-ending moment of trying not to throw up.

There was no humor in it now.

Cat made it to the door. Her ears were pierced with the angered thwaps of bare feet behind her.

The ooze of blood and unhealthy sweat sliming Cat's hands assassinated her attempt to leave. Her eyebrowless face was a warped mess of emotions and desperation and she spun in failing to twist the knob and fell to her back against the front door.

Melinda swelled in her vision, a looming specter of death.

Cat was powerless.

The knife rose in two hands as if the witch of a woman was making a ritual sacrifice, aching to disembowel her as she had the poor wolf-like dog, finally bringing full circle what diseased web hatred had spun in her heart toward Sarah.

Cat's body was flushed with senseless heat. The feeling of falling from a rollercoaster as it separated from the tracks bloomed within like a drug high.

It was a dream, a bad dream, a cruel nightmare she had no one to blame for but herself. She could've been in LA, unhappy but alive. And Loeb, poor Loeb, she'd brought him into this mess; Loeb whom she loved she'd ruined with ulterior motives and hidden desires.

Where was he now? It was all her fault.

She shut her eyes.

In her memory, the green skin of the Aurora gilding the dark sky of looming winter flowered within a stilling comfort and hushed her hurried breath.

Melinda took a broad step to plunge the knife into Cat's thinness and her bare feet caught bloodied mess of clothes on the floor. Her legs spread as she slipped. Her powerful frame attempted compensation.

It was the second step that ruined her, her thick thighs driven by the evil hunger to press forward. A bare foot sealed to the stickiness of the bloody cotton squealed along the floor and Melinda pitched unevenly with features of dismay. For half a second, if it was an eternity, her curvy body became horizontal in the air, two and a half feet from the ground.

The last breath of life within her puffed from her cruel, sensual lips in the blink of an eye. Equilibrium lost had buried the knife in her stomach all the way to her spine, where it nicked the bone.

Melinda West was instantly paralyzed. Her body tented and her hands were caught beneath her. Her blood soaked the floor and Cat couldn't fight the revulsion welling within her.

Cat tried to shrink into the door, slowly pressing herself upright.

The cold eyes of deep blue lake water stared at Cat, *into her.*

What's the difference between us? What did I do wrong?

Melinda was a psychopath, pure and simple. Cat willowed as she stood tall. The hallway danced and spun.

Life was senseless, death even more so. Long ago Melinda West had chosen her fate, and it had finally come upon her.

Even though the subtle terrorist of a woman had murdered the only connection in Cat's heart to nurturing love, to summer sun and warmth, to coziness in the dead of winter and hands that knew no bounds of affection and understanding, Cat couldn't deny the pity sinking like a stone down the well of her throat.

What a waste.

Of beauty.

Of life.

But life was a gamble as much as it was a game plan. One could only choose with what one had to choose from.

So some disease had infected Melinda's blood at a young age, some quiet kill of character, of the soul.

She'd only courted it, embraced it, thought its thoughts as a parasite host and submitted to its desires as it ever so slowly began to possess her body and ruin her life.

Cat forced air from flared nostrils and slogged outside.

Alaska was giant, broad and forgiving. The northern lights were gone and the chill was crisp, dry and cooling against her skin.

The gurgling whine of a small motor buzzed in the distant hush of the forest. Cat jogged a scuffing thing to the nearest outbuilding. Her breath was a cloud stifling her sight and she stopped. New snow had filled in the truck's tracks but their end hinted at the garage door of the shake-roofed structure.

Cat tried the door and it was locked.

The buzzing continued and what began as an insignificant fly in her strung out ears progressed into a chainsaw and finally a snowmobile. Cat rushed to the black dot of a vehicle as it slowly wove through the treeless property. Her feet sank in the snow and a hundred yards from it and its pale cascade of a headlamp Cat tripped on the hidden lump of a tree root. Frosty wet snow stung her skin and she scraped to her elbows to call out to the rider.

The black snowmobile veered to the right and the rider leapt from it, rushing to Cat, removing the shiny black full-faced helmet as she did so.

A thick cord of braided red hair flopped from the protective covering and Katie West tossed her helmet to the ground.

"My God, Cat, what happened?" Katie fell to the snow to roll Cat to her back. Katie's round hazel eyes jittered over Cat's body and the sight of so much blood made her hands tremble with fever. She bent down to cradle Cat's head in the crook of her arm and held the young woman's limp thinness.

"The garage." Cat said. "Save Ericson."

"What?" Katie's cute, girlish features were drawn together and wrinkled. Cat had no strength left. The night was so cold, but she didn't feel it.

She didn't feel anything.

"Melinda tried to kill me…"

"Oh my God…" Katie whimpered and bobbled Cat's head, the combination of hearing such a horrid thing and holding the witness of its actions jabbing its own knife into her belly.

The hazel eyes blurred.

"…call the police…"

Cat's neck slackened and her breath was thick and laborious. Katie let Cat's body flop in the snow and bolted for the split-level house and the light spilling from the open door.

Cat stared into the sky as a vesper of color began to weave through its infinite and uncontrollable darkness, its limitless depths of perfection.

Out there in space, Cat thought, *everything's okay. All the stars shine like they should, all the planets spin the way they're supposed to.*

I'm okay with it.

A new Aurora streaking the sky with a dusky blue brilliance reminded Cat of Loeb's eyes, the darkness of the pupils and the softness of his pastel blue irises, spread and smeared across the inexhaustible ink of space.

In the great beyond there was no end of beauty, no writer's block, no ache of separation.

Cat smiled as she lay in the somnolent peace of the snow, letting the living splashes of blue comfort her like the freshly squeezed orange juice of a new sunrise.

I'm okay with it...

I'm okay...

30

Echo Park

It was nearly sixty degrees outside. Loeb squinted up into the brightness sitting somewhere behind rippled bands of white clouds and took a swig of soda, the can still cold from a vending machine. The plastic shopping bag swished in the grip of his opposite hand and his steps were broad on the easy route back from the neighborhood mini-mart to the narrow two-story sun-bleached Spanish plaster and orange terracotta roofed-house that was his home. Bushy green trees congested the ground floor windows from the street and the quarter of an acre that came with the skinny Spanish rectangle was fenced from its tangle of neighbors. The yard to the right of the building was an overgrown knot of weeds and bushes and Loeb threw a glance to the white curtains still pinched together behind the black tic tac toe bars of the second-story window. A smile spread across his face, fueled by a gesture of heat from the sunlight against the back of his neck.

It was almost one o'clock.

Loeb opened the chain link gate and scuffed up three flat steps.

It wasn't until he made it upstairs to the small bedroom that he made a showy entrance of heavy steps and bag rattling.

Cat sat up from a lumpy mass of white sheets rumpled across an ebony-colored mission-style bed, her left hand palming a wearied face of half-snarled lips and thick brown eyebrows, suggestively twisted. They were make-up model's eyebrows, God knew why she ever shaved them, and the timeless simplicity of her face and her large eyes continually struck Loeb with unadorned loveliness.

She was Cat. Fun, vibrant, simple, blunt, thin, never again homeless.

Never again *fractured*.

She could cover her arms in tattoos, get ten pounds of piercings, have a baby and gain forty-five pounds but she'd still be Catriona Cohen, the woman who he was only beginning to understand but felt like knew him inside and out.

It was the journey of it all that he would cherish, the partnership, the destination.

The mystery.

Now and forever.

Loeb pressed his knee to the bed to bend toward her and kissed the gold ring on her finger.

"Still sleeping?" He said. "You can't stay in bed all day."

Beneath Cat's eternally brown eyes, puffy crescents begged for rest. The night before had been long in love and after returning from the painful dirge of Alaskan snows and the tedious aftermath of Melinda West's murderous reign as the Queen of Quill Creek, their January wedding up in San Francisco had taken whatever was left in their tanks. So for the honeymoon they'd left everything behind but the clothes on their backs, a handful of credit cards and an old beat up Guild twelve string and picked a nondescript place in Echo Park to start their new life.

Together.

"I'm not...but I thought writers kept vampire hours."

"They use typewriters, too. And chain smoke and drink whiskey sours and drive convertibles up and down along the highway looking for dark-cornered diners to write in and strange people to talk to."

Cat laughed a chuckling cough. She'd since quit smoking. And Loeb in a convertible? That would be the day. If Loeb ever owned a car, Cat would know the end of the world was nigh.

Loeb set his can of soda on a settee and kicked off his sneakers before snuggling up next to her on the bed.

"Solderman's happy with the rough of *Wind, Water, Fire and War.*" The writer pulled his wife close. "But he likes my bang bangs so much I wouldn't know if it's any good or not."

Cat yawned.

"It's not."

Loeb disregarded her sarcasm and began to ramble.

"I opted for the sadder ending of the two, by the way. I want to keep continuity with the genre. Remember, I was talking about it last night at dinner, the part where the hero..."

"Have you heard anything from Katie?" Cat yawned again. "Excuse me...I didn't mean to cut you off." The yawn flipped into a smile because she secretly did. It was funny how Loeb hadn't changed much since marriage. He was still Loeb and she loved every square inch of him for it.

"No." Loeb stared at the blankness of the walls and thought how blankness was a nice thing in a city so engulfed humanity's diverse colors and flavors. "But I'm sure she's okay. She's got our number here at home and I've told her I'd put in a good word with Sods and Pearle if she wanted to make a break for Hollywood. She's got the looks. I'm sure he'd get her a spot in a daytime soap no sweat. She could even do cosmetic modeling, shampoos and what not. I just hope her life takes a turn for the best, you know?"

"I bet her Dad's taking good care of her." Cat slithered her left hand in his right. Loeb's ring was silver, and well complimented his artistic mop of very dark hair. And his watery eyes. "Especially since Ericson died. In some ways, though, I wonder if Ericson was okay with dying, like he was tired of spinning his wheels. When he was beating you up I was scared for you but the more I thought about it as we talked it over with the police, the more I thought that he was just taking out his frustrations because he was impossibly stuck. We never got to ask him what he thought of Melinda…it makes me feel bad for him, knowing she was so rotten."

"Yeah." Loeb took a sip of soda, wanting its cloying sweetness to remove the bitter memories of Alaska's dark possibilities. "And Virgil Fox wasn't as gruff and mean as he made out to be. He took it really well. I thought he wasn't going to let go of you when he gave you that hug in the airport…I guess he really loved Sarah, way back when. It must've felt good for him to finally know the truth about what happened. For all of them to know, I guess. The whole town, the police, everyone. It must've been like getting a new lease on life, like a thick fog just…burning off. Especially with Quill Creek being annexed, it'll get to finally change and shed that old skin. Katie took it really well, too, considering. I could only imagine what a basket case I'd be if my mother was such a horrible person."

Cat's thick eyebrows danced and one nearly sat on top of the other as she eyed Loeb sideways.

"Really Loeb? Did you forget the wedding?"

Loeb playfully pulled at her nose and she blocked it and pressed into him, sliding her hand up his shirt and nestling into the crook of his shoulder and his neck. Sleepiness was still gripping her and she was trying to let its syrup seep into him.

"I guess you're right. Why was she so fastidious about the pictures?"

Cat frowned as if she'd smelled something sour.

"Fastidious? Who on earth says *fastidious?*"

Loeb grabbed her roughly and flipped her over, trying to lie on top of her back and she was slick in evading him and nimbly took an advantageous posture. One arm snaked around his neck, the other arm was at his chest and then her legs were vices around his core.

"Okay, okay. She was a fussy! See also difficult, taxing, exhaustive and problematic! Lemme go I can't breathe…"

Cat released the pressure of her legs as she sat against the headboard and began to run her fingers through his hair, taking small nibbles of kisses as he relaxed and leaned his head back into her chest.

"So whatchu gonna work on now?" She asked as both of them stared into the emptiness of the room, eyes glazed, focusing on nothing in particular.

"Maybe that one where the stock market gets hit by terrorists, or…that treasure hunt one in San Diego, where the pessimistic Navy SEAL washout dishonorably discharged for attitude issues teams up with the retired Hawaiian pro-surfer studying to be an oceanographer."

"Uh huh…"

"I'll weave in something about the cartels and throw in a wrinkle about one of the bad guys having killed her father or grandfather or her aunt's dog or something…"

Cat kissed his head, smelling the light fragrance of shampoo. Her lips were snarled in the slightest.

"It won't be as good as what I wrote."

Loeb paused to think, and when he realized she was serious he bent in half. His symmetrical features burned with the shock of a man hearing his wife was having a baby.

The sentiment drew across the width of his mouth, and Cat's face became a mirror.

"You wrote something?"

"Yeah." Her snarl spread and her head tipped toward her shoulder as her married hand idly curled his hair. Her eyes swelled with light. "I wrote it for you."

"Can I see it?"

"Let's go for a walk."

"I want to read it."

"In bed?" Cat frowned with childish gruffness to mock him, and her voice was attempting to be low and staccato like his. "You can't stay in bed all day."

Loeb stole a kiss from her.

"Says you."

Even though Echo Park was only a few blocks from their place and Loeb loved to stare into the lake Cat insisted on walking all the way to Elysian Park and Loeb held her hand to stop her satchel from thumping against her side. Or to be closer to whatever Cat had written. In the Chavez Ravine Arboretum they found a shady tree and settled in. Nearly two football fields away a small production company was attempting to film a tearful sequence between two tween actors, perhaps a breakup. A production assistant was dousing the girl with hairspray while the director coached the boy's wooden delivery of dialogue and a DP in baggy jeans was splitting squints between the banded streaks of clouds and a heavy-looking Nikon camera.

Loeb could barely contain himself as Cat sat down and kicked her feet together, digging through the pale brown satchel as if it was bottomless.

"I've got tickets to tonight's Dodgers game in here." She said.

"Cat, it's January."

"Just checking."

Her baby was a black, three-subject college ruled notebook. Like her it was something generic and plain and easy to pass by with no second thoughts on the outside when in truth, each page would be a mystery of enigmatic attraction; compelling, charming and full of new inspiration. Loeb received it from her with respect and from the moment the baby passed from hand to hand, Cat was already blessed.

"There may be some typos, but it's all handwritten. It just started as little tidbits here and there but it should make a cohesive story. I think. You're the writer, though…be kind to my first attempt at greatness. Granted, it's not finished yet. I might need your help with the ending."

Cat's wry smile was at herself as much as Loeb, the man who'd talked her ear off about *the craft* and who, like a chronic of any kind, wouldn't be able to stop himself.

Ever.

"I almost don't want to read it yet." Loeb said, wide-eyed and glowing. "It's like a Christmas present you really wanted but never had the guts to ask for."

"Loeb, you're Jewish."

"It's an analogy."

"Just checking." Cat winked.

Then Cat stretched back in the cool grass under the shade of a sprawling tree she didn't remember the name of and closed her eyes as her husband read the opening line of the book she'd written for him, as he'd written *Fractures* for her.

Loeb was a writer.

All gratitude goes to God; for the miracles of life, love, and for the untold blessings of perseverance! All things work together!

Thank you faithful readers for your thoughtful and honest feedback and your zealous support of whatever I write; you special few are a true blessing!

Thank you Laura for the perfect cover for this project once again!

And thank you very much for reading this book. If you enjoyed it, you'll be pleased to know Cat and Loeb have more stories ahead of them. They're so much an amalgamation of real life that I can't deny their right to be in print.

Until next time,
Luke Taylor

www.ingramcontent.com/pod-product-compliance
Lightning Source LLC
Chambersburg PA
CBHW030532270626
47155CB00024B/2794